I0817733

BRIDGE OF STORMS

OTHER SCHOLASTIC BOOKS BY PHILIP REEVE

THE MORTAL ENGINES QUARTET

Mortal Engines
Predator's Gold
Infernal Devices
A Darkling Plain

ALSO IN THE WORLD OF MORTAL ENGINES

Night Flights
Thunder City

THE FEVER CRUMB TRILOGY

Fever Crumb
A Web of Air
Scrivener's Moon

PHILIP REEVE

BRIDGE OF STORMS

A MORTAL ENGINES NOVEL

Scholastic Press
New York

Copyright © 2026 by Philip Reeve

All rights reserved. Published by Scholastic Press, an imprint of Scholastic Inc., *Publishers since 1920.* SCHOLASTIC, SCHOLASTIC PRESS, and associated logos are trademarks and/or registered trademarks of Scholastic Inc.

The publisher does not have any control over and does not assume any responsibility for author or third-party websites or their content.

No part of this publication may be reproduced, stored in a retrieval system, or transmitted in any form or by any means, electronic, mechanical, photocopying, recording, or otherwise, or used to train any artificial intelligence technologies, without written permission of the publisher. For information regarding permission, write to Scholastic Inc., Attention: Permissions Department, 557 Broadway, New York, NY 10012.

This book is a work of fiction. Names, characters, places, and incidents are either the product of the author's imagination or are used fictitiously, and any resemblance to actual persons, living or dead, business establishments, events, or locales is entirely coincidental.

Library of Congress Cataloging in publication number available

ISBN 978-1-5461-3826-6

10 9 8 7 6 5 4 3 2 1 26 27 28 29 30

Printed in Italy 208
First edition, February 2026

Book design by Steve Scott

For Philippa Milnes-Smith, with love

CONTENTS

1

Hawkshead

It was not Tamzin's fault.

All she did was duck. It was instinct — that was all. She barely even saw the beer mug come flying at her, just caught the movement from the corner of her eye. But that was enough to make her Arcade fighter training kick in. So she ducked, and the mug sailed harmlessly above her head. The man standing behind her should have ducked too, but his instincts weren't as sharp as Tamzin's. The mug hit him squarely on the nose, breaking both.

That was when it all went sideways. The broken-nosed man bellowed in pain. He lunged for the mug-thrower, but, blinded by anger and spilled beer, grabbed the wrong man. His victim let out an indignant yell that summoned all his shipmates to his aid, and the little tavern was suddenly full of windmilling fists, thrown chairs, squawking barmaids, breaking glass, and furious aviators intent on thumping anyone who came within reach. Tamzin dodged a swung bottle, dived beneath a table, surfaced on the far side, and went to help her friends.

Oddington Doom was the veteran of more brawls and battles than he could remember, and had adopted a fighter's stance, fists clenched, lashing out with cool, scientific violence at any piece of sky trash who came near. Max Angmering, far less experienced, had snatched up a chair to defend himself from a knife-wielding Uighur aviatrix who had taken a dislike to him for no reason he could understand. Hilly Torpenhow, who had been a history tutor until very recently and thought of herself more as a thinker than a warrior, snatched a heavy wooden tray from a neighboring table and applied it tactically to the Uighur's head. The aviatrix grunted and toppled backward through the pane of smeared plastic that served as the tavern's only window, landing hard on the balcony outside and rolling. Max and Tamzin both went after her, stopping her before she could smash through the flimsy-looking balustrade at the balcony's brim.

They caught her just in time. Below the balcony were the town's engines and propellers, and below those an awful lot of empty sky.

The Uighur lady did not thank them for saving her. Stumbling to her feet, she cursed them loudly in her own tongue and ran back inside to rejoin the fight. Tamzin and Max stood looking at each other. When they had set off with Hilly and Doom aboard the airship *Fire's Astonishment* in search of adventure, this was not quite the sort of thing that either of them had had in mind.

And as they stood there, listening to the din of battle spilling from the tavern, one voice suddenly rose above the rest, shrill and terrified. "Revenant! Revenant! Run for your lives! There's a Revenant loose!"

❁

Oddington Doom had warned them that Hawkshead was a rough little place. "A nest of villains," had been his exact words when they'd first sighted the air town, dangling from its patchwork cloud of gasbags somewhere above the Central Hunting Ground. A bundle of balsa-wood buildings and bamboo gantries, lashed together with rags of old envelope fabric, it had the off-putting look of something built by insects. But the *Fire's Astonishment* was running low on fuel, and it seemed more efficient to dock at Hawkshead than to descend to the next city that passed by upon the ground.

It had been Hilly's idea to visit the tavern once the *Astonishment*'s tanks were filled. "After all," she said, "we paid that sky-high mooring fee — we might as well look around a little. I have never been aboard an air town, other than Bad Luftgarten."

Bad Luftgarten was an elegant spa town. Hawkshead was a less classy sort of place entirely. Half the aviators who docked there were smugglers or sky-pirates, and the other half looked as though they would be happy to help out if the smugglers and pirates were short-handed. Dubious characters lurked in dingy doorways, trying to interest passersby in unsavory things. A parpsichord was hooting and wheezing inside the Hawkshead Tavern, but the music stopped when the crew of the *Fire's Astonishment* walked in. The conversations that had been in progress stopped with it. All heads turned to stare at the newcomers, except for those that belonged to folk too drunk to care.

"What a dump!" murmured Max.

"Oh, it does not look too bad," said Hilly brightly. She glanced around and caught sight of two men sitting nervously at a table near the window: an old man and a young one, dressed in robes of ginger tweed. "There," she said, "not all the clientele are miscreants or ne'er-do-wells. Those gentlemen look like scholars. Let us go and introduce ourselves."

It was as they picked their way between the crowded tables that someone called out, "Tamzin Pook!"

Tamzin glanced around. She didn't know the drunken airshipman who was pointing at her, but a lot of people Tamzin didn't know knew her. She had grown her hair a bit since leaving Margate, and wore aviator's clothes, but anyone who had watched one of her fights in the Amusement Arcade would recognize her. This fellow clearly had. He rose unsteadily from his seat and shouted, "You owe me thirty silver cogs, Tamzin Pook! I had a bet on Eve Vespertine to beat that hedgepig machine, and you went and let it kill her."

Tamzin hesitated, then decided to ignore him. She had carried the guilt of Eve Vespertine's death with her for a long time, and had left it behind her at last; she was not going to let this hairy oaf remind her of it. She looked away. By chance, her eye fell upon a yellowing page of newsprint serving as a tablecloth. *Where Is Mortmain?* asked the headline, beside a picture of a smug, bewhiskered face that Tamzin knew too well.

The hairy oaf who had yelled at her did not like being ignored, or perhaps he really did blame Tamzin for the loss of his money. He belched, then hurled his beer mug at her, and Tamzin ducked, and so everything went south until Tamzin and Max found themselves on the balcony outside the torn plastic window, listening to panicked voices take up the shout of "Revenant!"

It occurred to Tamzin that she had ended up in trouble aboard Bad Luftgarten too. She did not have much luck on air towns.

2

NEKROTEKNIK!

Revenant!" most of the tavern's denizens were shouting, although a few shouted the Germanic name, "*Todt-jaeger!*" or the Airsperanto one, "*Nekroteknik!*" One or two yelled, "Stalker!" which was rather a silly term in Hilly Torpenhow's opinion.

There was nothing silly about Revenants. Armored, undead soldiers created by the nomad empires, most had been destroyed hundreds of years before, but they still stalked the nightmares of the north. The Revenant animals Tamzin had fought in the Arcade had been flimsy contraptions compared to the Stalkers of old, but even they had been deadly enough. The thing now stomping along the creaking bamboo walkways of Hawkshead was human-shaped, and altogether more terrible. The bruised and battered drinkers pouring out of the tavern collided on the platform outside with a gaggle of townsfolk retreating before the Revenant. Forgetting their differences in the face of this horror, they all stood and gawped at it together.

The Revenant had blue armor with a chromium trim, speckled with brass patches where dents and bullet holes had been repaired. It had lost an arm somewhere, although the remaining one, with its massive steel hand, looked dangerous enough. It wore no helmet, so everyone could see its dead, gray face, and the green light that flickered like a bottled aurora behind its heavy goggles. It wore, for some sinister reason of its own, a rainbow-striped woolen bobble hat.

As the horrified aviators and townsfolk backed away from it, the Revenant suddenly stooped and scooped up something from the shadows behind the bins outside the Silverfish Grill. The something turned out to be a small black cat with white mittens. A few of the more sentimental onlookers cried out in pity, afraid the poor animal was about to meet a dreadful end. But the cat just jumped up happily on to the Revenant's armored shoulder.

The Revenant seemed to notice for the first time that it had an audience. The green light behind its goggles flared eerily.

Oddington Doom raised his voice. "It's all right, everyone. She's with us."

Tamzin, shoving her way roughly through the throng, ran to where the Revenant stood. "Vespertine," she scolded, "we told you to stay aboard the ship in case people saw you and . . ." She gestured at the horrified faces of the crowd. "Well, in case of *this*."

"Small Cat escaped," said the Revenant in her voice like dry-paper rustling. "I came to find him."

"Well, I don't suppose it matters," said Tamzin. She patted Vespertine's armored arm. This Revenant, the last and most sophisticated to be built in Margate, had been made from the body of Tamzin's dead team friend Eve Vespertine. Despite her size and strength, she felt to Tamzin like a little sister.

"Maybe it's good you showed yourself," Tamzin admitted. "Those sky trash will think twice before they try starting anything with us again." She took Vespertine's massive, metal hand in hers and said loudly for the onlookers to hear, "She's safe. She's a friend of ours."

But there were fewer onlookers by then, and soon there were almost none at all. The crowd was draining away: slinking into nearby shops, or down to the air town's lower decks, or hurrying back to their airships and starting up their engines. No one believed a Revenant could be safe. No one wanted to tangle with anybody who was friends with one.

Pretty soon, the crew of the *Fire's Astonishment* were all alone on the platform, except for the two tweed-clad scholars, who watched them warily from the doorway of the tavern. The older man seemed cautious, but after a few moments his younger companion edged closer and called out, "I say . . . do you really own this creature?"

"She travels with us," said Oddington Doom.

"Would you be prepared to sell her?" asked the older man.

"Indeed no!" said Hilly indignantly. "Vespertine is a friend of ours. She is not a mere contraption to be bought and sold."

"Pity," the scholar said, shaking his head. "Our city is in desperate need. A thing like this, capable of striking terror into the hearts of ruffians, might save it from a dreadful end."

"Then maybe we can do business after all," said Oddington Doom. "A few months ago, we liberated the city of Thorbury from the tyrant Gabriel Strega. Now we ply the Bird Roads as adventurers, looking for fresh challenges to test our courage and our wits. Striking terror into the hearts of ruffians is what we do best. Saving cities from dreadful ends is our specialty." He swept off his hat, adjusted his eye patch, and made the sort of elegant, theatrical bow that had won him scores of admirers in his younger days, but which now played merry hell with his lumbago.

The younger of the two scholars seemed delighted, but the older one was not convinced. "An old man, a woman not much younger, a youth, and a girl? What use could you four be to us?"

Doom grinned. "Don't let appearances deceive you, friend. I've been in more battles than I can number. Tamzin here is a fighter from the famous Amusement Arcade on Margate, where she battled machines bigger and deadlier than Vespertine here every night of the week, and twice on Saturdays. Max Angmering's family has ruled Thorbury since it was founded: The blood of warriors and heroes runs in his veins. And as for Hilly Torpenhow, why, she's brave as a she-wolf when the chips are down, and there's nothing she couldn't tell you about history or geography. She's the brains of our little outfit. So how about you buy us a round of drinks, and let's talk about this city of yours, and why it needs our help?"

3

The Men from Museion

The Hawkshead Tavern had shuttered its doors, but it opened them again when Vespertine tapped on the glass. The landlord did not want to serve a Revenant, but nor did he dare turn a Revenant away. He contented himself with glaring darkly from behind his bar while Vespertine and her friends sat down with the scholars at his largest table. Trembling barmaids served them ginger tea and brought a saucer of cream for Small Cat.

The older of the two scholars was a shortish, brownish, worried-looking man. His head was mostly bald, but — perhaps to compensate — bushy tufts of wire-gray hair sprouted from his large ears. "I am Professor Loomis," he explained. "My young assistant here is Rowan Bellweather. I am chief navigator for the city of Museion."

Hilly set down her teacup and said, "Museion? Goodness gracious! I feared it had been eaten years ago!"

"Indeed not, dear lady," said Loomis. "But it has fallen upon hard times. Hard times indeed . . ."

Hilly turned to her companions. "Museion is only a small city, but in its own way it is one of the very greatest. It was built by a committee of scholars from London, Paris, and a dozen other places. It does not wander as other cities do in search of prey or trade, but only in the pursuit of learning."

Loomis nodded proudly. "And we have learned wonderful things," he said. "For more than two hundred years Museion has roamed the world, seeking knowledge wherever it could be found, excavating Ancient sites, and amassing a vast collection of artifacts and books. Many bright young people came to study with us. Some returned to their own cities to found universities and museums of their own; others stayed with us and became important scholars, writers, and thinkers. But 'the times they are a-changin',' as the Ancient poet said. Not everyone in the Great Hunting Ground has the respect for learning that they once did . . ."

"Predator suburbs kept chasing us," explained Rowan Bellweather.

"So Museion sought shelter in an old city nest among the foothills of the Tannhäuser Mountains," Loomis continued. "There we have remained for the past year and a half."

"It's called the Frying Pan," said Bellweather.

"Now our dean and Senior Fellows have decided —"

"They are our equivalent of a mayor and town council," explained Bellweather, like a helpful footnote.

"We have decided," repeated Loomis, glaring at him, "that rather than waiting to be torn to pieces by savage towns, Museion should be devoured with dignity by a civilized city that understands the value of our work. We have made a treaty with London to that effect. London's Guild of Historians has agreed that when their city eats Museion, they will combine our collections with their own."

"A most sensible solution," said Hilly. "My own late father was a member of the Guild of Historians. I am sure Museion's treasures will make a wonderful addition to the London Museum."

"Unfortunately," said Bellweather, "we couldn't persuade London's council that it was worth coming all the way to the Frying Pan for a simple 'meet and eat.' They want Museion to travel to the Western Hunting Ground and rendezvous with London there."

"But that is a long journey," said Loomis. "And as soon as we leave the safety of the Frying Pan, we shall be beset by enemies."

"There's this nomad band called the Junkyard Dogs," said Bellweather excitedly. "They've already had two goes at raiding us. As soon as we move out onto open ground, they'll be down on us like a pack of . . . well, dogs . . ."

"Are they a big mob?" asked Doom.

"They lair in an upland valley, out of sight of our lookouts," said Loomis. "But they have dozens of armored vehicles, and a traction fortress they call the Hundberg. They must have hundreds of warriors."

"Then you'll have quite a fight on your hands," said Doom.

"But we have dealt with nomads before," said Hilly proudly. "They are nothing but bullies, who just need someone to stand up to them. And as civilized people we have a duty to help Museion in its hour of need. All those archives and collections! What a tragedy it would be if that great store of knowledge were to perish from the world. And what good fortune that we happened to stop in Hawkshead today. I believe the gods themselves must have arranged our meeting, Professor Loomis! Of course we shall come to Museion!"

4

The City Nest

The journey north and east was a long one, made longer by the fact that the *Fire's Astonishment* had to keep to the pace of Professor Loomis's airship, a tiny research vessel called the *Owl of Minerva*.

It was smooth, calm-weather flying, but Max felt uneasy. After the battle of Thorbury, he had thought it a splendid idea to set off in search of fresh adventures. Now that new battles lay ahead, he wondered if he was really suited to adventures after all. His memories of the fighting aboard Thorbury were just a blur of terror and confusion. Doom claimed he had the blood of warriors and heroes in his veins, but Max was keen to keep it there. What if, when the time came to fight again, he turned out to be too cowardly?

He tried explaining to Tamzin that he was not sure he had what it took to be a fighter. But Tamzin just snorted and told him he'd be fine. She had worries of her own. She was not sure she had what it took to be anything *but* a fighter. She was glad to be a part of the *Astonishment*'s crew, but Max and Hilly talked often about history and politics, which made her feel ignorant and uneducated, while Doom talked about everything, easily and cheerfully. It made

Tamzin realize how shy she was, how bad at talking, how bad at being part of anything. Perhaps all she had ever been good for was fighting Revenants in the Arcade?

Before they left the Hawkshead Tavern, she had helped herself to the faded news-sheet that had caught her eye before the brawl broke out. She read it again and again, alone in her little cabin while the *Fire's Astonishment* droned northward through the frosty nights. It was a story about Tamzin's former owner, Dr. Mortmain, the scientist-showman who had owned the Arcade. It was Mortmain who had built the Revenants that Tamzin used to battle. He had built Vespertine too, but Vespertine had turned on him and, in the chaos that followed, Tamzin had thought Mortmain killed. If this newspaper had it right, that might not be so. His body had never been found. Perhaps he had fallen overboard and drowned, since Margate was a raft city. But it had not been far offshore at the time, so there was talk that Mortmain might have swum to safety, and be selling his services to some other city.

"Just a silly rumor," Hilly said, when Tamzin showed her the article. "You can't believe everything you read in the papers, Tamzin." But what if it *wasn't* just a rumor? What if Mortmain was still out there somewhere, unpunished, alive, designing new death-machines to fight more captive girls like Tamzin Pook? Mortmain was unfinished business, a loose end she should have made sure was tied. The thought scratched like a mouse in the attic of her mind. She sometimes felt she should have parted from her friends at Hawkshead and gone off to hunt Mortmain instead. But maybe, if the people on Museion knew as much as Hilly claimed they did, one of them might know where he had gone . . .

❁

A thousand feet below, towns and cities drew their wakes of torn earth across the plains of the Central Hunting Ground, stopping sometimes to trade, or to eat one another. But as the two ships flew north and east, the towns grew smaller and fewer, and the cities were left behind altogether. The dull brown plains below were desolate, pocked with old craters and flooded track marks. On the skyline ahead loomed the Tannhäuser Mountains — the Walls of the North — going up in crag upon crag and cliff upon frowning cliff until their heights were lost in cloud and vapor and eternal snow. The legends said that the god Odin had raked the gaze of his dreadful eye across the earth, and the restless Tannhäusers had sprung from the fiery gash it made. Far off, a few were burning still. The badlands at the mountains' feet had been the birthplace of proud cities once. When the long light of morning or of evening lay across the plains, it showed up steep-sided earthworks ringed by deep-cut ditches. Hilly explained to her companions that these were "stadtsnesters" or "city nests," built long ago by towns and cities trying to keep predators at bay while, safe within those earthen walls, they rebuilt themselves in mobile form.

Hilly was having a wonderful time. She could not think why she had never taken the trouble to go traveling before. It was one thing to learn about the world from books, yet quite another to fly above it and see it all spread out before you. But in her younger days she had been too busy tutoring Max and his sister. And travel would not have been the same without Oddington Doom as her companion.

On Thorbury, once their first adventure was over, she had begun to find herself feeling very tenderly toward Mr. Doom. He was such a wise and kindly man, despite his rough manners, and really quite good-looking in a craggy way. It was most peculiar how he was always in her thoughts, and how absurdly happy she felt when she was with him. She had done her utmost to ignore the feeling. She had always thought love a rather silly business, probably invented by poets to give themselves something to write about. She told herself that she was far too old to be swept away by such foolish emotions. And what would a man of the world like Oddington Doom see in a dried-up old stick like her anyway?

But the feelings only grew stronger. And one remarkable evening while they were walking in the park — she would remember it always, Thorbury chugging past a string of lakes like sunset mirrors, and the musicians on the bandstand playing "Owl-Light Serenade" — she had somehow forgotten herself enough to hint at how she felt, and Oddington had picked up the hint and said that he felt exactly the same way about her.

Hilly had been so surprised and happy that she had kissed him, right there beside the municipal duck pond, with no thought at all as to whether any of her neighbors might see. And when Doom suggested they fly off together aboard the *Fire's Astonishment*, and when Tamzin, Max, and Vespertine agreed to come . . . Well! It was as though, after living her whole life alone, Hilly had suddenly acquired a loving family, ready-made.

So as she sat on the bench seat in the *Astonishment*'s gondola, with Doom's arm around her waist, pointing out interesting details of the scenery below, Hilly had never felt so lucky, or so glad. It was as if one of the gods had leaned down from the sky and bent the very tides of history to bring her what she wanted.

But she could not help remembering that gods had a cruel sense of humor sometimes. Now that she had found happiness, she wanted it to go on forever, but she knew that was not how the world worked at all. Sooner or later, something would happen to bring this golden time to an end.

❁

Which wandering city had emerged from the nest known as the Frying Pan, no one now remembered. It must have been a big one, for it had left behind a broad bowl of scrub and grassland enclosed by a steep, circular rampart. At its western end, a broad gap in the rampart showed where the newborn Traction City had smashed its way free long ago, dragging out two parallel ridges of rubble and churned earth to form the "handle" of the "frying pan." Across this opening, a barricade of rocks and felled trees had been built. In the center of the "pan," upon a patchwork quilt of fields, sat the city of Museion, with the late sunlight gilding its spires.

"It's like a toy!" said Max, looking down from his place at the controls as the *Fire's Astonishment* flew toward the former nest. He was delighted by the city's prettiness and its eccentric half-track wheelbase. All those gilded towers and spiky decorations reminded him of his own beloved Thorbury before Strega had modernized it. Then he noticed the big guns dug in along the ramparts of the Frying Pan, and a scatter of wreckage rusting on the northern slopes, which must have been debris from a nomad raid. A few miles farther north, where the first jagged ridge of the mountains rose from the plains like the spine of a sleeping dragon, he caught a flash of light reflecting. Up there among the crags, keen eyes were watching through telescopes or field glasses, and had noted the airships' arrival.

The *Owl of Minerva* had already begun her descent toward Museion's air harbor. When Oddington Doom came down the companion ladder into the gondola a few moments later, Max expected him to say the *Astonishment* should follow her down. But instead, Doom took the controls and turned the airship north, toward the ridge where Max had seen that ominous glint of light. "Might as well have a look at what we're up against," he said.

Figures could be seen running along the ridge's rocky summit as the *Fire's Astonishment* flew toward it. They were gathering around a rickety watchtower and two armored vehicles that were parked at its base. Some shook their fists, or waved spears and axes, as the airship's shadow went sliding over them. On the far side of the ridge, the land dropped steep and stony to a lead-gray lake. Along its shores, half hidden by the smog of campfires, dozens more vehicles were parked.

"Fascinating," said Hilly. "These Junkyard Dogs have not changed their ways since the days of the Nomad Empires. Before the first Traction Cities there were hundreds of bands like this, hunting the wains and wheelie-forts of their enemies across the northern plains. Those small armored vehicles are called 'kampavans.' And, look, there is a cluster of big old landships on the far side of the lake."

"There's an even bigger one behind them," said Tamzin.

"A typical motor-and-bailey castle," agreed Hilly. "That will be the traction fortress where the nomad chief lives. He is called their karn, or thane, or sometimes their ladmiral — a contraction of the term 'land admiral.'"

"It's those kampavans we mainly need to worry about," said Doom. "How many do you see?"

Max reckoned there were twenty of the fierce little machines parked up along the lakeshore; Hilly thought their number closer to thirty. Tamzin, meanwhile, was still looking at the traction fortress, and at the vapor that hung over the crags and screes behind it. There seemed to be the opening to another valley there, and it was filled with mist or smoke. Could an even larger force of nomads be encamped there, out of sight?

She pointed out the smoke to Doom, but by then the nomads on the ridge had overcome their surprise at the airship's arrival. White pom-poms speckled the air around their two parked kampavans. The *Fire's Astonishment* was flying too high for anyone aboard to hear the gunfire, but she was not quite high enough. Bullets began striking the keel of the gondola like hammer blows.

"Not bad shooting at this range," said Doom, grudgingly impressed.

He took the airship higher still, and swung her about. The ridge passed beneath her again and fell behind, with the nomads all jeering and gesticulating. Tamzin moved to the stern window to get a better look at them, but they were already almost out of sight, tiny figures lost in the chilly grandeur of the landscape. Then Oddington Doom was telling her to stop daydreaming and lower the mooring cables.

The *Fire's Astonishment* swept in low over the friendlier guns that lined the ramparts of the Frying Pan. Ground crew on the quay that jutted from Museion's upper tier caught the ropes Tamzin dropped to them. They attached the airship to a small, solid-looking vehicle, which towed it gently into a huge hangar as if it were a dog going into its kennel for the night.

5

Too Many Professors

Museion's quay was called the Air Staithe, and a crowd had gathered there to greet the new arrivals. A cheer went up when they emerged from the hangar, although some of the children present were horrified by Vespertine and hid behind their parents, who looked pretty horrified themselves. An honor guard of amateur soldiers wearing red sashes and antique helmets presented arms, rather clumsily. A large lady wearing a blue robe embroidered with golden wheels welcomed the travelers in the blessed name of Peripatetia, goddess of mobile cities. Finally, from a group of tweed-robed dignitaries, a small, fussy, harried-looking man detached himself and came to make his bow before the guests.

"Welcome to Museion," he announced. He had the bushiest eyebrows Tamzin had ever seen, and gray curly hair clustered thickly on the lower slopes of his bald head. "I am Professor Blissland, dean of this unhappy city. But . . ." He looked at Doom, then Max, then Hilly, down at Tamzin, up at Vespertine, and then past them, as if he expected the rest of their company, more impressive and heavily armed, to emerge from the hangar behind them. "Where are the rest of you?" he asked.

"It is just the five of us, I'm afraid," admitted Hilly, curtseying politely. "But Vespertine is worth twenty men."

"And there is Small Cat too," said Vespertine, holding him up for the dean to see.

"Meow," said Small Cat.

"Oh dear, oh dear," sighed the dean. "When Loomis told me he had found fighters to aid us, I rather assumed . . . Well, I was expecting someone a bit more . . . But I suppose we are lucky you got here at all. When you flew off over the mountains, we felt sure those nomad blighters would shoot your airship down in flames."

"They tried," said Doom cheerfully. "They even made a few holes in the envelope and rudders, but nothing your people can't easily repair. And I reckon it was worth the risk, for we got a good look at this mob you're up against."

"And what do you think?" asked the dean. "Is there any hope?"

"There's always hope, dean," said Hilly.

"Yes," Doom agreed. "I reckon we can get you out of here and safely on your way."

An excited murmuring broke out at this. The other dignitaries gathered around, all eager to contribute something. "We must go soon, if we are to leave before the snow comes," said one. "My observations lead me to believe there will be bad weather from the north before the week is out."

"Professor Pringle, our meteorologist . . ." the dean explained.

"But we cannot leave before we have made the proper prayers and offerings," protested the lady in the wheeled robes.

". . . and Professor Pott-Walloper, religious studies," added the dean.

"And we shall have to fetch our cannons down from the emplacements on the Frying Pan and bring them aboard the city," said a very tall, very serious-looking man in camouflage-pattern robes.

"Dr. Twyne, professor of military history," said the dean, and then, carried away, began introducing all the others too. "You have already met Professor Loomis, of course, but here are Professors Waghorn, Von Hinkle, Al-Mansour, Thickett, Bhattacharya, Quincey, Standish, Studge . . ."

"That's too many professors!" said Doom, holding up a hand to stem the tide of names and titles. "I've forgotten half their names already. Isn't there somewhere we can sit and talk tactics? And maybe get a bite to eat while we're about it?"

The dean blinked, unused to such blunt speaking. But Dr. Twyne, excited at the thought of talking tactics, took charge. Clapping his hands, he ordered the onlookers to stand aside, and asked the dean to lead the way to the Senior Common Room. His squad of amateur soldiers set about clearing a path through the onlookers.

"Vespertine," said Doom, "would you mind staying here with the ship tonight? On a city in this much trouble, someone might be tempted to nick it and get away."

"I will guard it," promised Vespertine. "And Small Cat will help."

❋

The light was fading fast as the travelers went with the dean and Senior Fellows across the top tier, but twilight suited Museion. It was a city that had been born in the bright morning of the Traction Era, and now evening was drawing on, and its fading splendor was both sad and beautiful. A broad park lay at the tier's heart, and around it towered buildings whose names Hilly murmured in a reverent undertone. "There is the Great Hall, the Temple of Peripatetia, the Museion Library, the Archaeological Collection . . ." High, stately buildings, with ivy creeping up their walls and over their shingled roofs.

The grandest of all stood near the city's bows, beyond an ornamental lake where autumn leaves scudded like little russet-sailed boats on the still water: a circular tower, six stories high, topped with a copper dome. Its white walls glowed in the last light of the dying day.

"The Ivory Tower!" said Hilly. "I have heard so much about it!"

"I'll send down to the kitchens for some refreshments," said Dr. Twyne as they climbed the steps to the tower's elaborately carved front door. "I would be glad of your opinion on my plans, Mr. Doom. Unlike you, I have no practical experience with the arts of war. My knowledge is all from books."

"I'd say your books have taught you pretty well," said Doom. "Your guns looked well sited to me."

Twyne beamed with pleasure, and held open the door for Doom and the others. But Tamzin lingered outside for a few seconds, looking out at the park and at the gaggle of professors hurrying up the steps behind her. Through gaps between the Ancient buildings she could see the ramparts of the Frying Pan and beyond them, in the twilight, the distant loom of the mountains. Out there in the frosty dusk, on that ridge where the nomads kept their long watch, campfires gleamed like the eyes of waiting wolves.

6

Stoat Dancing

There was dancing that night around the fires on the ridge. Stoat led it, because it was Stoat whose shooting had wounded the orange air machine. He danced hard, spinning and stamping, and his bare chest shone with sweat, and his long red hair swung out around his head like flames, and as he danced he howled high and hungry the wolfish war cry of the Junkyard Dogs.

The Dogs' armored column had been prowling the marches of the North since the firestorms of the Sixty Minute War went out. They were born to roam, and they longed always for new horizons and fresh hunting grounds. But they had been battered and humbled in recent years, hunted themselves by ferocious traction towns. Their failed attempts to take Museion had cost them dearly in men and vehicles. They had been forced to ask for help from the technomancers of a slinking suburb they called Bugtown, and now some grumbled they were little better than Bugtown's poodles. But their thane had sworn that they would stay and watch and wait until Museion ventured from its hiding place, and the thane was a hard man, who took the head of anyone who argued.

So for months, ever since their last raid on the Frying Pan had been driven off, they'd stayed in their camp by the lake dreaming of times long gone, while up on the ridge a few picked warriors kept watch over the prey. These were all lads like Stoat who had won their manhood killing townies in the fights at the Frying Pan, and they were itchy and restless, longing to taste battle again. It seemed to them the gods had stopped making new days and were just serving up repeats of previous ones: wet days and dry days and in-between ones, and none that featured anything of interest.

But that afternoon, at long last, something new had happened. An air machine had come, bigger than any they had seen before, bonfire-bright in the light of the westering sun. It was pretty, and pretty things always angered Stoat somehow: They made him want to smash them. Pauli, the captain of the lookouts, had said the ship was too high to hit and they should not waste bullets on it. But Pauli was dim and cautious, and only in charge because he was one of Thane Worrible's many sons. The others were all yearning for some action.

Stoat sensed their mood, and it gave him the courage to disobey Pauli. A heavy swivel gun was mounted on one of the 'vans. Stoat dragged the tarpaulin off it, fitted a drum of ammunition in place, and opened up on the air machine as it droned above the lake. Pauli screamed at him to stop, of course, but Stoat could not hear him over the gun noise, or pretended that he could not. Spent shells sprayed up all shiny in the sun. The other lads took turns peeing on the gun barrel to stop it from overheating. Stoat squinted through the steam and smoke and watched his bullets poke holes in the machine's hide.

For a giddy instant, he thought it might drop out of the sky like a shot snipe, but its skin was too thick. It rose higher and buzzed away toward the Frying Pan, and Stoat kept pumping bullets after it until the gun ran empty.

It was not exactly a victory, but it felt big somehow, like a sign from the war gods that the Dogs' bad luck was mending. The others cheered so triumphantly that Pauli had to cheer too, and pretend that he was the one who had told Stoat to start shooting. Stoat sprinted straight from the kampavan to the lookout tower, and reached the top in time to see the air machine descending toward Museion. He felt in his bones that it meant something. It was like the first drip of meltwater after a hard freeze: a sign that things were on the change.

Pauli sent one of the pups to tell Thane Worrible how he had wounded the air machine, and that night the lookouts broached a keg of wine and danced around their campfires on the ridge, shouting their war cries, singing the old songs, telling again the tales of their raid on the Frying Pan last summer and drinking toasts to the lads who had not come back. And between the dances Stoat paused, sweaty, panting, eyeing the distant lights of Museion. He wondered who had arrived aboard that orange ship, and what they were doing out there in the trapped city.

The messenger pup was back before midnight, scrabbling his way up the steep track from the lake. Stoat and Pauli went to meet him as he reached the top, both asking the same thing. "You saw Thane Worrible? What did he say?"

"He said you did good, Pauli," the kid said, reciting carefully in case he muddled the thane's words. "He said the air machine is called *Firey 'Stonishment*. It carries warriors the townies have hired to help them fight us. A man called Doom and his companions."

Stoat felt dizzy with the dancing and the drink. "How can Worrible know all that?"

"His Bugtown witch told him. She knows everything that happens in Museion."

The boy made the sign against evil as he spoke. So did Stoat. None of the Dogs liked Bugtown. None of them trusted the alliance their thane had made with Bugtown's bosses. And they were all afraid of the thane's new Bugtown technomancer, the woman they called Worrible's witch. But Pauli turned to the lads around the fire and shouted, "You hear that? The townies have real warriors to help them now. We won't just be fighting useless old men. We'll face real fighters, so there'll be honor in it when we take their heads!"

The Junkyard Dogs threw back their heads and howled. The fire was hot on their faces, the sparks went up and up into the night, and the antic shadows of their dancing jerked and flickered on the heather and the stones.

7

Museum Light

Tamzin woke late, and lay for a while wondering where she was, half convinced she was still dreaming. Morning sunlight shone on her through arched windows with a hundred tiny panes. There was a shelf of books beside her bed, and another on which weird Old-Tech trinkets were displayed. She wondered if she had fallen asleep in a museum.

But slowly it came back to her: the arrival on Museion, and the talk in the Senior Common Room, which had gone on late into the night. Most of it had flown over Tamzin's head. None of the learned gentlemen she had spoken with had even heard of Mortmain or his Arcade, so her hopes of finding a clue here to his whereabouts were dashed, but at least the food had been tasty and plentiful. Afterward, Rowan Bellweather had led the newcomers to this tall, narrow house, which was to be their home while they were aboard Museion. There was no shortage of good houses on Museion now, he said, since so many of the residents had fled. Hilly and Doom were on the top floor, Max was down on the ground level, and Tamzin had the whole middle floor to herself.

Throwing off the bedclothes, Tamzin set out to explore her new quarters. As well as a bedroom, she had a study, a dressing room, and a bathroom with a deep, white porcelain tub. The rooms were high-ceilinged, wide-windowed, and deep-carpeted. The previous resident, a lecturer in Old Technology, had fled Museion after the first nomad attack, and had left most of his clothes behind. Tamzin helped herself to a cream-colored shirt, which she wore like a tunic, rolling up the sleeves and belting it around the middle. His trousers were far too long for her, but her own brown breeches and tall aviator's boots looked well enough under the shirt. Studying herself in the mirror, she felt cautiously pleased. Her black hair hung almost to her shoulders now, softening the outline of her plain, brown face. She no longer looked like Tamzin Pook, the Arcade star. She took her nagging worries about Mortmain and locked them carefully away in a deep drawer of her mind. She was a new Tamzin for a new town.

Voices and a smell of fresh-baked bread lured her downstairs. The others were already sitting down to breakfast in the big, sunlit kitchen. The bread had arrived with Rowan Bellweather, whose family ran a bakery on the lower tier. "The last working bakery on Museion," he said sadly. Then he brightened and said, "Professor Loomis has given me the morning off. If you like, I could show you the collection."

He was looking at Tamzin when he said it, but Hilly said, "Oh, yes, we should love to!" before Tamzin could decide if she wanted to see the collection or not. (*A collection of* what? she wondered.)

"You do that," said Doom, touched as always by Hilly's enthusiasm. "That's what we're here to save, after all. I need to go below and talk with Mr. Voss, the chief engineer. I'd like you with me, Max. He's a prickly customer by all accounts, and I might rub him the wrong way. Your Angmering charm will win him over."

"Oh, I'm not sure about that," said Rowan Bellweather nervously. "I'm not sure charm works on Luka Voss. I wish Mr. Troutbeck was still in charge down there. Troutbeck was chief engineer till a couple of years back, and a nice old fellow. But he was killed in a fall and the engine district workers chose Luka to replace him. I'm sure he's a good engineer, but he's — well, you have to make allowances for him, that's all."

"He sounds most mysterious," said Max, wishing he were going with Tamzin and Hilly instead.

"What about Vespertine?" wondered Hilly.

"Would it — I mean she — be interested in the collection?" Rowan asked doubtfully.

"We wouldn't want her to feel left out," said Hilly. "We should call in at the Air Staithe on our way, and ask her to join us."

❁

They called at the Staithe, and Vespertine came with them, crossing the park in the morning sunlight with Small Cat perched on her shoulder like a pirate's parrot. The park was called the Quadrangle, Rowan said. From the tall buildings all around, empty windows looked down on them.

"This place was crowded once," said Rowan. "Professors, researchers, students from the finest cities of the Hunting Ground, and a whole town of folk to cook and clean and keep things running for them, and bake their bread, and bind their books. Now there are barely a thousand souls aboard. That's how I ended up a navigator, instead of a baker like my dad. My sister, Barley, works in the navigation suite too: Professor Loomis says girls must do their bit now as well as boys."

"I should hope so," said Hilly approvingly.

The collection was housed in a large building on the starboard side of the Quadrangle. At first it seemed dull: aisle upon aisle of glass cases filled with corroded lumps of soil and metal, each with a handwritten label beside it. But Hilly cried out in wonder and ran from case to case delightedly, like a child let loose in a toy shop. That made Tamzin look more closely at the exhibits, and she found that what had seemed just clots of rust were actually the remains of computer-brains, goggle-screens, and some of the other miracle-machines with which the Ancients had filled their world.

She started to understand why Hilly thought it important to save all this stuff. It had been lost for so long, and then dug up with such care. How could they be so *old*, that blue glass bowl, that battered plastic shoe? They had been just everyday things once, but they were touched now with the magic of deep time. To look at them was to be connected in some way with people who had made and used them thousands of years before. And Museion itself had something of the same quality. The elegant old architecture, the way the sunlight lay in the big rooms, it all felt solemn and mysterious, filled with a high seriousness Tamzin could not explain.

"There is a great deal more," said Rowan, almost apologetically, for Tamzin and Vespertine were so quiet that he feared the tour might be boring them. "And there is the library too, and the Natural History Collection . . ."

"It is marvelous!" said Hilly. "Oh, Rowan, it is better than anything I had dreamed of! So much knowledge, and so many treasures! The sooner we can help Museion leave this place and carry it all safely to London, the happier I shall be."

They moved on through the collection. One small case held finds from North America, that accursed continent where no one had dared venture since the Sixty Minute War. Although *someone* must have, Tamzin realized, because they had brought back a few mobile phones, which looked just like the mobile phones from other lands, and a faded, melted plastic sign on which the word "WENDY'S" could dimly be deciphered. There were coins bearing the faces of the old Kings of America, and a brass medallion with a smiling sun embossed on it, so familiar that Tamzin almost passed it by . . .

With a shock of recognition, she came back to look more closely. The medallion was almost exactly like the one she wore around her own neck, the one thing she owned that had belonged to her unknown parents.

"What's this?" she asked, bending so close to peer at it that her nose bumped against the glass. There was no writing on her own medallion, but on this one letters curved above and below the sun-face, blurred by time but still readable. "THURSDAY" they said, and "APOLLO NUEVO."

Rowan consulted a handwritten list next to the display. "It is a religious medal."

"Who is Apollo Nuevo?"

"I'm not sure . . . Sorry . . . Oh, but, look, here comes Professor Stanislaus! He's sure to know!"

A man was walking along the aisle toward them, carrying a bundle of leather-bound notebooks. He wore the ginger robes of a Senior Fellow, but Tamzin had not seen him in the welcoming committee at the Air Staithe the night before. He was a very thin man, and although he was not terribly old he was terribly *gray* — not just his hair, but the pale skin of his face and hands too, as if he were a black-and-white photograph that had been magicked into life.

He seemed surprised to find visitors in the collection. His eyes met Tamzin's as he drew near, moved to Hilly, narrowed a little as he tried to work out who they were, then widened as he looked past them and saw Vespertine standing in the shadows like a suit of haunted armor. He stopped then, and almost dropped his pile of books.

"What is the meaning of this?" he asked. His voice sounded gray too, and rather peevish.

"Professor Stanislaus," said Rowan, "may I introduce —"

"No, Mr. Bellweather. No, you may not! No! How dare you bring this . . . this . . . this *thing* into the collection?"

"This is the Revenant Vespertine," said Tamzin, stepping between Vespertine and the professor. "She's going to keep you and your collection safe when you bust out of this Frying Pan."

"Vespertine is part of Mr. Doom's team, sir," said Rowan. "They are here at the dean's invitation."

Professor Stanislaus seemed to accept that he was defeated. "Then . . . Then at least keep the monstrosity out of my sight!" he muttered, and, turning, stalked away.

"He does not like me," said Vespertine, calmly stroking Small Cat, who had fled onto the top of her head when the shouting started.

"Poor old Stanislaus," said Rowan. "He's been very ill, they say. Don't take any notice of him. I don't suppose he means it."

Tamzin patted Vespertine's hand. "He'll be glad enough of you if the nomads jump us."

Rowan looked nervously at her. "Do you really think you can beat them?"

Tamzin shrugged.

Hilly said, "If anyone can, it is Oddington Doom."

8

Below Decks

Oddington Doom had been exploring the pantry of his new quarters and discovered a rack of wine bottles that the previous resident had forgotten to take with him. He wiped the dust and cobwebs from one and handed it to Max, who carried it as they made their way down a broad staircase into Museion's depths.

Museion's base tier was much like the base tier of any other town or city. In the residential districts farther forward, skylights let down shafts of sunlight from above, but as they walked toward the city's stern Max and Doom entered a world of shadows, where the city's massive engines slumbered, waiting to be roused. They seemed in good condition, far cleaner than the engines of Thorbury, which were the only other city engines Max had seen up close. The pistons gleamed, the brass balls on the governors showed him spoonily distorted reflections of his own face, and the red-overalled workers in the engine halls all seemed to know their jobs and to be doing them efficiently. The only things that looked out of place were the bundles of herbs and heron feathers that hung above each engine, and the shrine under the main heat exchanger, wet with the blood of a freshly slaughtered chicken.

"That's how Luka likes it," said the foreman, who directed Max and Doom to the main control room. "A load of old nomad superstitions if you ask me, but don't tell Luka I said that. He follows his mother's gods, and he likes to keep 'em happy."

"Is Mr. Voss a nomad, then?" asked Max as they went aft.

"Half the world were nomads once," said Doom. "Up in these northern marches the old ways die hard."

Maintenance work was going on nearby, and the din of hammers and buzz saws made further talk impossible. It seemed troubling to Max that Museion's chief engineer still honored the nomad gods. If things came to a fight, would he not be as likely to side with the Junkyard Dogs as with the people of this little city?

They found him enthroned in a vast leather swivel chair in the control room. He did not get up to greet them. Only when Doom said, "It's time to talk about getting this old place moving" did Voss even bother to spin his chair around and look at them.

He was surprisingly ugly. That was the first thing Max noticed about him — that bony face with its wide mouth, small black eyes and pale skin, framed by lank black hair. But Voss was also surprisingly young: not much more than twenty, barely older than Max himself. How could he possibly know enough to keep a whole city moving?

Voss looked his visitors quickly up and down, and did not seem much impressed by either of them. When Max held out the wine bottle, he ignored it. When Doom took it and set it on the deck beside his chair, he went on ignoring it. "Has the dean told you I am not ready to start the engines?" he asked. "Does he think I don't know my job?"

"No," said Doom. "Nothing like that. In fact, the dean spoke very highly of you."

He was trying to be charming. There were very few people Oddington Doom could not charm if he put his mind to it. Unfortunately, Luka Voss seemed to be one of them.

"Thing is," Doom went on, "we're being watched. When Museion gets going, it'll need to go fast."

"You think I don't know this?" sneered Luka Voss. "I read every memo from the Ivory Tower. When the order comes to move, we will move, and we will move very fast. But to get up steam will take three, maybe four hours."

Doom nodded. "That's good. That's quick. Could we do it at night, so the nomads won't see the smoke?"

"They will see the fire from our furnaces. They are not stupid, even if you are."

Voss's arrogance was beginning to infuriate Max. "Don't you know who this is?" he asked. "Mr. Doom has saved better towns than this from worse foes than the Junkyard Dogs."

Luka Voss's beetle-black eyes, which had glanced with so little interest at him earlier, found Max's face again, and this time lingered. "Yes, I know who he is, and I know who you are, Max Meringue. I know about your airship, and your tame Stalker, and your girlfriend."

"Tamzin is not my girlfriend, and my name is *Angmering*," Max said, then realized Voss had been baiting him. "What if we were to set fire to the stubble in the fields?" he suggested. "And the gorse on the slopes of the Frying Pan? I've seen farming towns do that, clearing brush, at this time of year. The fires would hide the smoke from your engines and the glow from your furnaces."

Voss raised an eyebrow. He was silent for a moment. Then he said, "Well, you may only be a meringue, but you are not entirely stupid. I like this idea."

❁

"What a twerp," Max muttered angrily as they climbed back to the upper deck.

"He has a chip on his shoulder — that's all," said Doom. "He expects people not to like him because of how young he is and how he looks. He acts all tough so nobody can hurt him. But he's a good engineer by all accounts. The engine district people swear by him. And your idea about the fires is a good 'un. He was impressed by that."

Max blushed with pride. "But what about the nomads? They'll still see us when we move."

"Not if we blind them."

"How?"

"If a couple of us creep up on to that ridge and knock out that lookout post right before Museion moves off, their friends camped around the lake may not know a thing about it."

"A couple of us . . . ? You mean Vespertine?"

Doom shook his head, pausing for breath halfway up the stairs. "Revenants are terror weapons — they're not built for sneak attacks. Those glowing eyes of Vespertine's would give us away."

"Then . . . me?" asked Max.

Doom gave him an unreadable look and said, "Most likely."

He went on up the stairs, and Max followed. He felt fiercely glad that Doom would trust him with such a mission, but also terrified that he would be called upon to do such things, and so soon. Was it not cowardly to sneak up upon the nomads in the dark, rather than facing them in a fair fight? He wondered how it would feel to kill someone. On Thorbury, the fighting had mostly been a matter of firing guns wildly into the shadows, and he had never been sure if he'd actually hit anyone. This night attack of Doom's would mean knives, he supposed. And the nomads had guns and axes . . .

"Come on, Max!" Doom yelled, already out in the sunlight at the top of the stairs. "We have work to do!"

9

Pringles for Breakfast

Everyone aboard Museion had work to do in the next few days. Under Doom's direction, the little city began to stage a sort of play or conjuring trick, whose only audience was the watchers in the nomad lookout post.

Each night, gangs of men went up to the artillery emplacements on the ramparts and swapped the guns Dr. Twyne had stationed there with replicas built from junk and painted cardboard. The real guns were carried back one by one into the city and installed on the balconies that lined the edges of the upper tier. Each day, down in the shadows between the tracks, out of sight of hungry eyes, Dr. Twyne's militia trained. They practiced cleaning, loading, and aiming their hodge-podge of hunting rifles and antique firearms, though very seldom actually firing them. Lead was being stripped from rooftops and gutterings all over the city to mold into bullets, but ammunition was still in short supply. The militia contented themselves with shouting "bang" instead.

Meanwhile, the folk of the city's farms took in the last of their harvests. Up the ramps into the city they led as many of their livestock as they reckoned could survive the journey.

The rest were slaughtered, and the meat smoked or salted.

There was still time, between her various duties, for Tamzin to explore. Hilly insisted she visit the Art Gallery, where each gilded frame was like a window, giving her a glimpse into other places and other ages of the world. But Tamzin preferred those parts of Museion she discovered on her own, by accident, like the old stairway near the bows where the bannisters were decorated with carvings of whales, elephants, and a little dog, or Dark Park, near the front of the lower tier. She had found her way to the park on her third day aboard Museion, and liked it so much that she took to slipping down there whenever she felt the need to be alone. Shafts of daylight reached down into it through light wells in the tier above, and wherever the light fell, flower beds had been planted and benches arranged. But between the beds and benches the park really was dark, and there in the shadows stood all the statues Museion had collected on its travels, like a conclave of ghosts. There were tall, stern-looking men and women who must have been important before time wore away the legends carved upon their pedestals, and winsome, weeping girls from ornate tombs. Most were likenesses of real people, Tamzin supposed, and what would those people have thought if they could have known that a hundred or a thousand or two thousand years after their deaths she would be standing in the Dark Park, studying their faces?

"Don't you worry," she told them. (It was easier to speak to statues than to real, live people.) "We'll make sure you get safe to London." And, if no one was around to see, she would pat their stony feet or hands or, if she could reach, use a damp handkerchief to clean the pigeon droppings from their hair.

❁

Each evening there was a meal in the Great Hall. The students and Junior Fellows ate at long tables, while the Senior Fellows and their wives and guests sat at the High Table, on a raised dais under the hall's splendid rose window. Before anyone could take their seat, the dean walked three times around the hall and declared that all present were friends and fellow scholars. Then everyone said, "Huzzah!" three times, and sat down to eat. It seemed like a lot of pointless fuss to Tamzin, but Hilly explained that it was an old tradition, and that traditions were important for binding a city together and making its people feel part of something bigger than themselves.

"We'll be part of something bigger than ourselves once London eats us," said Professor Waghorn, Tamzin's neighbor at her first such dinner. His robes were corduroy, not tweed, and his spectacles had square black plastic frames. Tamzin thought his bushy ginger sideburns made him look like a monkey. "I expect you find all this pomp and circumstance as absurd as I do, Miss Pook?" he asked her.

But the food was so good that Tamzin didn't really mind the fancy dress and rituals that went with it. Nor did she care that the conversation at the High Table went mostly over her head. She ate and watched and half listened while the Fellows grew excited discussing things she had never heard of. Hilly was in her element, debating the causes of the Second Wheeled War and the poems of Lady Zhou. Max chipped in with an opinion sometimes. Doom looked on fondly, convinced that Hilly was the wisest person in the world and more than a match for Museion's dusty professors. Tamzin just kept quiet and waited for dessert.

Afterward, when the diners were nibbling cheese and crackers to fill up any remaining gaps not already filled with beef, suet pudding, and jam roly-poly, the dean would stand up to ask in a theatrical voice, "Are we well fed?" and one of the Junior Fellows would reply,

"We are well fed indeed!" while Professor Waghorn rolled his eyes and sighed to show that he was too sophisticated for such nonsense. Then Professor Pott-Walloper would offer thanks to Peripatetia, and Professor Pringle would announce the next day's weather.

Pringle was a small, round, sandy-haired man with a small, round, sandy-haired wife, and together they had devoted their lives to rediscovering the Ancient art of weather forecasting. Pringle delivered his predictions in the proper, Ancient manner, standing in front of a large wall map to which Mrs. Pringle enthusiastically applied cut-out paper symbols to represent sun, rain, snow, and wind. The forecasts were seldom very accurate — it often rained on days when the Pringles said it wouldn't, and failed to rain on days when they said it would — and the Senior Fellows paid little attention. But Oddington Doom always listened carefully.

❁

One morning, coming downstairs into the shared kitchen of their house, Tamzin found that Doom and Hilly had invited the Pringles for breakfast. The table was covered with their complicated charts. "There is a hard winter coming," Pringle said. "The birds of the north began their migrations far earlier than usual, and there are other signs. They all point to a prolonged cold snap. Perhaps even a new ice age, like the one that put an end to the Raffia Hat Era . . ."

"When we were young," said Mrs. Pringle wistfully, "Professor Pringle and I would hike right up high into the mountains, making our observations. It is not always possible to predict when a shower will start, or when the sun will shine, but when it comes to the long-term trends we are almost always correct."

Doom rubbed the graying stubble on his chin, as he often did when he was pondering a problem. "So if Museion doesn't leave the Frying Pan soon, it could be snowed in here till next spring at least. When do you think it will start, this cold snap of yours?"

The Pringles looked at each other. "It is hard to be certain . . ." said the professor.

"Perhaps within the next few days," said his wife.

Doom grunted, and looked thoughtfully out the window. In the Quadrangle, Dr. Twyne's militia were busy training. Students clad in antique armor hollered unconvincing war cries as they took turns to bayonet a dangling burlap punching bag, while others shot crossbows in the general direction of a target, or pointed rifles at a line of cardboard nomads and yelled, "Bang!"

"Ready or not, we need to get going," he said. "Tonight."

"Tonight?" said Max, turning pale.

"Tonight?" said Hilly. "Oh, Oddington!"

Doom hugged her. "Don't fret, Hilly. We came here to save this place and save it we will. We'll light some smudge fires in the Frying Pan this evening, and tonight I'll pay a call on the Junkyard Dogs. There weren't more than half a dozen blokes on that ridge that I could see."

"But you cannot fight them alone!"

"I don't intend to fight 'em. I'll have surprise on my side, and I'll tackle them one by one. Bind and gag them if I can, kill them if I need to. And I won't be alone. I reckon I'll take Tamzin with me."

"Tamzin?" Max felt terribly relieved, and then terribly disappointed and ashamed. "I thought you said it would be me? I will go!"

Doom shook his head. "Are you up for a fight, Tamzin?"

Tamzin nodded. She didn't have to think about it. She didn't much care for the idea of killing living people, but if that was what had to be done to keep her friends and this city safe, she reckoned she could do it.

"I'll come," she said.

"Good girl," said Doom, and laughed at all their worried faces. "It'll be all right. Ain't this what we came looking for when we left Thorbury behind? Adventure and a chance to set the world to rights, or at least some small part of it? I'll go straight over to the Ivory Tower and let Prof Twyne and the dean know."

"I still think I should come," said Max, catching up with him as he set out across the Quadrangle. "Three is better than two."

Doom turned and looked into his flushed, earnest, almost fearful face, then laid a hand on his shoulder. "You're not ready, Max. Young Tamzin's been in a hundred fights and come safe and sound through all of 'em. You've just seen one, and it was nothing like tonight's outing. It's not that I don't trust you. It's more I don't trust myself to bring you home in one piece."

"You mean Tamzin can look after herself," said Max bitterly. "And I can't — is that it?"

"That's about the size of it," Doom agreed. "Not yet, anyway. You'll stay here, and run messages down to Voss and his people in the engine district. He likes you."

"No, he doesn't! He calls me 'Meringue.'"

"That's just his idea of friendly banter, I reckon. Anyway, I need you to keep an eye on Hilly for me. If things do go wrong, you'll have to fly her safe away. You can handle the *Fire's Astonishment* better than any of us."

Max nodded, but he knew Doom was only trying to make him feel better. He had to turn away then, because, appallingly, he felt tears coming. What was he doing here? He was no use to his friends, or to Museion, or to anyone. He wished he had stayed behind in Thorbury.

10

The Night Attack

Fires were being lit on the inner slopes of the Frying Pan when Doom and Tamzin made their way up to the ramparts that evening. The smoke rose straight up into the still and cloudless sky, forming a screen that would hide Museion from the watchers in the north.

Doom led the way along the rampart to the eastern redoubt. The replica guns there looked comical when you saw them up close, made from old packing crates with lengths of drainpipe for barrels. The gunners looked comical too, in their makeshift uniforms and antique helmets. But the burned-out skeletons of the assault vehicles they had destroyed during the last nomad attack lay half buried in the grass on the outer face of the Frying Pan. Tamzin noticed a late butterfly perching in one of the wrecks as she went after Doom down the steep slope and out on to the plain.

They moved quickly across rough, tussocky ground and into an old track mark that some passing town had made decades before. The mark ran roughly north toward the mountains, and its once-sheer walls had slumped and crumbled so that it was not hard to scramble down into it. Alder, willow, and birch grew there, clustering around deep pools from which ducks sometimes rose as Tamzin and Doom pushed their way through the thickets.

They went in silence, each busy with their own thoughts. Tamzin was thinking of Max, who had been so distant and unhappy when they said goodbye. She knew it had been hard on him, not being chosen for this expedition. He must feel like a coward, and young men hated that — she had seen it often with her fellow fighters in the Arcade, and she knew it could be deadly, making them take silly risks to prove themselves. Max did not need to prove himself to her. She wished she could have told him that, but she could not think of a way to say it that would not sound false. She wished now that she had tried anyway.

Doom's thoughts were mostly focused on what lay ahead, but from time to time a memory of Hilly distracted him. It was a constant surprise to him, to find himself so deeply in love at an age when such things had seemed far behind him. A brave, brittle old bird, he'd thought when he first set eyes on her. Now he could not understand how he had not noticed her surprising beauty. Hilly had a stern face, but when she smiled Doom could see what she had looked like as a girl. And she made him feel like a boy again, like a little child sometimes, safe and snug. There was a gentleness in Oddington Doom that he had hidden long ago, and kept hidden through many hard and dangerous years, but it came out when he was with Hilly. It made him wistful sometimes, to think of the life they might have shared if only they had met when they were young . . .

But at least the gods had brought their paths together now. And they would have a few years yet, he reckoned, as long as he stopped letting his thoughts wander so. He would need his wits about him tonight. *Concentrate, Doom* . . .

It was slow going along the track mark, and the way was often barred by fallen trees and sprawling masses of brambles. By the time they reached the place near the foot of the ridge where the mark curved away eastward, the sky was growing dark and the first stars were showing. They stopped for a swig of water (Hilly had made Doom promise to drink nothing stronger when he was working). Then, trusting the gathering dark to hide them, they climbed out of the track mark and set off across open country.

Behind them, the lights of Museion's taller buildings glowed above the black rampart of the Frying Pan. Ahead, the ridge rose, very close. Tamzin could see no sign of the nomad's nightly camp fires, and guessed they must be hidden among the crags on the top. But the stars were old friends of Doom's, and he said they would guide him straight to the target.

"Look," he said, pointing out constellations as they walked. "There is the Pole Star, and that bright one is the Hamster Wheel. There is the Mankini. And those three stars in a line there are the Ladder of Beyoncé . . ."

A frost was settling, and the long grass through which they pushed their way was crisp and cold to the touch. For a long time, they barely seemed to make any progress at all. Then, quite suddenly it seemed, the ground was rising. Above them, black against the near-black sky, Tamzin thought she could make out the spindly shape of the nomads' watchtower, and a dim light showing in the wicker crow's nest at its top. She touched the hilt of the knife in her belt, just to be sure of it. She touched the sun disc that hung around her neck for good luck. Her body was readying itself for what was to come, muscles tensing, adrenaline surging. It was the feeling that had come to her always in the Arcade, waiting backstage for a show to begin. She realized that she had missed this feeling.

A sudden movement to her left made her start, but it was only deer, a small herd of them, flashing their white tails in the darkness as they went bounding away. She drew her knife, and started up the slope.

❁

Movement! Down there where the screes ended . . . Stoat crouched, waiting, scanning the dark below, until the running things moved across a pale patch of grass.

"Just deer," said one of the other Dogs, waiting beside him.

Stoat nodded quickly, still watching. Just deer. But what had set them running?

A pup had come up from the Hundberg earlier that day with a message from the thane. Museion was trying something: There would be people coming. No one bothered to wonder how Thane Worrible knew this secret. They all knew he must have heard it from his witch, who had heard it from her friends in Bugtown. The Bugtowners spoke with spirits. Some said they kept a chained demon to mind their engines.

Stoat did not know if he believed that, and he knew he did not trust Worrible's witch, but the warning could not be ignored. Even stupid, lazy Pauli knew that. He might be the thane's own son, but the thane had plenty more sons and he would still have Pauli's head if he slipped up and let the prey town get away. He had kept his little outfit tight and ready all day, forbidding the bantering and napping with which they usually filled their time up on the ridge.

In the late afternoon, smoke had begun to billow from the Frying Pan, and they had thought at first that Museion was firing up its engines. But the excitement was short-lived. It looked as if the townies were just burning off scrub or stubble, preparing their scanty fields for next year's sowing. Which meant they planned to stay a few more seasons, and the Dogs would have to overwinter here. The lookouts grew irritable, dismayed by the prospect of cold months in camp, the lake frozen hard, food scarce. Stoat felt the same, but he kept watching. Someone would come. Something would happen. Worrible's witch had foretold it.

"Deer," said Yanna, creeping through the heather, crouching down beside him with her bow. He could smell her sweat. Yanna was Stoat's girl, for now at least. She was a squat, solid, dangerous girl, and the others mocked him sometimes for sticking with her, but she was the best kampavan driver in the whole pack. "We should go after them, Stoat," she whispered. "Tell Pauli. We'll need meat for winter. Warm hides too. They'll be far away by morning."

"Ssst!" hissed Stoat, holding up a hand for quiet. The darkness down below was blacker than the Pits of Czilkay, but Stoat sensed something moving in it. Something sly and cautious. A fox, maybe? A polecat?

"There!" he said, glimpsing for a moment a shape that was surely human. And the frustrations of the long day vanished, and the Dogs were scrambling for their kampavans and howling their war cries.

❁

Tamzin was crouching halfway up the steep slope when the shouting started. She had stopped to wait for Doom, who had fallen behind, grumbling softly about his aching knees and how he was not as young as he once was. She was waiting for him to catch up when that chorus of howls broke out above her. Sudden light swept over the screes. Tamzin dropped behind a boulder as the bright beam came rushing at her. Ten yards downslope, Doom dropped too, but he was stiff after the long hike from the Frying Pan and he did not drop quite fast enough. The shouting grew fiercer, with a sound of triumph in it. Tamzin heard an arrow whisk through the dry grass heads nearby with a sound like a terse sigh.

"They've seen us," she hissed, slithering her way downhill to Doom. "What do we do now?"

"Retreat," ordered Doom, starting to wriggle away. But an engine snarled, and when Tamzin bobbed her head up to look she saw two vehicles barreling down the slope with bow waves of loose stones bounding ahead of them. The searchlight was mounted on the front of one. The ground ahead of it blazed white, and black shadows raced and danced among the rocks.

Tamzin considered her knife, comparing it with the larger and more impressive weapons being waved by the silhouettes who clung like apes to the tops and sides of those vehicles. *No way out of this one*, she thought, and felt not fear so much as a dull disappointment. There were just two choices now: fight and die, or surrender and hope to escape later, if the Dogs did not just kill her out of hand.

"There's too many of them," she shouted to Doom, and stood up in the full glare of the lamp, raising both arms, spreading her fingers wide.

She had been afraid Doom would try to fight it out, but after a moment he rose too, grunting with the effort, and tossed his gun and knife into the grass. "They must have been keeping a good watch," he said. "Like they knew we were coming. But how?"

It did not seem to Tamzin to matter very much. Bouncing

stones hammered at her shins and ankles as the lead vehicle swerved past her and stopped just below. The other waited above so that she and Doom were penned between the two vehicles. The kampavans were armored clumsily with rusty steel. Figures came scrambling down from their roofs and out of hatches on their sides. Shots were fired, but just into the air. Someone knocked Doom down. "Leave him!" shouted Tamzin, and was knocked down herself by a wiry young man who knelt on her chest before she could get up again. He took her knife and gun and checked her for other weapons.

"How many are you?" He spoke in Anglish with a hard northern accent. "Where are the others?" His whole weight was on Tamzin's chest, and the stench of his unwashed body all around her. She could barely breathe, let alone answer. Night-flying insects whirled like snowflakes through the beams from the lamps. She heard more shouting nearby and wondered what was happening to Doom. She gurgled something. The nomad seemed to understand the problem and eased some of his weight off her. "How many?"

"Just us two," croaked Tamzin.

The nomad grabbed her face and wrenched it toward the light. "This one's a girl!" he shouted.

"It's just a girl and an old man," said one of the others.

"Can't be!" scoffed a third. "Search around! Find the rest! The townies wouldn't send a girl and an old man against us, not alone."

"Maybe girls and old men are all they've got left, Pauli," said the one kneeling on Tamzin. The lamp had swung away and she could see him now as well as smell him: an underfed youth with cruelty and cunning in his pale-blue eyes. He had reddish hair, long, tied back. His leather jacket was branded with a battle logo in the shape of a spiky black dog. When Tamzin looked sideways, she saw the same dog on the others too, here as a hat badge, there a tattoo. A bunch of the nomads had gathered around Doom, who was down in the grass.

"Leave him," she said again, not expecting them to listen.

"Who is he?" asked her captor. He stood over her and poked her in the ribs with the toe of his boot. "Who are you? You from Museion? Come to kill us, did you?" There was a scratchy wildness in his voice. "They wanted us gone so they could move their poxy town out without us seeing!" he shouted to his friends. "They thought a girl and an old man would be a match for the Junkyard Dogs!" He let out a doglike howl, and others joined in.

"We're not from the town," said Tamzin loudly and firmly, hoping to calm him. She had seen Arcade fighters get like this before a show, working themselves up toward violence. "We're travelers," she told him. "Adventurers."

"You're the ones who flew over in that air machine!" said the nomad, treating her to a jagged grin. "I put holes in that. Now I'll put holes in you." He used his knife to cut the leather cord around her neck, and pulled the sun disc out from inside her shirt.

"That's mine," said Tamzin.

He hit her hard, and the hilt of his knife gashed her cheek. He held the sun disc up in the light from the kampavans and peered at it. "Mine now," he said, knotting the cord and looping it over his own head.

"Leave her, Stoat!" shouted one of the others. He came out of the shadows. Bigger than Stoat, his head was shaved except for a long horse tail of blond hair hanging from the middle of his scalp. The black dog was stenciled badly on his breastplate. "The thane might want to question them. You take them down to the Hundberg. Take Yanna and a couple of lads with you. The rest of us will stay here and keep the watch."

"Eat dung, Pauli!" the one called Stoat yelled. "I ain't your errand pup! I'm staying here. If the fun starts, I don't want to miss it."

Pauli did not answer, but a few young nomads who seemed loyal to him reached for their weapons. Tamzin hoped for a second they might all turn on one another, and maybe in the fighting she and Doom would have a chance to slip away. The wind blew the grass, and the hot metal of the two kampavans ticked as it cooled. A few last stones went rattling by in search of resting places farther down the scree.

"All right," grumbled Stoat, backing down. "Yanna, Krowbar, Hound, you're with me. Get the townies aboard *War Baby.*"

Rough hands dragged Tamzin to the smaller of the two kampavans. An armored door slid open and she was thrown on to a hard deck. Oddington Doom landed beside her and lay still. *If he's dead*, thought Tamzin, *Hilly will never forgive me.*

But how would Hilly ever know? For already the kampavan's engines were running and it was turning, tilting alarmingly on the steep slope as it prepared to scramble over the ridge, down to the lake and the main encampment of the Junkyard Dogs.

11

Miss Torpenhow, in the Library, with the Dagger

Along the starboard side of Museion's top deck there ran a broad strip of parkland called the Library Gardens. There, in the deepening twilight, Hilly walked, and looked toward the north, and worried for her friends. She had no appetite that evening, and she had felt unable to contribute much to the conversations about the coming journey, which was all anyone wanted to talk about at dinner. After half a bowl of soup, she had excused herself, hoping that fresh air and a brisk stroll would settle her nerves.

They did not. Again and again she felt her eyes drawn northward, although there was nothing to see there. The smokescreen from the smudge fires in the Frying Pan hid the nomads' hills from her as surely as they hid Museion from the nomads, and by that time the city's engines were waking up, and fumes from the smokestacks were adding to the fug.

She was about to leave when someone called her name. She turned to see Rowan Bellweather coming toward her.

The young navigator had seen her walk out of the Great Hall, and guessed at once what was troubling her. "I am worried for them too," he said, peering northward just as she had, trying to pierce the veils of smoke.

"No need to worry," said Hilly brightly. Whatever she might be feeling privately, she felt it was bad luck to say such things aloud. "Oddington Doom is more capable of looking after himself than anyone I have ever known. He has survived hundreds of such adventures, many of them far more perilous than tonight's expedition. He and Tamzin will be back in an hour or two, full of pride at a job well done. Then Museion can be on its way."

Rowan nodded, happy to believe her. "She is very brave, isn't she?" he said after a moment.

"Tamzin? The bravest. I must tell you at some point about the way she fought Strega's stalkers on Thorbury. And the Revenant in Paris — now *that* was an adventure . . ."

"Do you think she . . . ?" said Rowan. "I mean, I was wondering if I . . ."

"You would like to ask her out?" asked Hilly, and beamed at him. Now that she was in love herself, she wanted everyone else to be as happy as she was. "I think that is a splendid idea," she said. "Tamzin is as sweet a girl as you could hope to meet, but she is desperately shy. I think she had to build a sort of wall around herself to survive all those years in Mortmain's horrible Amusement Arcade. She is really not sure how to handle ordinary life at all. I think a friendship with a young man like yourself — a gentle, respectful, kind young man — would do her the world of good. You must certainly ask her when she is back aboard. I shall be sure to put in a good word for you."

Rowan had turned very pink, and they stood in silence for a while, feeling the deckplates vibrate underfoot as Luka Voss and his people tried out the engines down below. Then Rowan said,

"Shall I show you the library? There was not time the other day."

"Is it not locked up at this hour?"

"I have a key. Senior staff have passkeys to all the main buildings."

"It seems strange to think of one so young as senior staff. But why not? I should love to see the library, and I don't think I shall be able to sleep tonight. I must be wide awake when Tamzin and Oddington return, so that I can make them a nice pot of tea, and hot baths. Oddington tends to forget that he is no longer a young man. It leads him to overstrain himself."

❁

They entered the library by its rear door, which opened directly onto the park. Deep shadows lay within, filled with the comforting, dusty scent of many books. Finding their way by what dim light came through the windows, they walked to the front of the building, where the librarian's desk stood deserted, facing the main door across an expanse of polished parquet floor. Rowan flicked the light switches, and the electric lamps came on in green glass shades. Aisle upon aisle of bookshelves stood waiting to be explored. *One could spend a lifetime here,* thought Hilly.

She left Rowan by the desk and went wandering between the stacks, down one aisle and up another, quickly losing herself in a booky labyrinth. There were treasures beyond counting here, arranged according to a system she did not quite grasp — she would have to ask the chief librarian about it, she thought. She brushed her fingers over the spines of a leather-bound set of all twelve plays by Shakespeare, and peered at the embossed ideograms on a whole bay of books from Shan Guo, wishing she had found time to learn the lovely language of that land. She opened drawers and looked upon etchings by Walmart Strange and Ruan Solent. And while she was studying them she heard — or thought she heard — soft footsteps in a neighboring aisle.

"Rowan?" she called out, thinking he must have grown tired of waiting for her. She closed the drawer she had been looking into and went to look for him.

The neighboring aisle was in shadow, and as she turned down it someone came charging at her, so fast and sudden that she cried out in alarm. She caught a glimpse of a long, dark robe, the deep hood shadowing the face of its wearer. His shoulder struck her, throwing her backward against the shelves. She almost lost her footing. Something heavy hit the floor nearby. Then the stranger was gone. Footsteps went pounding away between the stacks. Down at the front desk, Rowan Bellweather gave a quick cry of surprise, and then the big front door opened, and slammed shut with an echoing boom.

Hilly caught her breath, and turned to look at the thing the stranger had let fall. It was a book — the operating instructions for some kind of Old-Tech machinery, by the look of the spidery diagrams on the pages that had burst from its binding when it hit the floor. It was hardly Hilly's idea of a good read, but she hated to see a book damaged, even a dull one.

"I say!" she called indignantly, and went after the stranger. But the silence and the shadows had swallowed him, and she took a wrong turn and ended up deep in the theology section.

She retraced her steps and picked up the fallen book, hoping it could be repaired. Carrying it as carefully as if it were a wounded bird, she started back toward the front desk, wondering if Rowan had seen the careless stranger. *Such bad behavior should certainly be reported to the chief librarian*, she thought, and wished she had managed to get a look at the stranger's face.

"Rowan," she called as she emerged from the stacks, "did you happen to see —?"

Rowan Bellweather lay on the floor, halfway between the librarian's desk and the main door. He lay on his back, looking up in a puzzled way at the ceiling. Jutting from his waistcoat was the hilt of a knife.

"Oh no! Oh dear!" said Hilly, dropping the book and running to him. Her first thought was to pull the knife out, but as she knelt over him and her fingers closed upon the hilt, she remembered reading somewhere that to remove the blade from a wound in such circumstances might cause the victim to lose more blood, and Rowan had lost such a great deal of blood already, a wide, spreading, crimson pool of it.

And then she realized that it would make no difference whether the dagger was in or out, because it was very clear that the poor young man was dead.

"Oh, Rowan, my dear," she said. She hesitated a moment, and then, steadying her shaking hands, pulled the dagger out of him. It had looked so undignified, sticking from his chest like that.

There was a flurry of sound on the steps outside. Hilly looked up in alarm. It had not occurred to her that the killer might come back.

The front doors of the library burst open. There stood Dr. Twyne, with several other gentlemen of the faculty and a couple of nervous students armed with crossbows.

"Oh, Dr. Twyne!" gasped Hilly. "Thank gods you're here! There is a murderer loose aboard your city!"

Twyne and the others did not answer. They stood on the threshold like startled statues of themselves, staring at Hilly as she knelt all atremble in the widening pool of Rowan Bellweather's blood, clutching the dagger that had killed him.

12

King of the Underworld

Max had been sent downstairs before dinner. Professor Loomis had prepared new charts of the country Museion was to travel over, and he wanted copies delivered to Luka Voss, with his compliments. "You take them, Angmering," he had said, pushing the rolled-up maps into Max's hands. "Voss told me he'd throw me into the main furnace if I showed my face down there again."

Max was annoyed at being treated as an errand boy, but secretly glad that he had something to take his mind away from what his friends were doing out there in the nomad-ridden night without him. So he took the charts and spent the next hour blundering through the complicated warrens of the lower deck, where Voss's people were making ready to move the city out the instant Tamzin and Doom returned.

Voss himself proved hard to find. He was moving from one part of the engine district to the next, checking that pistons were oiled, fuel lines clear, drive chains free from every speck of rust. He certainly took pride in his job, Max thought, as he followed the young engineer's trail past turbines and engine blocks that gleamed in the oily shadows like burnished idols in a subterranean temple.

He found Voss at last under the main drive shaft, with a bevy of his staff looking on respectfully as he carefully tapped the housings with a small wrench. He was taller than Max had realized, and his body was as ugly as his face, lanky and hunched, long in the leg and short in the torso, as if he had been assembled from parts that did not quite fit.

Tap, tap, went the wrench against one of the big nuts that held a drive shaft housing together. Voss scowled, listening to the echoes fade like a piano tuner gauging a note. "You see?" he said to the men and women who stood watching. "A bad engineer will look at the checklist and it will say 'check all nuts every two days.' But each time he checks them he maybe tightens them a little bit, and then after a month, boom, the nut shears off, and a new one must be fetched and fitted. We don't have spares to waste that way. A good engineer knows if a nut needs tightening or not by looking, by listening, by knowing."

He handed the wrench to one of his staff and came over to where Max was waiting. He had an odd, lurching walk as if his legs were different lengths, or jointed differently to normal legs. "It's the Meringue boy," he said.

"I've told you before, my name is Angmering," said Max. "But you can call me Max. That sounded smart, about the nuts. Did the old chief engineer teach you that?"

That seemed to throw Voss. He hesitated, as if trying to think of some new insult, then said, "My mother taught me. She was technomancer aboard a little marsh town in the Rustwater. The town was eaten. My mother became a slave aboard the town that ate it. One day that town stopped to trade with Museion, and Mr. Troutbeck saw her, and guessed from her tattoos that she was someone who knew her way around an engine. He was a good man, Mr. Troutbeck. He did not dismiss the old ways and the nomad gods the way most city engineers do. He did not mind what my mother was."

"A nomad, you mean?"

"A nightwight," said Voss, and bared too many sharp white teeth in a smile designed to unsettle Max.

It worked. "Nightwights are just things in old stories," Max said, trying to sound scornful. "Like werewolves, or vegans. Nightwights live in caves. They drink blood, and can't go out in daylight."

"I live in a cave," said Voss, gesturing at the iron roof above them. "Daylight hurts my eyes, and the sun burns me easily."

"And the blood?" wondered Max.

Voss ignored him. "There aren't many of us left now. 'The mutation died out' — that's what the clever fools upstairs would tell you. Nightwights and normal humans do not make babies together easily, and those babies they do make are unhealthy and do not often live. Maybe my mother was the last full-blood nightwight. Yartra Vithili Shanta Voss was her name. She was descended from Vixen of the Oakwall, who was trained by Fever Crumb, who was technomancer in the long-ago to the blind queen of Arkangel herself."

Max shrugged. He reckoned Voss was pulling his leg. He gave him Loomis's charts and explained what they were.

"New maps. Good," said Voss. He unfurled the charts and glanced at them. "It will be a hard journey, but my engines will make it. One last run before the end." For a moment he looked proud and rather wistful, and Max could see that he truly loved these great engines, even though he seemed not to care about the city they drove. Then he furled the charts again and snapped his fingers to summon one of his underlings. “Take these to the main control room.” He looked Max up and down. “You are not as completely useless as the other people up above.”

Max started to say that he was glad to hear it, but Voss was gone, lurching off to his next task with his loyal assistants hurrying after him.

“Don’t mind his manner,” said a worker Max passed on his way back to the stairs. “He’s the best engineer any of us have ever seen. We’d follow him anywhere he asked. If anyone can get us safe out of this country, Luka can.”

“Is it true he’s a nightwight?”

The woman shrugged. She was older than Voss, and kindly-looking. “Luka’s mom was a nightwight. It looked good on her, though. It wasn’t just her skills as a technomancer that made old Troutbeck rescue her.”

“You mean she and Troutbeck . . . ?”

“He married her. Luka is their son. They agreed he’d keep his mother’s name ’cause that was the way among her people. Luka was helping them with the engines from the moment he could walk, so it was natural he’d take over after they were gone. It’s in his blood, you see. Luka’ll get us where we’re going, all right. He doesn’t care much for the learned gents up top, nor all the dusty things in their museums, but he’ll keep these engines running through thick and thin, to honor his mom and dad.”

That was why the engine district people were so loyal to Voss, thought Max, as he climbed back up the stairways, stopping on the middle tier to buy a pasty from the Bellweather bakery. He had grown up among them, and they loved him. Max felt rather jealous. He himself was an aristocrat, born to rule Thorbury, fit and educated and not bad-looking, but he knew he didn’t have an ounce of Luka Voss's authority. Nobody would follow *him* anywhere he asked.

He finished his pasty and climbed the next flight of stairs. On the upper deck the night air was cool and refreshing and the sky was clear. He forgot Voss and wondered what was happening to Tamzin and Doom in the Out-Country. Would they have reached the watchtower yet? It seemed hard to believe that they might be fighting for their lives. And shameful to be stuck here, acting as a messenger, while they were in danger . . .

He barely noticed the group of students and Junior Fellows hurrying toward him until they had him surrounded. They wore the red sashes of Museion's militia, and several carried rifles.

"Put your hands up, Angmering!" said a young man who wore two red sashes to show he was their leader. He pointed his rifle at Max in a slightly apologetic way. "Don't move!"

Max stared at him. "Well, which is it? Don't move, or put my hands up?"

"Er . . ."

"And what will you do if I don't do either? Shout 'bang' at me?"

"You are under arrest. Your friend Miss Torpenhow was found in the library. She had been stealing Old-Tech manuals from the stacks. Poor Rowan Bellweather must have disturbed her. She has murdered him."

13

Stanislaus and the Stalker

Murder? On Museion? It sounded most unlikely to Professor Stanislaus. His neighbors had woken him, talking overloudly on the landing, and when he went to see what all the fuss was about, they told him the gory details. Poor young Bellweather! But Stanislaus did not really think Miss Torpenhow capable of murder. He had met her only briefly, but she had seemed a sensible sort of woman, despite the outlandish company she kept. She did not strike him as a thief, either. He said as much to his neighbors, but they would not listen.

"Bellweather must have stumbled across her while she was pinching that book from the stacks," said Professor Al-Mansour, the astronomer from the apartment below. "She knifed him to keep him quiet. But murder will out! They have her locked up, and they have captured her young accomplice, Angmering."

"And what about her friends who went north?" asked Mrs. Evenholm, a nervous musicologist from the floor above. "Gone to warn the nomads of our plans, I'll warrant!"

"Young Angmering has been taken before the dean in the Great

Hall for questioning," said Al-Mansour. "Perhaps he will reveal the details of their wicked plan."

"If we hurry, we can hear him!" said Mrs. Evenholm.

"And what about the other member of their company?" asked Stanislaus. "What about the Stalker?"

But no one was listening to him: They were busy pulling on cloaks and hats and scurrying down the stairs and out into the Quadrangle. Stanislaus sighed, and went back into his rooms. But he could not stop wondering about Vespertine. The Stalker had been on his mind ever since that first day, when he had run into her so unexpectedly in the collection and made such a fool of himself in his surprise. That grim, gray face, like a *memento mori*. What was a creature like that not capable of? What would it do when it learned that its masters had been arrested?

At last, he threw his greatcoat on over the top of his pajamas and went out. He did not go toward the Great Hall, as his neighbors and everyone else on the city seemed to be doing, but walked as quickly as he was able to the Air Staithe. It seemed only proper that he should be the one to tell Vespertine the news. The doctors at Museion's infirmary had given Stanislaus six months to live, and that had been six months ago. Who better to talk to the dead than a man who would soon be dead himself?

The hangar door was unlocked, but no lamps were lit inside. The thing guarding the *Fire's Astonishment* did not need light, Stanislaus supposed. He could dimly see it standing on the deck below the tethered ship: a looming silhouette against the faint green glow from its own eyes. It was making small movements, and as Stanislaus went cautiously nearer he saw a little cat on the deck at its feet. The Stalker would turn its head, and the light projected from its eyes would move, and the cat would chase the light and pounce on it. It was teasing the cat, Stanislaus realized. He watched for a while, half expecting it to crush the poor creature under one of its steel-shod feet, but it did not. It simply seemed to be playing.

Stanislaus tried and failed to imagine why a Stalker would do such a thing. It seemed so engrossed in the game that if he had been carrying a weapon he could easily have struck it down. But he was unarmed, and unsure if there were any weapons aboard Museion capable of damaging a Stalker, so he just stood there dumbly watching until it became aware of him.

The green eyes turned toward him, and it stooped and gathered up the cat and held it protectively in its one big hand.

"Who are you?" it asked.

"Gilbert Stanislaus," he said, wondering uneasily if it would remember their meeting in the museum.

"What is happening? I heard shouting. I was expecting Miss Torpenhow or Max Angmering to come and tell me its cause."

"You did not think to go and see for yourself?"

"Oddington Doom told me to wait here and watch the airships, so I wait and watch. Are my friends safe? Is there news of Tamzin Pook and Oddington Doom?"

"There is no news," said Stanislaus. "Not of them . . ." The Stalker had come closer as it spoke. He could see its dead face staring at him from beneath that absurd woolly hat. He backed away a little. "But Miss Torpenhow and Max Angmering have been arrested. People think — Well, Mr. Bellweather has been stabbed. Murdered. In the library. People think Miss Torpenhow is the killer."

The Stalker hissed. Anger, Stanislaus supposed, and wished he had not come here bearing bad news. Hastily he said, "I do not believe it myself. I think it is all a mistake. It will be sorted out. That's what I came here to tell you. In case you . . . In case you heard it from someone else, and decided to do something hasty. That would only make things worse for them."

The Stalker considered this. The cat writhed free of its hand and climbed on to its massive shoulder, mewing. The Stalker said, "Miss Torpenhow and Max Angmering are my friends. I must free them."

"Please," said Stanislaus, holding up his hands. "Wait and see what morning brings. This whole business may be sorted out by then."

The Stalker tilted its head on one side. Stanislaus sensed it was unconvinced.

"Stay here," he told it, trying to sound commanding. "Stay here, as Mr. Doom instructed you. I will return the moment I have more news. I promise."

"Very well," said Vespertine.

Stanislaus left it standing there and closed the hangar door behind him on his way out. As if a mere door could stop a Stalker! Why had he told it he would return? Why had he spoken to it at all? He had felt sorry for it, he realized. He had felt sorry for *her*. As if she were a real person.

Climbing back to the top deck, he became aware of the slow, pulsing pain in his side. It had been there since he'd woken, as it always was, but he had not noticed it till now. In all the excitement, he had forgotten for a little while that he too was one of the walking dead.

❁

"Silence! Silence!" shouted the dean at the top of his reedy voice. He banged the flat of his hand on the High Table, which had been pressed into service as a judge's bench. "Oh, *please* don't all talk at once, or we shall get nothing decided at all! Silence!"

They heard him at last. The gaggle of faculty and students who had crammed into the Great Hall fell quiet. The dean turned his attention from them to Max, who stood in front of him, flanked by armed guards.

"Well, Mr. Angmering," he said. "What have you to say for yourself? Did you know of Miss Torpenhow's plan to rob the library? Are you part of her schemes? How do Doom and the Pook girl fit in to it all?"

Max, looking up at him, felt as if he were in a dreadful dream. "It's all nonsense," he said. "I have known Miss Torpenhow since I was six years old. She would never harm anyone . . ."

"Yet she is a mercenary, and part of your band of mercenaries. Isn't it her job to harm people?"

"Yes, but Miss T is not very good at it. I mean, not at that part of it. Anyway, she would never have hurt Rowan!"

The crowd around him all started talking at once again. Max could not hear what any of them were saying, but the general gist seemed to be, "Oh yes she would."

"Then how do you explain," shouted the dean, "how do you explain that Twyne found her crouched over poor Bellweather's body with the murder weapon still in her hand? And how do you explain the book she had taken from the stacks? How do you explain that, sir? Eh?"

"What book?" demanded Max.

"Operating instructions for an Ancient machine called a 'radar,'" said Professor Quincey, the librarian. "She had torn out several pages. And it turns out that we are also missing several other valuable Old-Tech works. Purloined by Miss Torpenhow on an earlier occasion, no doubt."

"Miss Torpenhow knows nothing about Old-Tech," said Max.

"Aha!" cried Blissland, his eyes lighting up. "The missing books seem to have been chosen at random, as if by someone who knows nothing about Old-Tech. That explains it! Doubtless Miss Torpenhow thought they looked valuable and planned to sell them to a dealer. Young Bellweather must have disturbed her as she was helping herself to the Radar grimoire. I expect the rest are concealed aboard that airship of yours."

"Search it, then!" shouted Max. "I promise you'll find no stolen books."

"This lad's no more to be trusted than the old woman!" said Professor von Hinkle. "Loomis should never have brought these people here. Thieves and murderers, the lot of them. They should be cast out at once!"

"You cannot blame me!" complained Professor Loomis indignantly. "Fetch mercenaries, I was told. I said at the time it was unwise. I said at the time we should overwinter here . . ."

The crowd all started shouting again. Some agreed with Von Hinkle that Hilly and Max should be cast out. Others thought the safest thing to do with thieves and murderers in times of war was to kill them out of hand. Some grabbed hold of Max and began pulling him toward the High Table, where a few enterprising students had fashioned a noose from curtain cords and were proposing to hang him. Max struggled between them, afraid that he would be pulled in half before either faction could put their plans into effect. The dean shouted for calm, but this time his voice could not cut through the hubbub.

Another voice did, however. "Leave him be!" it ordered.

All heads turned toward the door. The spectators there were shuffling aside to make way for the tall, ungainly figure of Luka Voss, who stalked gracelessly up the center of the hall in his oily red overalls. He had put on tinted spectacles, as if he thought the light of the top tier might hurt his eyes even by night. He glared coldly through blue lenses at the Senior Fellows.

"Voss!" said the dean, managing a smile. "What an unexpected pleasure . . . We so seldom see you on the upper decks . . ."

"But I hear what goes on up here," said Voss, stopping next to Max and scattering his captors with a glance. "I heard about Bellweather. I don't know if the Torpenhow woman killed him or not, but I know Meringue boy here didn't. He was below decks with me when it happened."

"That doesn't mean he's not an accomplice," Professor Waghorn pointed out.

Voss's gaze swung toward him like the beam of a haughty lighthouse. "Your fancy robes don't mean you're not a fool, yet still they let you prattle away up here, filling people's heads with froth and fluff."

"I'll have you know I'm a highly respected figure in my field," Waghorn protested, but Voss had lost interest in him.

"All this panic, all this foolishness," he declared, "is distracting you all from what must be done. If we cannot trust the Torpenhow woman, then we cannot trust Doom or Tamzin Pook. Have they really gone north to kill the nomad lookouts, or to tell them of our plans? We have to assume we are betrayed. We must leave this Frying Pan now, tonight, at once."

"We can't!" shouted Max. "Tamzin and Doom wouldn't betray you! We can't leave until they get back . . ."

"And we can't wait to learn if they are coming back," said Voss.

"If we wait, we may never leave. So we leave now. Have you not noticed? Have you not heard, over the sound of your own voices, the voice of your city singing?"

The crowd listened. The noise was faint here on the upper deck, but someone opened the doors again and they all heard it clearly, that steady rumble, like tame thunder trapped beneath the pavements.

"I have woken the engines," said Voss.

"This is most irregular," Professor Loomis complained. "It is not the chief engineer's job to decide when the engines are to be turned on or off . . ."

"Someone had to," said Luka Voss. "I will give the order to move off too, if no one else will. Or will you do it, dean? Shall Museion go, or will it stay here until the snow comes and the Junkyard Dogs grow hungry enough to attack again? I do not think we can hold off another of their raids."

The dean opened and closed his mouth for a while without making any very useful sounds. He regretted very much now that he had ever put himself forward for the post of dean of Museion. Why oh why could he not have been content to remain a simple professor of mathematics? That had been such a nice, safe job, and no one had ever looked to him for life-or-death decisions. They were all looking now: his students and his colleagues, and the Angmering lad, and young Voss. Oh, what a dreadful bother it all was!

He cleared his throat, and said in a whisper, "Yes," and then in a louder voice, "Yes. You shall have your orders, Mr. Voss. Tell your people to move west as soon as possible, at full speed."

14

Worrible the Horrible

The kampavan *War Baby* lurched and wobbled, scrambling down the near-vertical track toward the nomad camp. Tamzin, tied to a bucket seat in the crew compartment, was terrified that it would tip over end and go somersaulting down into the lake. But the studded tires kept their grip upon the slithering scree, the slope shallowed at last, and the *War Baby* crunched over a few last reefs of stone and stopped. Stoat leaped up to slide the side door open.

The engine had stopped, but the engine noise seemed to grow louder. As they untied her from the seat and bundled her out into the cold, Tamzin saw that was because the *War Baby* was surrounded by other vehicles, and all of them were starting up their own engines. Fur-clad figures hurried about in the muddy spaces between them, lugging crates of ammunition, pumping tires, and fitting rattle-guns on to the mountings that jutted from the kampavans' backs and flanks. The Junkyard Dogs were going to war.

"It's my fault," said Doom as he was bundled out to stand beside Tamzin. She was glad to see him conscious and upright. He looked ruefully at her through a mask of drying blood. "I'm sorry, kid. I've gotten too old, and too slow. If I'd dropped a bit faster up on the hill, they'd never have seen us . . ."

"Shut it," said Stoat before Tamzin could reply. He shoved the prisoners forward, his friends walking on either side of them. A landship came grinding by, with a big wolf-toothed grin painted on its armor. Stoat waited for the vehicle to pass, then shoved his captives onward, cursing them whenever they slipped or stumbled in the deep mud.

Ahead, the traction fortress thrust its sharp spires at the moon. It was called the Hundberg, Tamzin remembered. A spiky, timber-built affair, squatting on twelve huge armored wheels, it looked absurdly old-fashioned, but the large engines at its stern had been ripped quite recently from some traction town, and the spiky appearance was largely due to the guns that poked out of ports and turrets all over it.

"It's not your fault," Tamzin whispered to Doom, while Stoat was explaining himself to the guards at the entry hatch. "They were waiting for us, like you said. I heard them talking on the way down here. They knew we'd be coming."

"How?" asked Doom.

But Tamzin had no answer for that, and no time to answer anyway. Stoat turned and signaled for his friends to bring the prisoners inside, and she and Doom were shoved roughly up the boarding ramp and in through the hatchway.

Near the summit of the fortress lay the Heart Chamber, throne room, and council hall to the thane. Red-painted pillars held up its vaulted roof, and the walls were hung with dusty tapestries showing the long-ago wars of Mad Mick Madrigal, the Hundberg's legendary founder. There on a raised dais, upon a chair taken from an Ancient ground-car, sat Thane Worrible. He had red hair, amber eyes, and a proud, hawkish face that would have been handsome were it not for his brutish nature, which Tamzin could sense the moment she and Doom were thrust in front of him. He wore a leather tunic with a thick fur collar, and chains of gold and silver hung about his neck, bearing jeweled medallions and the precious hood ornaments from Ancient ground-cars. His booted feet rested on the back of a bony old man who crouched on all fours in front of his throne. Around him stood guards, massively muscled, heavily armed. The women of his household sat on cushions and beanbags, all young, meek, and decorative. But an older woman in a red gown waited in the shadows behind his chair, dark-haired and dark-eyed, and she seemed stern and slyly watchful. Tamzin remembered one of the nomads mentioning a witch, and guessed this must be her. She had never seen a real live witch before, but she could not imagine anyone much witchier.

"Stoat," said the thane, narrowing his eyes.

"Hail, Thane Worrible," said Stoat. "Hello, Uncle Eagle," he added.

"Wotcher, Stoat!" said the scrawny little man who was acting as Worrible's footstool. "How you doing?"

"Quiet!" growled the thane, jabbing the old man hard in the ribs with a heel. "Stoat your business, State. I mean . . ." He looked dimly thoughtful, and Tamzin realized he was drunk. "What's all this about, boy?"

"Captured two townies, up on the ridge," said Stoat. "Pauli said you'd want to question them."

Worrible looked at Tamzin, then at Doom.

"We are adventurers, your honor," said Doom. "Soldiers of Fortune. Hired to help Museion, but the slickness and snobbery of those city folk turned our stomachs, so we came looking for real men to fight alongside. Our swords are at your service."

Nothing was more calculated to please a proper, old-school nomad than hearing city dwellers be called slick and snobbish. The guards' eyes glittered under the iron eyebrows of their helmets. The women tittered. But Worrible seemed displeased. "I am Worrible the Horrible," he slurred, and took a swig from the goblet he held in his right hand. "I am Master of the Hounds of the Gods of War. I don't need no help from soft southerners."

"Southerners we may be," admitted Doom. "Soft we ain't. And we can tell you things about that nerd-town that you'll need to know. Like how many guns they've got."

Worrible leaned forward, interested. But the woman in red who stood behind his throne said, "Lies." She took a step forward, and the light fell upon her pale, clever face and night-black hair. Her left hand crept like a white spider on to the thane's shoulder. The other wore a long black glove, glittering with silver wires. A cogwheel, painted red, was bound to her forehead by a strip of leather.

"I have spoken with the Powers of the Air," she said. "The spirits see all that passes aboard Museion. They warned me that a sneak attack was coming, and now here are these two fools. They have told me too that Museion will break out of the Frying Pan before dawn." She smiled a cold smile. "It is time to unleash your dogs."

Worrible belched. He gestured with his goblet at the prisoners. "And these two?"

The woman looked at Tamzin. "You are Tamzin Pook?" she said. It was only half a question, as if she already knew who Tamzin was and was only interested to see if Tamzin would deny it. Tamzin nodded cautiously.

"The girl is mine," said the woman. "As for the man, he was a warrior once, and there is still strength in him. His blood will bless the tracks, so that the war gods will look kindly on your hunt."

"No . . ." Tamzin started to say, and tried to writhe free of the young nomad who gripped her arms, but he was far stronger than her, and held her easily.

Then the old man who was Worrible's footstool spoke. "No need to kill him! If there's strength in him, send him to the slave holds. That will keep him out of trouble. The war gods favor you already, bold Worrible. If they didn't, you would not be our thane. Besides, we need all the stokers we can get."

"The Thane of the Junkyard Dogs does not take orders from slaves," snapped the woman.

"Nor should he take orders from women," said the old man. "Who leads this pack, wise Worrible? You? Or this Bugtown witch?"

"Quiet," growled Worrible. Tamzin could see his brain trying to work, slowed by drink and probably not quick to start with. After a moment, he nodded. "Uncle Eagle speaks well. This is my pack, and I don't take no orders from nobody. If your spirits spoke truthful, Sister Rothrock, we'll have no time for sacrifices, and no need neither. The war gods won't desert their faithful hounds."

The woman did not like being disobeyed, but she shrugged and said, "Do as you wish, then. It is of no importance. But the girl is mine."

Worrible rose unsteadily to his feet, kicking his human footstool aside. "To your vehicle, fool!" he roared at Stoat. "We're moving out. A wild hunt, like in the days of old! Our kampavans and breach buggies will seize the prey and hold it till we can bring up our landships and the Hundberg. Stoke the furnaces! Load the guns! Start the engines!"

The red-robed woman caught Tamzin by the wrist and drew

her away from her guard. "You are coming with me," she said, and led her quickly past the dais to a small door in the wall behind it. Looking back, Tamzin saw Doom being dragged away through another door. He caught her eye before it closed behind him, and nodded. Tamzin took the nod to mean "good luck." Later she would wonder if it had only meant "goodbye."

15

Out of the Frying Pan . . .

All night, Max had been waiting to hear that his friends had returned. He kept reminding himself that Doom and Tamzin were more than a match for a bunch of Out-Country ruffians. They would be back any moment to sort things out. They would make the Museion folk understand that these ridiculous accusations against Miss Torpenhow and him could not possibly be true. They would let Hilly out of whatever cell the dean had locked her in.

Max knew he was lucky not to be in a cell himself. In the chaos in the Great Hall there had been many voices calling for him to be imprisoned as a traitor, and a spy, and an accomplice to murder. But to his surprise Luka Voss had shouted them all down, and said that he would take Max to the engine district, where he promised that he would do no harm and come to none. As chief engineer of a city with a long journey ahead of it he had a certain power, and the Senior Fellows decided to humor him. Max had gone with him gratefully. He had even managed to sleep for an hour or two on the narrow bunk in one of the curtained alcoves where workers on the night shift took their breaks.

When he woke, the city's engines were churning loudly. For a moment, he thought Museion was on the move. He put a hand on the wall behind his bunk and felt it trembling with the rhythm of the engines. But there was none of the side-to-side swaying or up-and-down jolting he would have expected if the city was traveling, so he guessed it was still safe in the Frying Pan, getting up steam.

Footsteps came hurrying along the corridor outside his cubbyhole. Max drew the curtain aside and stepped out into the path of a startled messenger carrying orders for the auxiliary engine captains. "Any news of Miss Pook and Mr. Doom?" he asked. The girl shook her head, dodged past him, and ran on.

It was like a blow to the heart. If his friends had not returned, Max knew, it meant they were most likely dead. Or *prisoners,* he thought wildly — *nomads took prisoners, didn't they?* He would organize a rescue mission. He would take the *Fire's Astonishment* north. He and Vespertine would cut their way through whole hordes of nomads till their friends were safe . . .

The jolt as the city released its brakes threw him off his feet. He scrambled up and ran to the main control room, shouting for Luka Voss.

He found the chief engineer enthroned on his chair, listening impatiently to messengers from different corners of the district who kept running in to bring him reports about steam pressure, torque, coolant levels, and other matters with which Max had never bothered to concern himself. He had never much cared *how* cities moved, only that they did. Or, in the case of Museion at this particular moment, that it did not.

"Stop the city!" Max shouted, remembering as the words spilled out of him that he had given the same command to the engineers of Thorbury when he helped seize it from Gabriel Strega all those months ago. But he had been carrying a gun then, and backed up by a band of armed rebels. His demand had been obeyed without question. Now, all he achieved was to make Luka Voss glance up from the maintenance lists he was checking.

"Go away, Meringue. We are busy."

"They might be captives!" shouted Max. "You leave if you must, but I'm going north!"

"There is no way off Museion now," said the engineer. "The cargo ramps are raised and locked, and all stairways to the ground have been barricaded. If you show your face above decks, Twyne's fools will clap you in irons before you can get anywhere near your airship. And if you make a nuisance of yourself down here in my realm, I will clap you in irons."

"But —"

"Get him out of here," said Luka Voss to the men and women who stood waiting for his orders. And as they took hold of Max and led him firmly from the control room, Voss leaned over to the brass mouthpiece of the speaking tube beside his chair and shouted, "All engines: full speed ahead."

❁

Museion had remained for so long in one place that it seemed at first to have forgotten that it was a Traction City. It stirred slowly, as if Voss's order had confused it, as if it were no more capable of movement than those Ancient static cities whose ruins its archaeologists had made such efforts to unearth. Then, groaning with the effort, it rocked backward and forward a few times, and finally, with a lurch, tore its massive wheels and tracks free of the mud and vegetation that clasped them. A colony of bats that had made their home in the wheel arches fluttered into the sky like scraps of burned paper.

The city rolled forward slowly until it reached the earthen barrier that sealed the exit of the Frying Pan. The barrier had been deliberately weakened in the preceding days. Big, angled plates bolted to Museion's prow pushed easily through what remained, scattering rocks and soil. First the forward wheels and then the tracks went grinding over the rubble. Everyone who was not busy making the city move or manning its defenses hurried to the observation balconies to watch as Museion emerged at long last on to the open plain.

How drear and inhospitable it was, that land beneath the ghost light of the westering moon! How scarred by the furrows that other cities had carved across it in forgotten years! But Museion went safely over the furrows, and across the narrow, deep-cut valley that a little river had made, snaking down from the mountains. Up in the navigation suite on the top floor of the Ivory Tower, Professor Loomis consulted his charts and issued orders that his junior staff scribbled on scraps of pink paper, tucked into brass and leather cylinders, and sent whooshing down vacuum tubes to the control room, where Voss and his assistants read them, and issued orders of their own.

Museion backed its starboard tracks and swiveled its bulk clumsily toward the northwest. Five hundred miles westward, a spur of rugged peaks called the Golgan Hills reached south from the Tannhäuser Mountains, barring the way to the Western Hunting Ground. But between their northern end and the main body of the Tannhäusers stretched a broad, level scab of ancient lava known as the Ravnina Gap, which had been a highway for cities since the dawn of Traction. Museion pointed her prow toward it, and ran on. The deckplates throbbed to the beat of the engines, banners of smoke flew from the exhaust ducts, and the dark land rolled by at an increasing speed. On the steps of the Temple of Peripatetia, Professor Pott-Walloper and her acolytes sang hymns, although no one could hear them over the engine noise. People lining the observation balconies cheered and waved goodbye to the Frying Pan as its ramparts dwindled astern.

But from the nomad lookout post that had been their nosy neighbor for so long, a signal rocket rose, and burst, and the smoke of it hung in the sky for a time, drifting slowly southward with the wind.

❁

"So they know that we are leaving," said Hilly Torpenhow to herself.

She had been shut in a room on one of the Ivory Tower's lower floors. It was quite a pleasant little room, intended for visiting scholars, with a bed and washbasin. There was even a small selection of books, for the Senior Fellows thought it cruel to lock someone up without a good supply of things to read. The door that let out on to the balcony was locked, as if they were afraid Hilly might shimmy down a drainpipe and escape, but through her window she had a good view of the passing scene, and of that ominous rocket rising on its stalk of smoke and blooming like an evil flower.

Until that moment, Hilly had still half hoped that Oddington and Tamzin might have succeeded in their mission. Now all hope left her. If there were still nomads in that lookout tower, capable of shooting off rockets, it must mean that her friends had failed and were likely dead.

She could not quite believe it. She did not think she would ever believe it. Poor Oddington, who was more alive than anyone she had ever known — how could he be gone? Would she really never see him again? And Tamzin, whom she thought of as a daughter, or at least a sort of honorary niece . . . How could such a thing have happened? They had all set out from Thorbury together with such hope, imagining that years of travel and excitement and wonder lay ahead, and now their very first brush with adventure had ended in calamity, and their happy little fellowship was sundered . . .

Hilly sat down on the bed and put her head in her hands. She did not care anymore that she was a prisoner. She did not care about proving her innocence. She did not care if they found her guilty of poor Rowan Bellweather's murder. She did not think she would care much even if they hanged her for it. Oh, why ever had she insisted on coming to Museion?

16

The Black Glove

The signal rocket from the watchtower had burst while Stoat and his crew were hurrying back along the lakeshore. The nomad camp was in uproar by then. It would take an hour or more to get the fortress moving, but the kampavans, breach buggies, and monster trucks that formed the spearhead of the Dogs' armored column were already setting off, each crew determined to be first to reach the prey. Battle banners fluttered from their flagstaffs, black against the starry sky. The young, unmarried women of the pack zoomed about in speedy half-tracks, tossing fuel cans to each kampavan and shouting encouragement. Landships tested their turrets, swinging their big guns to and fro, while technomancers made last-minute checks and spattered the blood of sacrificial chickens on their tracks. The motorized shrine — a top-heavy, three-wheeled vehicle that carried gruesome idols of the war gods on its flatbed — was picking up steam. The idols had been carved from huge trees back in the days when there were still huge trees to carve, and they bristled with the rusted blades of the Dogs' defeated foes. They were supposed to bring luck in battle.

Stoat dodged and wove his way through the chaos and

scrambled aboard the *War Baby*. "Get to the front!" he shouted at Yanna as she clattered up the ladder to the driver's cupola. Krowbar and the Hound started slamming ammo into the side guns. Yanna was switching on the engines. They spluttered for a moment, and Stoat felt a jolt of pure terror. What if the *War Baby* would not start? What if, after all these months of waiting, he missed his chance at glory because of a blocked fuel line or a dirty carburetor? And behind that fear his other fears came crowding in — what if he failed, what if his courage left him, what if, despite all his bragging, he turned out to be a coward?

Then the engine caught and roared, the *War Baby* sprang forward, and all Stoat's fears went scattering downwind with the exhaust smoke. Yanna had parked where the slope steepened at the foot of the lookouts' ridge. The rest of the pack was clogging the flatter ground below, a traffic jam of muddy armor all jostling to reach the western end of the lake, where a narrow gorge led down on to the plains. Tilting alarmingly, the *War Baby* raced along the hillside above them. Ahead, Pauli's kampavan *Beserker* was scrambling down the steep track from the watchtower in an avalanche of displaced scree. The *War Baby* shot past it before it could join the rest of the pack, and Hound and Krowbar opened the top hatches and leaned out to whoop and jeer at Pauli and his crew.

Stoat climbed up into the driver's cupola and flung open the hatch cover. His hair streamed out behind him and he shouted for joy. The kampavan was scrabbling its way over the boulder field at the end of the lake. The waterfalls were loud, but not loud enough to drown out the roar of the massed engines, or the klaxons, or the skin drums and bone glockenspiels of the priests aboard the mobile shrine. This was the stuff of songs and stories, and if Stoat was driving to his death he did not care, because the speed and the glory of it would be worth dying for. This was how the world was meant to be. This was how it *had* been, before men started making mobile towns instead of roving free like men were meant to. This was how it would be again, if Stoat had any say in things. He started to chant aloud the war-rap of the Junkyard Dogs, and the others in the cabin below him and in the vehicles behind heard him and joined in, knowing that a new verse would be written about their deeds this day.

Out of the north in the centuries of night
Madrigal marshalled us, mighty in battle.
Hunters of nightwights, hewers of Scriven,
Fierce on the blood-scent, foes fled before us.
At Burgh on the Longshore, we bulldozed the wyrd wall.
The kings of the Birkenmark cowered at our coming.
High rose the Hundberg: We harried the fuel lands,
Toppled the troll towers, guzzled the gas wells
Hounds of the war gods, wolves of the North Wind!

A narrow stairway, steep as a ladder, zigzagged down between the Hundberg's decks to a port in its belly. The guards there stood aside fearfully when Sister Rothrock came stalking down the stairs, driving Tamzin Pook ahead of her. One man hastily unbarred the hatch and swung it open. The witch pushed Tamzin out and stepped down after her. Their feet sank through a rime of frost into the shin-deep mud between the Hundberg's wheels.

"Our last night in this mire, thank the Head," Sister Rothrock muttered as she squelched through the filth.

Tamzin looked left and right, wondering which way to run

when she made her break for freedom. But it was surprisingly busy under the traction fortress. Mechanics were greasing the axles, while a whole shantytown of tents, makeshift huts, and duckboard walkways, which had sprung up between the wheels, was being hastily cleared out of the way. Under the overhanging gun deck at the stern, a light kampavan was waiting. Sister Rothrock shoved Tamzin toward it, calling out to its crew to start their engine.

They seemed to know where she wanted them to go without being told. They heaved Tamzin aboard like luggage, and Sister Rothrock climbed in and took a seat, glancing distastefully at the mud on the hem of her robes as the vehicle moved off.

It seemed strange to Tamzin that they were leaving the traction fortress just as the chase was about to start. She wondered if Worrible liked to keep his witch safe aboard another vehicle — one of the big land barges that carried the pack's women and children and took no part in battles. But this seemed unlikely if she was his technomancer. Did he know she had left the Hundberg at all? A faint little butterfly of hope opened its wings inside her somewhere. Was this woman helping her to escape? Was she somehow a friend?

The kampavan had turned away from the camp altogether, and seemed to be climbing the slopes on the north side of the lake. "It is regrettable that we have to make use of these animals," said Sister Rothrock mildly, looking out of the window. She stroked her own face thoughtfully, and the silver wires on her glove glinted cold in the moonlight. "We are strong, but we are not yet fast. It was decided that the nomads could be of use to us in that regard." She glanced down at Tamzin. "When Museion moves, the Dogs will chase it, and catch it, and we shall follow them, and then it will be ours. You picked the wrong side this time, Tamzin Pook."

So not a friend, then. Tamzin, jolting around on the deck at her feet, wondered again how Sister Rothrock knew her name. There had to be a spy inside Museion, feeding information to the nomads. She needed to warn Hilly and the others. But first she had to find Doom. And before she could do either, she had to get away from this woman.

She wrenched at the rope that Stoat's lads had bound her wrists with, and was pleased to feel it start to give. Not so good at knots, these Junkyard Dogs. And Sister Rothrock seemed to be carrying no weapons. Maybe she reckoned everybody was so scared of her witchy vibes she wouldn't need any. But she did not scare Tamzin.

The kampavan stopped. One of the crew slid the door open. It was cold outside, and the moon had come right out from behind the mountains and was painting everything silver and gray. Tamzin was dragged roughly out and set on her feet. She looked around. She was on the hillside behind the lake, and she remembered suddenly how she had seen smoke there, in the mouth of a high canyon or hanging valley, on the day she arrived. The smoke was there still, but she was standing now in the canyon's mouth, and she could see what made it.

A town was hidden in the canyon. It was small, and it seemed to be made in articulated segments, like one of the Ancient trains Hilly had told her about. They gave it the look of a snake or a bloated worm, curled around the buttresses of rock that projected from the canyon walls. Each segment was shielded by an armored lid, which made Tamzin think it must have come down from the Ice Wastes, where towns covered themselves up like that to keep their heat inside. And each segment had two banks of caterpillar tracks, one on each side, sticking out on stanchions from beneath the cowling. Lights showed here and there. On the foremost section there were mouthparts, and clusters of green lamps shone above them like the eyes of a hunting spider. Tamzin had a curious feeling that the place was watching her.

"Welcome to the Experimental Suburb of Crawley," said Sister Rothrock with a chilly pride. "People in the north call it 'Bugtown,' but its true name will be known everywhere soon enough. Walk on, girl."

The kampavan drove off. Tamzin and Sister Rothrock were alone. They started walking toward the town. Tamzin could see an open door in its forward section, and a group of people waiting at the top of the gangplank that led up to it, but they were fifty yards away, and it was night, and even if they had rifles she doubted they could hit a moving target. She would work her way around above the lake. On the way, with luck, a plan for saving Doom and warning Museion would arrive in her mind.

She swung around and ducked, driving her head hard into Sister Rothrock's midriff. "Ooof!" went the witch, going down with a satisfying thud. Tamzin stumbled over her and started to run, struggling free of her bonds as she went. But Sister Rothrock, with surprising speed, sprang after her. Her gloved hand closed on Tamzin's elbow.

Then Tamzin was lying on the ground, and not entirely sure how she came to be there. There had been a sound like bees, she remembered, and then something hit her like a hammer blow, jolting her bones, unstringing all her muscles. Even now her limbs kept making jerky little movements she had not asked them to. She had wet herself, and steam was rising from her sodden breeches. Sister Rothrock stood over her. The black glove buzzed until she touched something at her waist and the buzzing stopped.

"Electricity is greatly undervalued as a weapon," said Sister Rothrock. "I shall set the glove to full power if you disobey me again, and roast you like meat on a griddle. One of my colleagues aboard Crawley is eager to speak with you, but personally I don't care if you live or die. I have had enough of the company of barbarians."

Tamzin lay there feeling like a broken puppet, weeping helplessly for her friends and the danger they were in. The witch smiled coolly down at her, and from the waiting town the witch's friends came running in their long white coats.

17

Into the Fire

Hanging above the bunk in Max's cubbyhole was a set of the red overalls that all Museion's engine-district workers wore. When Luka Voss's people escorted him back there, Max waited until they had gone, then put the overalls on over the top of his own clothes. They made him feel bulky and shapeless and unlike himself, but that was the idea. He had noticed a line of hard hats hanging on a rack in a nearby passageway, and he went there and helped himself to one. It was made from ridged metal with a wide brim that shaded his face. A leather cap was riveted to the inside, with dangling flaps that hung down on either side of his head like the ears of a basset hound. No one looked at him as he went forward through the hot and fume-filled streets. Everyone was too busy going about their allotted jobs, clinging to the safety lines that ran along the walls to stop themselves being thrown off their feet each time Museion went bucketing through another old track mark. Max heard someone say that the city was moving at almost twenty miles per hour.

There was a stair halfway down the port side that led to the upper tier. Max felt more conspicuous up there, but luckily there were fewer people about. A group of lads went by, laughing, wheeling trolleys of powder and ammunition to the gun emplacements. On the far side of the Quadrangle, Professor Loomis hurried sternward with a logbook in his hands, a telescope under his arm, and a preoccupied look on his face. He did not so much as glance at Max. Somewhere below, terrified cattle were bellowing their disapproval in one of the farm sections. Above the spires of the collection, the stars were fading as dawn began to gray the eastern sky.

At the Air Staithe, Max found the rear door to the *Astonishment*'s hangar and unbolted it. But as he stepped inside, calling out to Vespertine, he saw that the Revenant was not alone. Professor Stanislaus turned to stare at him with a look that was half alarm and half annoyance. Or maybe one part alarm and three parts annoyance.

"Max Angmering," said Vespertine, as if she were announcing his arrival at a swanky party.

Max pulled off his tin hat. He nodded to Stanislaus, whom he had seen a few times in the Great Hall, but to whom he'd never spoken. "Vespertine," he said, "we have to fuel the ship and get out of here. Tamzin and Mr. Doom may still be alive. We must fly north and find them . . ."

"But what about Miss Torpenhow?" asked the Revenant.

Max hesitated. He wondered if it would be possible to rescue Hilly before they took off. He supposed that with a Revenant on his side almost anything was possible. Vespertine was the most powerful weapon in Museion, and she was Max's to command. But what about old Stanislaus? How would they keep him from raising the alarm? Max did not want to have to hurt him, and that made him realize that he did not want to hurt anybody else either, which might make rescuing Hilly tricky.

"If I may interject, young man," said Stanislaus, "your proposal is unsound."

"What? Why?"

"Because it is unlikely that you could fuel your airship without the crew who man the fuel tanks noticing. Even if you could, the whole of Museion would see you leave, and they would look unkindly on such an abrupt departure. Some might take it as proof that you really are in league with the Junkyard Dogs, and are flying away to join them. Dr. Twyne's guns may be old, and his gunners inexperienced, but I'd imagine even they are capable of hitting a bright orange airship at close range. Vespertine might survive the ensuing explosion, but it is unlikely you would. And where would that leave your friends?"

The old chap was right, Max knew. It was infuriating. "I have to do *something!*" he protested. "Why are you here anyway?"

"I came to speak to Vespertine," said Stanislaus. "She was concerned about Miss Torpenhow. I promised to keep her abreast of any developments."

"Have there been any?"

Stanislaus shook his head. In the faint light that came in through the high windows of the hangar, his face looked as gray and gaunt as Vespertine's. "Everyone has been busy with other things. But if Miss Torpenhow is not responsible for Bellweather's death, then it is important that we find out who is."

"Of course she's not responsible!" said Max. "Hilly wouldn't hurt a fly. Well, maybe a fly. And she may have shot a few people when we took Thorbury back from Strega, but that was only because they were shooting at her."

Stanislaus seemed tired. He sat down on a crate at the foot of the *Astonishment*'s boarding ramp and ran a hand through his thin hair. "You should return belowdecks, Mr. Angmering. There are plenty of folk up here who would lock you up too if they could — or worse. Young Voss will keep you safe down below."

Max laughed bleakly, remembering how the engineer had just treated him. But he knew Stanislaus was right again. Now that the city had been moving for a while, the novelty would wear off, and people would be drifting away from the observation platforms. If they caught Max lurking around upstairs in his engine-district disguise, it would confirm all their suspicions about him. He took one last, wistful look at the *Fire's Astonishment*.

"We will save them, if they are alive to be saved," Professor Stanislaus promised. "But we must clear Miss Torpenhow's name first."

"Professor Stanislaus will find out the truth," said Vespertine, sounding very certain about it.

Stanislaus looked up at her. He could not help but feel pleased that she had so much confidence in him. A strange creature, but clearly not as mindless as he had thought, and capable of kindness, it would seem. She was nothing at all like the Stalkers he had read about. Even her ashen face did not disturb him as it had at first.

"Come," he said to Max, and raised himself stiffly off the crate. "I shall walk with you to the top of the stairs. Then I shall go and take a look around the library for clues."

They left the hangar and walked for a while in silence, each lost in his own thoughts. There was still no one about in the trembling streets, although the sounds of laughter and a tinkling piano drifted from a café that had stayed open to serve tea and sandwiches to the city's defenders. Someone in there was singing

"A Roving Town for Me," an old music-hall number that Stanislaus remembered from his youth.

He bade Max goodbye when they reached the stairs, and stood for a moment listening to the song, until it was drowned out by a new noise — a steady, high-pitched clanging. For a moment, Stanislaus wondered if something might have gone wrong with one of the engines. But no — this new din was coming from the observation balconies on the city's starboard side. The lookouts were ringing Museion's alarm bells.

18

CAPTIVES

The Hundberg plowed its way across the plains, already miles behind the racing kampavans. The overseers in its engine rooms had learned there was no point in trying to make their voices heard over the long thunder of the engines. If they needed to urge their stokers to work harder, they used the long leather whips they each carried. As for the stokers, they had no time to do anything but stoke. Over and over, like components in some terrible machine, they thrust their shovels into the side of the mountain of coal, brought out a portion, and flung it into the fiery maw of the nearest boiler. The coal mountain never dwindled, because more coal kept coming down the chutes from the bunkers as fast as they could dig and fling it. The air was a fog of coal dust. The faces of the stokers were black with it, and shining with sweat, and their clogged lungs labored, and sweat soaked through their ragged clothes, and the whips lashed any who faltered or fell.

Oddington Doom was starting to feel that he had always been there, shoveling and slinging coal in that red light, and that everything else that had ever happened to him was just a fading dream. Every part of him ached with the effort. Even he had to admit that he was far too old for work like this. But he knew there was no use begging the overseers for a break. He must not even let them see that he was flagging. The Hundberg had no use for the weak. A man on a neighboring crew had collapsed earlier, and Worrible's men had picked him up and tossed him into the furnaces. So Oddington Doom shoveled and slung, shoveled and slung, and consoled himself with the hope that his work was helping to drive the Hundberg south, and bringing him nearer to Hilly.

At last a new shift of thralls was brought in, and Doom's crew was allowed to hand over their tools and stagger aside into an alcove roofed with steam pipes where there were splintery wooden benches to collapse on, and metallic-tasting lukewarm water in tin cups. Drinking, he looked at the faces around him — blackened, sweat-sheened, glassy-eyed — hoping to find in one or two of them a spark of rebellion he might fan into a fire. He reckoned that with a few strong blokes to back him he might be able to gain control of the engine room, and force Worrible to abandon his raid on Museion. But the men around him had been in the Hundberg longer than he had, and the spirit had been beaten out of them long ago. Besides, most of them were Oster-Rus, or Uzbeks, and spoke no Anglish. Doom had led some shabby outfits in his time, but even he did not see how this wretched lot could be turned into a fighting force.

An old man came in, dragging a pot of thin stew on a trolley. It was the same poor old fellow Worrible had been using as a foot-rest. He had stripped to the waist against the heat, and across his scrawny back a tattooed eagle spread its wings and talons, as beaky and crazy-looking as its owner. Doom levered himself up and limped over to join the queue.

The stew was not worth really queuing for, but as he gulped it down he found the old man watching him, cunning blue eyes under thick white brows.

"Thanks, friend," Doom said. "For earlier. You saved my bacon."

The old man snorted. "I never had no one thank me for sending him to the slave holds before. But it kept the Worrible's witch from having her own way. That's all I did it for."

"Stoat called you Uncle Eagle," Doom said.

"That's my name," the man replied. "Technomancer to Thane Worrible himself. Leastways, I was, till the witch came aboard."

"Who is she?" asked Doom. "Where has she taken my friend? Young Tamzin Pook. You seen her?"

Uncle Eagle shook his head and busied himself serving stew, but when his pot was empty he looked sideways at Doom and said, "'Sister Rothrock' she calls herself. She comes from Bugtown. A creeping beetle of a place that came crawling over the high passes last springtime. We thought it might be prey at first, but its armor and its magic make it strong, so we parlayed. The Bugtown people sent Sister Rothrock to help us. She knows her engines — I'll give her that — but that's not all she knows. She's enchanted Worrible with her wiles. He takes his orders from her now, and she takes *her* orders from the demon that dwells in Bugtown."

"A demon, eh?" asked Doom.

"That's how those Bugtowners got so clever," said the old man. "They have dealings with demons. They have a tame one chained up in their boiler room. That's where Worrible's witch has took your girl. She'll be sacrificed to the demon, I expect. Nothing pleases demons better than the blood of a brave girl."

The brief break was already ending, and the overseers were cracking their whips and ordering the workers back to their places.

Doom licked the last traces of stew from his tin plate. Nasty as it was, he wished there had been more. He considered what Uncle Eagle had told him. He did not believe in demons, nor in witches. But if Tamzin was no longer on the Hundberg, that was bad news indeed.

❁

When the Hundberg had set off after its pack, and the land barges and landships had followed it, and the abandoned fires were dying down in the valley by the cold lake, Crawley came creeping from its canyon. Its many segments and outrigger track units made it look more like a vast centipede than a suburb as it scrabbled its way along the lakeshore and started down toward the plains, following in the scumbled wheel ruts of the Junkyard Dogs.

Somewhere inside it, Tamzin sat on a hard, black bunk in a hard, gray room. The room had no windows, and she had been too groggy when they brought her there to know in which segment of Crawley she was imprisoned. From what she had seen on her way from the entry port, all portions of Crawley looked the same anyway. All mobile towns were machines at heart, but most tried to disguise the fact by making their upper tiers as decorative and as homely as possible. Crawley seemed proud to be a machine. Tamzin had seen no streets, only corridors; no houses, only numbered cabins. There had been none of the shops or pubs or public squares or any of the other things that made Thorbury and Bad Luftgarten and Margate feel so busy, and so human. The corridors were dimly lit, roofed and often walled with snaking ducts. The only decorations were large stenciled slogans: *The Head Sees All: The Head Hears All: The Head Knows All*. The people seemed silent and serious: men, women, and little solemn children all dressed alike in white coats or overalls, and all with shaven heads. At every intersection, green lamps glowed like watchful eyes.

There was a green light on the ceiling of Tamzin's cell too, shining like an emerald beside the bright, softly buzzing panel that gave her light to see by. Not that there was anything to look at. Along with the black bunk she had a bucket to do her business in, and a plastic bottle filled with metallic-tasting water. She studied her bruised reflection in the bottle's surface and saw that in the course of her capture someone had thought to put a bandage over the gash on her cheek. The bandage was a cheerful pink. It looked as out of place on Tamzin's brown face as Tamzin felt in Crawley.

She could feel the town moving, and dimly heard klaxons and shouted orders echoed in the corridors outside. It must be pursuing Museion, but how fast it was going, and what lay outside, she could only guess. She thought it had been traveling for several hours when the door opened.

Sister Rothrock peered in. She had changed her red robes for a long white coat, and scrubbed the makeup from her face. She had also removed her long, black hair: Tamzin guessed it had been a wig. Without it, her face looked even more angular and severe. Tamzin did not recognize her at first. She did not recognize the man who waited out in the corridor, either, just as bald and dressed identically. But something about him nudged at her memory.

"Here she is," said Sister Rothrock, speaking to the man behind her. "Tamzin Pook. I knew her name from your debriefing, Brother. I thought you should be the one to interrogate her. My gift to you."

"Now, now, Sister," said the man, "you've been too long among barbarians. You're sounding whimsical, and you know our Head doesn't hold with whimsy." He came into Tamzin's room as he spoke, Sister Rothrock standing aside to let him through.

Tamzin knew him then. His appearance had changed a lot, for he had shed his beard and whiskers, and lost his fancy turban and his expensive, shiny clothes. He seemed a smaller man entirely, and his scalp was shaved to a faint gray stubble, but Tamzin would have known his voice anywhere.

"Well," he said, beaming down at her. "This is an unexpected meeting! An unlooked-for reunion! I had not expected to see you again until we eat Museion. Well, well, well. Tamzin Pook!"

It was Mortmain.

19

The Dogs of War

Max was on his way back to his cabin in the engine district when Museion's alarm bells started their neurotic clamor. He hesitated in a passageway outside the control room, wondering what was wrong and whether there was anything he should do about it. Before he could think of anything, someone opened the control-room door and Luka Voss saw him standing there. Max's disguise did not appear to fool him. "Meringue boy!" he shouted. "Make yourself useful! Go outside and see what's gotten the old men upstairs tinkling their jingle bells."

Max waved in acknowledgment and hurried off, glad of an errand. Out on the tier's edge there were openings that led onto a juddering iron walkway that ran along the city's flank, a few feet above the speeding tracks. The air out there was cold, and filled with up-flung grit and a kind of misty salad of mashed foliage. Max rummaged in the pockets of his overalls and found a pair of standard-issue goggles. Pulling them on, he edged out along the walkway, clinging to the handrail with one hand while he held his tin hat in place with the other. Beyond the veil of debris, brown ground was rolling by at speed in the cold morning light. He saw tussocks of winter grass; cold pools; small, stunted trees. Northward, the foothills of the Tannhäusers stood unmoving, the higher peaks behind them buried in ominous-looking clouds.

Max stared at the clouds for a moment, recalling Professor Pringle's forecasts and wondering if those could be what had set the lookouts sounding their alarms. Then the sun lifted itself out of the pall of low mist that hung behind the city, and lit up strange, pale scarves of smoke or dust that were rising from the plain between Museion and the mountains. Fires, Max thought at first, or maybe the smoke of fumaroles. Was Museion blundering through an active volcanic zone? But no. In the base of each cloud the sun found steel to gleam on, weapons and whirling wheels.

Museion crashed through a patch of swamp and Max was drenched and blinded by dirty water. He wiped his goggles clear and looked again. What he had thought were just a few vehicles was actually a fleet — fifteen, twenty, two dozen kampavans — all racing along much faster than the city, on a course that would soon bring them together. Max could see them more clearly now. Speedy, ramshackle things, with big wheels and outsized engines. Their hulls were covered with crudely welded armor. Some had fierce teeth painted on their prows, or bloodred banners streaming from long poles. Some had turrets that stabbed quick spurts of flame, testing the range.

But the old guns on Museion's upper tiers were answering. The city had no forts or weapons turrets, because the scholars who designed it had never imagined fighting anyone. But on some of its outer walkways and observation balconies Dr. Twyne had supervised the building of semicircular sandbag emplacements, and in those he had positioned all the working guns from the city's historical collections. There were twelve cannons of various sizes, some heavy machine guns, an age-old nomad siege mortar like a fat iron pot and a reconstructed Tien Shanese catapult called the Ultra Donker. The gun crews still shouted "bang" from force of habit as they pulled the lanyards of their guns or set slow matches to the touchholes. Muzzles spat fire, gunners leaped nimbly aside to avoid the recoil of their weapons, and the Ultra Donker slung its first payload of burning oil into the midst of the kampavan swarm. One of the 'vans flipped over, bounding end-over-end across the rough ground until it burst in a sudden blossom of orange flame, with others bunching up behind it or colliding with one another as they tried to swerve around it.

Max grinned as the cheers of the gun crews came faintly down to him from above. He clung to the handrail and watched the running battle unfold. It was a pretty one-sided affair. The kampavans could not get close enough to do any damage without coming in range of Museion's guns. Max saw half a dozen of them hit. He started to feel that the Junkyard Dogs might not be quite as dreadful a threat as they had been painted to be.

But, as so often happens just when things seem to be going well, fate had a surprise in store. From somewhere astern there came a *boom*, and then a dreadful scraping, rending sound that went on and on. Museion slowed abruptly and swerved off course. The shock threw Max off his feet, and almost off the city's edge. A dense spray of earth and stones, flung up by the tracks, hung for an instant in the air between the city and the kampavan swarm like a dirty curtain. Then it crashed down, half burying Max, the larger stones battering and bruising him, rattling like round shot against the city's side.

By the time he'd fought his way clear of the debris, it was not just stones striking the metal walls above him. Veering wildly,

Museion had drifted into range of the kampavans' guns. The nomads were aiming at the gunners on the higher levels, but their aim was haphazard and quite a few stray rounds were hitting the tracks and the catwalk where Max crouched. He stood up, keeping low, and scurried back into the safety of the engine district.

He expected to find chaos there. But although there was a sense of urgency, there was no sign of panic. A woman whom he recognized from the control room hurried past and Max stopped her to ask, "What's happened to the engines?"

"Nothing," the woman said. "Something's gone wrong astern — we've fouled some wreckage, or a deckplate's come loose and started rubbing on the tracks . . ."

"Can I help?"

The woman looked doubtful, but she did not stop Max from following as she ran on. They passed down the shuddering alleyways around the central engine block to the door of the starboard cargo hold. There, in towers of crates and huge containers stacked neatly against the metal walls, spare parts for the engine district were housed alongside artifacts that would not fit in its museums. The hold was a dark place usually, like all the warrens of the engine district, but as Max's companion slid the door open a blaze of sunlight dazzled them, streaming down the broad, clear aisle between the stacks. The giant loading ramp that normally formed the rear wall of the hold had been lowered. It was scraping along the ground behind the city, acting as a drag anchor.

"No!" screamed the woman, aghast. "Oh no! Who has let the ramp down?"

"Maybe it just came loose?" shouted Max. He had to shout to be heard. The hold was a vast echo chamber, filled with the screech of the metal ramp dragging over the ground, the steady holler of the engines, the threshing metallic song of tracks and axles.

The woman was shaking her head. "We checked it was secure only last night. Luka inspected the bolts himself . . ."

Something shot up the ramp, adding its own shriek of engines and stressed metal to the general din, flashing a sudden shadow that made Max look up in time to catch it still airborne, cresting the top of the ramp. It was one of those janky armored jalopies, and it landed hard on its six huge wheels in the center of the hold. It swerved to a halt there, tires smoldering, painted cartoon dogs baring their red teeth on its flanks. A red-headed maniac clung to its roof, waving a spear and screaming bad poetry.

❁

How the Dogs had howled when that big ramp came down! It had looked touch and go till then. They had been driving flat out for hours. They had chanted the hundred verses of the war-rap five times over, until their throats were raw from shouting. But still the prey outran them. Museion was moving faster than Stoat had ever thought a city could, and Yanna kept yelling about the fuel running low, and none of the 'vans could get close enough to do much damage with their guns. The *War Baby*'s fuel was running low, and when Stoat looked around for the nearest fuel maidens, he was just in time to see a lucky shot from Museion's guns turn their half-track into a rising ball of oily flame, speckled with tumbling scraps of metal and maiden. He looked back at the city, tears in his eyes, sensing the bright hope of victory slip away . . .

And that was when the war gods worked their miracle, and that big ramp at the rear came crashing down. The city slowed abruptly, as if some giant foot had pressed a giant brake pedal. It slewed off course, and kampavans went racing alongside to shoot their guns at it while the defenders were distracted. But Stoat was more interested in that ramp, dragging along on the ground between the city's track marks. It wasn't just an anchor to slow the prey. It was his road to glory.

He reached down into the cupola, shook Yanna's shoulder, pointed. She understood at once and slung the *War Baby* hard left, jolting down into the slime and slither of the rut the city's starboard track had chewed, then up the other side. Stoat looked back. A dozen other 'vans and a monster truck packed with warriors had seen what he was planning and were following, but the *War Baby* was first. Stoat snatched a boarding spear from the rack on the kampavan's flank and started on the war-rap again.

"Hounds of the War Gods!" he roared. "Wolves of the North Wind!" And Yanna screamed and stood on the accelerator, and the *War Baby* shot forward in a last desperate sprint, somehow made it onto the ramp, and went screaming up it.

❁

Bullets were pecking and pinging at the doorframe as Max and the woman retreated from the hold. Max started to push the door shut, but other hands and other bodies were pushing from the other side. He threw his weight against it, and the woman joined him, but the nomads pushed back with an eager fury. Then suddenly Voss was there, running down a ladder from some walkway in the roof, and he added his own weight to Max's, and shouted for others to help, and men came running. The door slowly shut.

Max looked at Voss, and wondered what he was doing there. Why wasn't he in the control room? Did he just magically know wherever something was going wrong in his engine district? "Thank gods you were here," he said.

The door locked with a heavy bar, but that would not keep the nomads inside for long.

"Get upstairs! Tell them there are boarders in the hold!" Voss shouted at Max, and went hurrying off toward the control room. Max ran for the nearest stairway, yelling the news at everyone he passed.

The upper tier seemed deserted, except that from the edges of it came the sound of guns, and the hoarse shouts of their crews.

Vespertine spun toward the door when Max entered the hangar. Her eyes were flaring a brighter green than usual, as if the sounds of battle echoing through the city had excited her.

"Nomads in the hold," Max gasped, winded by his run. "They need you down there."

"But Mr. Doom told me to guard the airship, Max Angmering," said the Revenant.

"Mr. Doom isn't here and, if he was, he'd tell you you're needed downstairs. Please, Vespertine. It's just Voss and a bunch of workers down there; they can't hold off the Junkyard Dogs."

Vespertine considered this a moment. Then she picked up a lidded wicker basket and handed it to Max. "Please look after Small Cat," she said, and went striding from the hangar with her eyes blazing.

The basket jiggled in Max's hands, and annoyed cat noises came from inside it. He went after Vespertine, out into the empty streets. A student jogging by on some errand stopped to stare as the Revenant marched past. Max handed him the basket. "Look after this," he said. "Make sure you keep it safe, or you'll have Vespertine to answer to. Find the dean, or Dr. Twyne, or somebody: Tell them there are boarders in the hold!"

20

Bullets and Battering Rams

"I heard one of the loading ramps has come undone," said one of Hilly's guards a few minutes later, opening the door of the prisoner's room to answer her questions about what was happening.

"Good heavens!" said Hilly. "How ever did that happen?"

The guard did not know. Her name was Lamorna Fey and she had been a student of Ancient Literature and captain of the Museion Ladies Hockey XI in happier times. Now she was pale and trembling and her helmet kept slipping down over her eyes.

"Here," said Hilly, going to the little desk and fetching a few sheets of the writing paper that her captors had thoughtfully provided. She folded the sheets together to make a long, thin pad, and took off Lamorna's helmet.

"Hey . . ." said the girl, sensing that this somehow breached the rules of their guard-prisoner relationship. But she made no attempt to grab the helmet back, just watched as Hilly turned it upside down and wadded the paper into the leather band inside.

"There," said Hilly, placing it back on the girl's head. It still made her look like a military mushroom, but at least it did not cover her eyes anymore. "Now," said Hilly, "is there any possibility that I might be allowed to take a look outside? I give you my word I will not try to escape. I should dearly like to see for myself what is happening."

Lamorna thought for a moment, then shrugged. There was a narrow balcony outside the room, high enough that an old lady could not hope to jump from it. She locked the door behind her, unlocked the door that led on to the balcony, then followed Hilly outside.

They were high on the starboard side of the Ivory Tower. Below them, on the roof of the Great Hall, an eager crew was busy reloading one of the museum guns. Hilly clapped her hands over her ears just in time as it went off, and let her eyes follow the course of the shell out through the veil of smoke that hung above the front wheels. There was the blast and a plume of black smoke and upflung earth that fell behind as the city moved past. But it did not fall behind very quickly, for Museion was not traveling nearly as fast as Hilly would have liked. And there was the enemy: a swarm of vehicles so small that they were hard to spot at first, racing alongside while foolhardy youths clung to their roofs, ready to leap aboard the city if their drivers could bring them close enough.

"It is a scene from five hundred years ago," she said, and felt for a moment almost privileged to be witnessing such a spectacle. "Look, there is the nomad's traction fortress . . ." She pointed beyond the kampavans, where the gathering clouds above the mountains were casting a deep shadow on the land. Bright against it rose the exhaust plumes of the Hundberg, hastening to catch up with its hounds. And behind that, faint in the far distance, was another smudge of dust, smoke, and metal, which she supposed must be the rest of the nomad column, although it looked too big and solid somehow.

A series of sharp noises came drifting up from the street, like a lot of doors being hastily slammed. Hilly looked down. Through the space between her building and the next she saw people running. One stopped to raise a gun and shoot at something out of sight, then sprinted on. One fell upon his face and lay there while others ran around him. Hilly did not recognize any of them, and they were not wearing Museion clothes but raggedy leather and furs. More doors slammed, but she knew now that the sounds were not doors at all: gunshots were echoing between the Ancient buildings. Ricochets whined like hungry cats. Lamorna Fey gasped.

"Good gods," agreed Hilly. "Nomads! They have gotten aboard!"

Lamorna made no reply. Hilly glanced around and saw that the girl was swaying, looking down in some confusion at a hole that had appeared in the breast of her tunic. A wet, dark stain was spreading rapidly around the hole. The girl looked up at Hilly — a sort of pleading look, as if Hilly might have the power to undo what had just happened.

Hilly caught her as she fell, and helped her back inside. The bunch of keys on Lamorna's belt clanked as Hilly laid her down on the rug beside the bed. Hilly looked at them for a moment. She knew no real adventurer would let an opportunity like this go by. Oddington would expect her to make the most of this dreadful stroke of luck. Here was her chance to snatch the keys and make good her escape.

"I'm not even supposed to be here," Lamorna whimpered. "I was supposed to go home to Wheelchester in the summer, but the airship never turned up and now I'm stuck here and now I'm going to die here."

"No, you are not," said Hilly, very sternly, although she was quietly horrified by the amount of blood, and by the pinkish foam that the girl now began to cough up. Perhaps, when it came to it, she thought, she was not a real adventurer. She pressed the scared girl's hand to the wound, told her to keep it there, snatched the keys and ran to open the door.

"Help!" she shouted. "Help! Help!"

❁

The crews in the engine district had worked hard and fast to barricade all the doors out of the cargo hold, but the Junkyard Dogs did not particularly need doors. They scaled the towering stacks of crates inside the hold and found their own ways out through vents and air ducts.

"The control room! The control room!" yelled Stoat. "Get to the control room! Stop the engines!"

But the Dogs had never boarded anything as big as Museion, and they were not sure how to find its control room. Stoat's more raucous comrades were already growing bored with the engine district. Climbing the tier-supports, they swung like monkeys through the girders overhead until they found access hatches, which let them pop up through the pavements of the upper tier, causing panic among the defenders who had been braced for an attack from outside the city, not from within. Many of the Museion militia, confronted for the first time with enemies who were not cut out of cardboard or stuffed with straw, threw down their antique guns and ran to hide. For a time, the Dogs had the run of the Quadrangle. They barged into the Temple of Peripatetia and emerged laden with silver statues and golden candlesticks. They battered their way into the Archaeological Collection and, finding nothing worth looting inside, simply started smashing things. Their war-raps rang from the ivy-covered walls, and their clumsy machine guns nattered like vicious gossips in the stairwells.

Downstairs, Stoat got his bearings at last. With Yanna, Hound, Krowbar, and a few others behind him, he found his way to the control room. The doors were barricaded, but in a nearby storage shed Hound found spare piston rods the size of felled pines. Stoat and his followers lifted one between them and started using it as a battering ram.

❁

Max caught up with Vespertine as she entered the engine district. She had been displeased at first, but when he promised her that Small Cat was safe she seemed to accept his presence. He followed her, stepping over dead bodies, ducking under dangling ceiling panels, dodging around the plumes of steam that geysered from damaged pipes. Alarm bells were clattering. Terrified animals bellowed and bleated in the livestock sections. Whirling red alarm lights filled the narrow streets with their migraine flicker. At an intersection, Max spotted a rack of protective headgear and snatched down a heavy welder's mask for Vespertine, who put it on over her bobble hat. Max tightened the straps of his own hard hat and hurried on.

As they neared the control room, the noise of the battering ram came to meet them. "One, two, three, heeeaave!" and then a low, reverberating *boom* of metal on metal. "One, two, three, heeeaave! One, two, three . . ." — and then nothing, because one of the battering ram crew glanced up to find Vespertine watching, and the others noticed the look of horror on his face and turned and saw her too.

The welder's mask had a single square viewport. The glow of Vespertine's weird green eyes behind, it made her look like an armored cyclops. The battering ram, forgotten, clattered on to the deck. Several of the Junkyard Dogs turned and ran. Others pulled out guns and started shooting. Max, ducking behind Vespertine, heard the bullets play their noisy music on her armor. Vespertine ignored them and strode forward, leaving Max crouching there exposed.

Vespertine snatched Stoat up and hurled him bodily at his friends, who started to fall back in terror. Stoat staggered to his feet and tried to rally them, but Yanna shouted, "We can't fight it, Stoat! We can't kill it!" and he was too dazed to argue as she dragged him away.

So the siege of the control room was lifted. Max hammered on the doors to tell the defenders they were safe. If he had hoped for praise from Luka Voss, he was mistaken. "Stop grinning, Meringue!" Voss shouted when he saw him. "These bells — can't you hear them? We're on fire! Come!"

"But there may be more nomads . . ."

"Let your dead friend deal with them. She is better at fighting nomads than you. But fires need fighting too, and even a meringue can do that. Come with me."

He set off at an ungainly trot, with a few of the control room staff behind him. Max went with them. Vespertine made a circuit of the control room, decided that there were no more nomads on that level to fight, and set off upstairs, sifting through the complex soundscape of the stricken city for any sounds that spoke to her of battle.

❁

Lamorna Fey was a well-built young woman, and too heavy for her fellow guard, who had been stationed in the corridor outside Hilly's room and came running when she called for help. Since everyone else seemed busy with the battle, he and Hilly carried the unconscious girl to the infirmary between them, avoiding the war-torn Quadrangle and moving through empty alleys that echoed with the sounds of gunfire.

The infirmary was on the city's port side. Some of the students manning the sandbag barricade on its front steps came hurrying to help when Hilly and her companion appeared. Hilly wondered if she should remind them that she was a prisoner, and ask to be escorted back to her place of confinement — but that felt like taking fair play a little *too* far. Besides, she was worried that Lamorna might not get the attention she needed, given how awfully busy the infirmary seemed. There were already several trails of blood drying on the steps where other casualties had been carried in.

So she went inside, and used her best schoolteacher's voice on the nurses and orderlies until Lamorna was found a bed, and someone fetched the chief physician, a big, bearded, kindly, exasperated man named Dr. Jaffaji. It was only when he was bent over the girl, examining her wound, that one of the nurses looked at Hilly and said, "She is the traitor who killed young Mr. Bellweather! What is she doing wandering free?"

"She is not the traitor," said the young man who had helped Hilly bring Lamorna in. "Haven't you heard? The boarding ramp was dropped, and that happened while Miss Torpenhow was safely locked away."

"There could be *two* traitors," said the nurse, who was a keen reader of detective fiction. "She might have *accomplices*. She might have any number of accomplices! You should take her back to the Ivory Tower and lock her up!"

"Take her back, at least," said Dr. Jaffaji. "This is an infirmary, not a talking shop." But he looked up at Hilly and said, "Lamorna will live. You did well."

21

Stranger on the Shore

Five months earlier, on a dank beach at the marshy eastern end of the Anglish Sea, one of the clots of weeds that lined the foreshore had twitched, heaved, and risen to stand more or less upright, more or less man-shaped, mud-covered, and moaning.

A few hours earlier, Dr. Mortmain had flung himself off the raft city of Margate. His pleasant life as Master of Amusements had been taken from him so suddenly that he still could not quite believe it was gone. He even raised a hand to wave at the raft city, which was drifting aimlessly beneath a pall of dirty smoke a few miles offshore.

But no, Mortmain — no. The slaves whom he had sent night after night to fight and die in his Amusement Arcade had broken free, and thanks to the strict training and excellent diet Mortmain had given them, they were more than a match for Margate's dozy policemen and the Arcade's security thugs. The ungrateful hooligans would have the run of the whole town by now. And what of Vespertine, his rogue Revenant? She had already tried to murder him. The salt stung in the gashes he had received when she'd hurled him through the window of his private box.

Mortmain lowered his hand. Whining softly with the pain of his cracked ribs and many wounds, he started to limp westward along the coast. A whole gaggle of rusty little scavenger towns had been lured seaward by rumors that Margate was sinking. Disappointed to find their prey still afloat, they were trundling about in search of other scraps. Mortmain hid himself in ditches or cowered beneath windswept clumps of sea cabbage as they passed. The oafs who drove those ramshackle places would have no use for a down-on-his-luck genius, and Mortmain did not intend to end up in their slave holds. He would have to find his way aboard a larger city, one where he could use his charm and peculiar skills to begin afresh and build a new life. He had done it once before, after all . . .

He slept badly that night on a shingle slope. By dawn, Margate was just a pimple on the horizon far behind him. A white airship prowled the sky above the beaches, the mutter of its twin engines rising and falling on the breeze. Mortmain tried to encourage himself by imagining the new Arcade he would construct when he was safe on some new city. It would be bigger than the last, and devoted to the staging of battles even more violent and inventive . . .

The engine buzz grew suddenly much louder. A cigar-shaped shadow swept across the scrub. Mortmain stood watching as the airship settled on a rise a short way off. Surely it could not have come for him? But they were calling his name, the aviators, as they jumped down in their white overalls from their silvery gondola. They were striding purposefully toward him through the marram grass.

Mortmain started to run, imagining they had been sent to track him by the freed slaves of Margate. They overtook him easily, and barred his way. That was when he saw the red wheel printed on their sleeves and flying helmets, and knew where they had really come from. They spoke with the same accent of which Mortmain had spent so long ridding himself when he arrived on Margate. He remembered suddenly and vividly his miserable childhood: his mother scolding him about the drawings of mechanical dragons and basilisks he had hidden under his bunk.

"Brother Mortmain! Brother Mortmain!"

"Mom?" he murmured. But she was long since dead, of course. This was another woman with the same voice and the same disapproving scowl. No doubt she had the same bald noggin too, beneath that leather helmet.

"We were about to give up the search, Brother Mortmain. We hear things have gone badly for you aboard Margate."

"Badly?" said Mortmain, and laughed until he choked. "Badly?" he croaked. "I was Mortmain the Great! I was Mortmain the Magnificent! I was Mortmain the Master of Amusements! I was everything you lot would never let me be at home! I was a king!"

The aviators watched him as he stood, swaying, laughing there, covered with filth, crusted with dried blood, clad in the scarecrow tatters of expensive clothes, until his laughter turned to something more like tears. Then one said, "No more amusements for you, Brother Mortmain. You are to come back north with us. There is important work for you in Crawley. The Head has need of you."

❁

Tamzin, knowing none of this, sat staring at Mortmain while he fetched a little metal chair, set it down, and sat on it. "Leave us," he told Sister Rothrock.

The witch withdrew. Tamzin kept on staring. Mortmain seemed

smaller than before. The loss of his beard and whiskers had revealed a weak chin, and there was a hunted, furtive look in his eyes. He glanced up frequently toward the green light in the ceiling.

Tamzin could not believe it was coincidence that had brought her back into his grasp, all these many months and miles from Margate. But if it was not coincidence, then what was it? She supposed some god with a sick sense of humor must be determined to braid her fate with his.

"I hoped you were dead," she managed to say. "I wish you were."

"Come now, Tamzin," chuckled Mortmain, "that isn't very friendly! Aren't you glad to see me? I am glad to see you. I will freely admit there was a time when I blamed you for my misfortunes, and plotted all manner of revenge on you. But I have a new life now — or at least an old one back again — and I find that, yes, I am very pleased to see you. We are like old friends, don't you think?"

"No," said Tamzin. There was a time when his purring charm would have worked on her, but that time was long gone. She hated him so much. She wondered if she could overpower him, but she doubted it — even in this diminished form, he was still a big man, and she was small, very weary, and unarmed.

She said, "What are you doing here?"

Mortmain shrugged ruefully. "Believe it or not, Crawley is my hometown. When I was Master of Amusements, people were always inventing stories about where I had come from, and I let them. The more colorful, the better, I thought. But the truth is that I come from Crawley, where there is very little color at all. The things I dreamed of as a lad were all the things Crawley deems irrational. Adventure! Excitement! Show business! That is why I left, as a penniless young man, and found my way to Margate, where the skills I had learned here could be put to use in the service of Art."

"Is that what you call it?" muttered Tamzin, remembering the desperate fights she had endured, her weekly brushes with many-bladed death.

"Art is meant to be challenging," Mortmain assured her. "But of course one can't please everybody. After you and your friends put an end to my time there and I found myself alone again . . . Well, it turns out my former brothers and sisters here in Crawley had been keeping a close eye on my activities, even after all these years — it's rather flattering, really. They had followed all the advances and discoveries I made, and they came begging me to help them with a problem that no one but I, Mortmain, could solve. They said the Head needed me. How could I refuse?"

"Who's the Head?" asked Tamzin.

Mortmain's eyes flicked upward very briefly. She saw the green light glint in them. "The Head is our mayor. Jago Flint, Crawley's founding father. A very great mind indeed." He reached inside his white coat and took out a small book, pocket-size, which he tossed to Tamzin. "Here: a little light reading for you. All residents of Crawley are expected to know the Head's thoughts and sayings."

Tamzin caught the book and turned it over. It was printed on hairy, blue-ish paper. The title on its plain cover was *The Principles of Flintism*.

"How is Vespertine, by the way? I gather you have tamed her."

Tamzin shrugged and tossed the book aside. "Vespertine didn't need taming. She's a good friend to those she likes. And a deadly enemy to those she doesn't."

"I shall have to watch out, then!" laughed Mortmain. "I am looking forward to seeing her again when we take Museion."

"You'll have to catch it first. Museion has good engines. This place isn't moving fast enough."

"Oh, our hired help will do the catching for us. The Junkyard Dogs are a rowdy bunch, but they're useful in their limited way. The Head has been watching Museion for a long time. He thinks the papers and Old-Tech devices in its various collections are far more valuable than those fuddy-duddy professors realize. He means to grab the whole lot so that he can use the knowledge they contain to expand and strengthen Crawley, which is rather a sluggish little place at present, as you so rightly observed. It was designed for mobile research in the Ice Wastes, not for high-speed pursuit. That's why the Head chose to lair in the mountains and let the Junkyard Dogs act as our foot soldiers."

"Oddington Doom is aboard their traction fortress," said Tamzin.

"Your mercenary friend? Oh dear. Not much hope for him, then, I'm afraid. The Dogs work their prisoners hard, and throw them away when they break. Here in Crawley we are more enlightened. No slave-hold for you! I've put in a request for you to be my new personal assistant."

"Me? Why? Never! I'll kill you first . . ."

"Excellent!" said Mortmain cheerfully, as if she had said how much she would like the job. He stood up and carried his metal chair to the door. Before he went out, he glanced back at Tamzin and said, "I really am pleased to see you, Pook. I'm not just saying that. Having you here again brings back so many happy memories."

"Me too," said Tamzin. "I remember how stupid you looked the time Hilly fed you that drugged macaron, and the look on your face when Vespertine chucked you through a window. Those were good times."

He bowed. "I am happy to have entertained you. We'll talk some more once Crawley has caught Museion." He glanced at the ceiling again and added, "I may need your help to repurpose Vespertine."

"What do you mean, 'repurpose'?" Tamzin started to ask. But the door had closed, and she was alone again.

22

A Change in the Weather

Museion was still moving, but more slowly now. The loading ramp bounced and scraped along beneath it, ripping up divots of frosty soil, striking showers of sparks from buried boulders. It was hard for even the Dogs' best drivers to steer their kampavans on to the ramp, and harder still to drive up it while it bounced and twisted, but five had made it into the hold. The rest swarmed along on either side of the besieged city, shooting at tracks and steam pipes and any defenders they glimpsed.

In all the excitement no one paid much attention to the weather. An odd, brownish light hung over the plains, but who stops to ponder interesting atmospheric effects in the middle of a battle? The temperature was certainly dropping, but such things don't seem of much importance when you are trying to keep your balance on the roof of a kampavan as it drives too fast over rough ground just inches from a city's whirling wheels. In Museion's meteorology department the barometers showed a startling drop in pressure, but Mr. and Mrs. Pringle were sheltering in the Senior Common Room.

It may have been Thane Worrible himself who was the first to notice that the weather was on the turn. He had been watching the chase from an open observation deck on the Hundberg's roof. Heavier and slower than its kampavans, the old fortress was now many miles northeast of Museion and the rest of the pack. Every few moments Worrible leaned forward to bellow orders down the speaking tube that connected him to the control room. Mostly he shouted, "Faster!" but sometimes for variety's sake he would yell, "Faster, damn you! More speed! Or I'll feed you to the furnaces!"

It was not an idle threat, and the men in the control room did their best to obey. Lumbering old thing that it was, the Hundberg seemed in danger of shaking itself to pieces. The long banners streamed out in the wind of its passage. The barges and landships that carried the Dogs' wives, families, and supplies had been left far behind. Worrible was not worried about them. He was not even too bothered when the motorized shrine to the war gods, which had been plowing along ahead of the Hundberg, was overtaken. All he wanted was to catch up with his hounds and help them seize that city. For months Sister Rothrock had been telling him of the treasures it held. Catching Museion was all that mattered. The rest of the column could follow in their own sweet time, to share in what was left of the spoils. Then the Dogs would have all the fuel and loot they could carry. They could bid goodbye to Crawley, and go hunting fat traction villages in the green fields of the west. It would be just like the old days again!

But as the prey drew nearer, and Worrible strained his eyes to try to make out what was happening aboard it, there was a sudden, loud *flap*, like someone shaking out a sheet, and the banners that had been streaming astern began to billow forward instead. At the same moment, Worrible felt a chill breeze, as if someone with icy breath was blowing gently but insistently on the back of his neck.

He turned, and looked up, then up again.

The wall of cloud that had been slowly enfolding the mountains all morning had grown immensely tall. It covered half the sky now, black as night, except where it was lit internally by flashes of lightning. It appeared to Worrible to be toppling toward him. Already it had swallowed up the rear of his column. Now, turning his telescope on the war-shrine, he watched that ungainly vehicle swerve and topple as the wind hit, scattering priests and spiky idols in its fall. The wind came racing at him over the grass, faster than a speeding kampavan, faster than a city, faster by far than the poor, hard-laboring old Hundberg.

Why had his witch not warned him of this? She must have known! Worrible sensed that he had made a terrible mistake. He started to run toward the hatch that would let him back into the shelter of his fortress. But he never reached it. The strengthening wind caught him and held him like a huge, cold hand, and the storm broke over him, a shrieking blackness filled with knives of ice.

❁

When the storm shadow fell across Museion, it found Vespertine prowling the picturesque alleyways that branched off from the Quadrangle. She was hunting down the last of the nomad boarding parties. Some she killed, angered by the things they had done to the city or its people. Most, when they saw her coming, simply fled, and flung themselves wildly from Museion's side into the mud below — a long drop, but a fairly soft landing. Sometimes, if they hesitated, Vespertine picked them up and threw them over the side herself.

She did not notice the weather changing or the wind rising until a sudden gust blew the nomad she had just hurled overboard straight back in her face. It was a surprise for both of them. "Sorry!" the lad said nervously, and then, "Thank you!" and, "Aaaaargh!" as Vespertine picked him up and re-hurled him, harder this time.

She made her way back to the Quadrangle through streets strewn with tiles torn from the roofs of nearby buildings. The rushing air was filled with ivy leaves. In the Quadrangle itself, some of the militia, inspired by Vespertine's example, had bravely attacked a band of nomads. A body lay on the graveled path beside the fountain, and a man in professorial robes was struggling toward it against the battering wind.

Vespertine recognized Professor Stanislaus, and went to him. Even she was finding it hard to keep her footing by then. She caught him by the hand as a gust almost bowled him over, and helped him into the shelter of a nearby doorway.

"That poor boy is one of my students," Stanislaus shouted, trying to break free of her and return to the body on the gravel. "Enzo Rotola is his name. He may only be wounded! I must fetch help!"

Vespertine looked back at the body. Her eyes were better than human ones at such distances, in that dim light. She could see at once that Enzo Rotola was beyond help.

"He is dead," she said.

"Really? You are sure?"

Vespertine considered telling him what a nomad axe had done to the young man's head, but decided that it might upset him, and merely nodded.

Hailstones began to fall, very suddenly and startlingly loud. Vespertine shoved open the door and let them into the shadowy quiet of the Old-Tech Department. Reconstructions of Ancient flying machines hung from the ceiling on softly creaking cables: a helicopter and an X-Wing Fighter. (No one had ever managed to puzzle out how either of them flew.)

Stanislaus sank down on the plinth where a machine from the Blue Metal Culture was displayed. "It is so unfair!" he said. "I should have been killed, not Rotola. My life is over, but Enzo had sixty years ahead of him, perhaps, and who knows what discoveries and good works?"

"It is unfair," Vespertine agreed. She did not like what he had said about his life being over. She took off her welder's mask and squatted next to him. "You are unwell," she said.

Stanislaus shrugged. "Yes. It is not something I choose to advertise. All rather gloomy."

"The doctors cannot repair you?"

"No. Apparently not. They give me pills that help to control the pain. Not the fear, though." He smiled at her, a little ruefully. "It is a private matter, Miss Vespertine. Please don't mention it to anyone else."

Vespertine nodded solemnly. The hail beat like angry, armored fists against the windows.

The Ancients, thought Hilly, would have thought all this was simply weather. They would have pointed out that the atomics and Slow Bombs they had lobbed at one another in the Sixty Minute War were the sort of things that tended to leave a bit of a dent on a planet's climate, and unseasonal hyperstorms were just another of the long-lingering aftershocks. The Ancients had been very wise, and they had not believed in the old gods of the sky and the ice, or in their anger. Hilly found it calming to remember that, as the notice that the weather was on the turn. He had been watching the chase from an open observation deck on the Hundberg's roof. Heavier and slower than its kampavans, the old fortress was now many miles northeast of Museion and the rest of the pack. Every few moments Worrible leaned forward to bellow orders down the speaking tube that connected him to the control room. Mostly he shouted, "Faster!" but sometimes for variety's sake he would yell, "Faster, damn you! More speed! Or I'll feed you to the furnaces!"

It was not an idle threat, and the men in the control room did their best to obey. Lumbering old thing that it was, the Hundberg seemed in danger of shaking itself to pieces. The long banners streamed out in the wind of its passage. The barges and landships that carried the Dogs' wives, families, and supplies had been left far behind. Worrible was not worried about them. He was not even too bothered when the motorized shrine to the war gods, which had been plowing along ahead of the Hundberg, was overtaken. All he wanted was to catch up with his hounds and help them seize that city. For months Sister Rothrock had been telling him of the treasures it held. Catching Museion was all that mattered. The rest of the column could follow in their own sweet time, to share in what was left of the spoils. Then the Dogs would have all the fuel and loot they could carry. They could bid goodbye to Crawley, and go hunting fat traction villages in the green fields of the west. It would be just like the old days again!

But as the prey drew nearer, and Worrible strained his eyes to try to make out what was happening aboard it, there was a sudden, loud *flap*, like someone shaking out a sheet, and the banners that had been streaming astern began to billow forward instead. At the same moment, Worrible felt a chill breeze, as if someone with icy breath was blowing gently but insistently on the back of his neck.

He turned, and looked up, then up again.

The wall of cloud that had been slowly enfolding the mountains all morning had grown immensely tall. It covered half the sky now, black as night, except where it was lit internally by flashes of lightning. It appeared to Worrible to be toppling toward him. Already it had swallowed up the rear of his column. Now, turning his telescope on the war-shrine, he watched that ungainly vehicle swerve and topple as the wind hit, scattering priests and spiky idols in its fall. The wind came racing at him over the grass, faster than a speeding kampavan, faster than a city, faster by far than the poor, hard-laboring old Hundberg.

Why had his witch not warned him of this? She must have known! Worrible sensed that he had made a terrible mistake. He started to run toward the hatch that would let him back into the shelter of his fortress. But he never reached it. The strengthening wind caught him and held him like a huge, cold hand, and the storm broke over him, a shrieking blackness filled with knives of ice.

When the storm shadow fell across Museion, it found Vespertine prowling the picturesque alleyways that branched off from the Quadrangle. She was hunting down the last of the nomad boarding parties. Some she killed, angered by the things they had done to the city or its people. Most, when they saw her coming, simply fled, and flung themselves wildly from Museion's side into the mud below — a long drop, but a fairly soft landing. Sometimes, if they hesitated, Vespertine picked them up and threw them over the side herself.

She did not notice the weather changing or the wind rising until voices of the wind rose in a chorus of demented screams, and the hail bombarded the walls and roofs of Museion far more fearsomely than nomad guns.

But where were the Ancients now, with all their wisdom? Gone, gone, wiped away so utterly that no one even knew for sure how many centuries it had been since their dominion over Earth had ended. They had not believed in the gods, and now all that was left of them were rusty relics. So when half the windows on the starboard side of the Senior Common Room exploded inward under the pressure of the wind, and hailstones the size of cricket balls began landing on the hearthrug, Hilly offered up an earnest prayer to Peripatetia, and another to Clio, the goddess of History. She could not be certain that the goddesses were listening, but if they weren't, well, her prayers would have done no harm. And if they were, perhaps one of them could have a quiet word with the more boisterous deities who brewed up northern storms . . .

News of how she had saved Lamorna Fey seemed to have spread, and when she arrived back at the Ivory Tower the Senior Fellows had not shut her back in her little room. Word had reached them of the cargo ramp, which everyone was sure had been lowered deliberately in order to slow the city and to aid its enemies. Miss Torpenhow could not have been responsible for that, since she had been securely locked up when it happened. So perhaps she was not responsible for Bellweather's murder either? A few were still unsure of her, but most now felt they had been too hasty in accusing her, and they suggested she join them in the Senior Common Room, where all those who had nothing directly to contribute to the battle were sitting it out.

Hilly had accepted, feeling rather glad of a comfortable chair after her adventures. She had asked for a pot of tea, and had been about to pour herself a cup when the windows came in. The wind, screeching through the shattered panes, grabbed handfuls of papers from the wooden pigeon-holes inside the door and flung them about. Letters and memoranda whirled and flapped around the heads of the startled Senior Fellows as they struggled to close the heavy wooden shutters. Professor Pringle plucked a hailstone from the rug and stood holding it triumphantly aloft, while ice water ran down his arm and spattered his robes. "I *told* you there was bad weather coming!" he said.

"Oh, do stop crowing, Pringle!" snapped Professor Waghorn. "It is only a storm . . ."

From somewhere above them, faint beneath the din the wind was making, they heard a strangled cry, and a crash of breaking glass.

"That sounded," said Professor Pott-Walloper, "as if it came from the dean's office . . ."

They hurried upstairs: Waghorn, the Pringles, Professor Pott-Walloper, and Hilly. On the landing outside the dean's office they met Professor Loomis, who Hilly supposed must have run down from the navigation suite on the top floor. "Did you hear it too?" he asked.

Waghorn pushed the door open. The dean lay slumped over his desk, the window behind him shattered by the storm. There was a deep wound in his head, presumably made by the same hailstone that had smashed the window. It lay on the desk beside him, trundling to and fro as the city moved.

"Is he dead?" asked Loomis, watching as Waghorn ran to close the shutters while Hilly and Mrs. Pringle cautiously approached the lifeless figure at the desk.

Mrs. Pringle nervously reached out and felt for a pulse in the dean's neck. "No. Not quite. Not yet."

Everyone began talking at once.

"Lay him down!"

"Put a cushion under his head!"

"Loosen his collar!"

"Fetch him some brandy!"

"Does anyone have any smelling salts?"

No one had. They improvised by burning a feather from Professor Pott-Walloper's hat and holding that under the dean's nose, but he did not stir. Nor did he show any interest in the largeish brandy Professor Waghorn poured him.

"It looks bad," said Pringle.

"Someone should run to the infirmary for Dr. Jaffaji," said Waghorn.

"In this weather? We would be struck down the instant we set foot outside."

"We must make the dean as comfortable as we can here," said Professor Loomis. "We can send word to the infirmary as soon as the storm dies down. These north-country squalls don't generally last long, whatever Pringle says."

But the storm showed no sign of blowing itself out. Professor Waghorn shrugged, and drank the brandy he had poured. Hilly helped to make the dean comfortable upon the couch in the corner of his office. She could hear the wind howling outside, and the shutters rattled occasionally, but no hail struck them. Of course, the office was on the leeward side of the Ivory Tower, sheltered from the worst of the storm. How unlucky, she thought, and how odd, that one solitary hailstone should have shattered the window, and struck down the poor dean with the accuracy of a sharpshooter . . .

She went back downstairs to the Senior Common Room and looked out of the leeward windows there. Sure enough, rain and hail were still rushing past, almost horizontally, but none of it was hitting the windows on that side of the tower. She had a nasty feeling that Museion's enemy within had struck again, seizing on this awful storm as an opportunity to attack the dean. She wondered who to tell, and whether she would be believed.

And then she saw something that drove it from her mind. For beyond the rushing hail not all was darkness: She could see the sternward spires and rooftops quite clearly, standing out as black silhouettes against a pulsing red glow.

"I believe a fire has broken out," she said. "Oh dear, oh dear! It is just one thing after another. Poor Museion. This day has gone from bad to worse . . ."

23

Fires Were Started

The fire was Stoat's fault. After the Revenant attacked them, he and his followers had made their way back to the hold where they had left the *War Baby*. But while they had been busy in the city's depths, the dragging cargo ramp had finally torn free from its overstressed hinges and been left behind. Without it there was no way for the kampavans to leave.

More survivors of the raid crept in. Stoat did his best to rally them. He tried to convince them that one more push would make Museion theirs. But Vespertine had been moving so swiftly around the city that the scared and battered Dogs believed there might be two, or three, or half a dozen of her. No appeal to greed or honor could raise their spirits. No punishment Stoat could threaten was worse than the prospect of facing Stalkers.

To make things worse, Museion's militia had found their courage. They had been harrying the retreating nomads with antique muskets and a couple of highly collectible Widmerpool machine guns. Now, with the last of the Dogs penned in the hold, they took up positions outside it and yelled at them to throw down their weapons and surrender. That was not a word that often featured in the vocabulary of the Junkyard Dogs, but many of them now found it had a certain appeal.

"We could give ourselves up," said Krowbar nervously.

Stoat shot him dead. Krowbar had been his friend since they were pups together, but friends didn't let friends dishonor the war gods with coward's talk like that. "Who else wants to surrender to these townies?" Stoat yelled.

To his surprise, a fair few hands went up.

"We won't be slaves for long, Stoat," said Yanna. "These townies are too soft. We'll bide our time, and gather our strength, and start the fight again another day."

Stoat snarled at her, but all around him the weary, wounded Dogs were starting to mutter their agreement. "She's got a point, Stoat," one said.

"It is dishonor," said Stoat.

"It's the only way," said Yanna, and Stoat knew she was right, and hated her for it.

"Throw down your guns!" called the voices from outside. "Give yourselves up!"

"Hold on!" yelled one of the Dogs, backing toward the door with his eyes on Stoat. When Stoat did not attack him, his comrades started moving too. Soon they were all crowding to the doors, throwing down notched swords and empty guns, creeping out of the hold with their hands up and their heads down, to be grabbed and led away while Vespertine stood by to make sure no one changed their mind.

Soon Stoat stood alone in the hold. He looked at the battered, oil-seeping kampavans, the crates of loot he could not cart away, the body of Krowbar whom he now slightly regretted killing. He looked out through the open back of the hold at the empty land

and the weird, bruised sky. He could not grasp how a day that had begun in so much glory could be ending like this, in darkness and defeat. It made him sad. It made him angry. It made him weep hot tears of shame and pity.

"Come on, son," called a man's voice, kindly sounding, from just outside the doorway. "We know you're in there. Come out quiet and we'll not harm you."

Fuel was pooling on the deck between the kampavans, leaking from the *War Baby*'s fuel tank, which had been ruptured when she landed in the hold. A little stream of it was creeping across the deck toward the place where Stoat stood. Stoat breathed it in, that petroleum perfume. He threw away his empty gun. He threw away his sword. He threw away various small knives. He took out his lighter and flicked it to make a flame. "The Dogs took this town," he said, but softly, so only he and the war gods could hear. "If the Dogs can't have it, no one will."

He left the lighter burning and set it down in the path of the stream of fuel. Then he raised his hands high above his head and went out through the door like all the others, and as they marched him and his packmates aft he heard the *whooomph* of the *War Baby*'s fuel tanks exploding. It sounded like bitter victory.

❁

Hours later, the fire was still burning. Days later, it seemed to Max, for he had lost all sense of time as he worked with the rest of the engine district to try to stop the flames from spreading.

Yet spread they did. The fires had consumed everything in the cargo hold, and then set out to make new homes for themselves among the oily workshops and storerooms of the district, where they started raising families of excitable baby fires.

"It mustn't reach the fuel stores!" people kept shouting, as Max trained his fire hose on the flames, or on unburned bulkheads and partitions that they hoped to stop the flames from devouring. "If the fuel stores go up, Museion goes with them!" Max remembered someone shrieking at him, as if it were all his fault. Maybe that had been Luka Voss himself? He could not recall. People came and went as if he were in a dream. One moment he was helping a burly woman mechanic work the hose, the next she had become a bumbling professor, come down from the top tier to do his best to help. Everyone looked the same soon anyway: blackened clothes; soot-smeared faces; wild, red, bloodshot eyes. Most people wrapped dampened cloths around their nose and mouth, but the smoke and fumes still found a way into their lungs. They coughed and choked as they worked, and sometimes someone collapsed and had to be carried off to regions where the air was clearer. The rest labored on, moving mindlessly through the smoke and the jagged firelight.

The hoses had minds, though, or they seemed to. The thick canvas tubes writhed and twisted like captive snakes, constantly trying to escape the hands that held them. Sometimes they succeeded, and lashed about, spraying water uselessly over the firefighters rather than the fire, knocking people flat with their heavy brass nozzles, until they could be caught, and tamed, and pointed at the fire again.

Around midnight someone shouted at Max to take a break, and pointed him to a place where some ladies from the top tier had set up a tea urn on a trestle table. He stumbled to the table and took the tin mug they passed him. As he drank, he watched scared cattle being driven past, and one of the ladies told him that the barn the beasts had been housed in was threatened by the fires so they were being moved to Dark Park, to be stabled among the statues there.

The scalding, teak-brown tea was the best thing Max had ever drunk, and the stale biscuits that went with it were the best thing he had ever eaten. He handed the mug back and returned to his hose. The man who had been in charge before was gone, injured by falling debris, one of the others said. They seemed disorientated without him, so Max took his place, encouraging them forward to where the fires burned hottest, pulling them back just in time when more sections of the roof came down. The air was full of scraps of charred paper from a blazing office, whirling like the bats that had fled from Museion's wheel arches when it first set off. As they fell past his face, Max saw that the ink on some of the scraps was still glowing red, so that they were covered with fiery writing, but it always faded before he could read it.

He knew he should be scared. He was in far more danger now than he had been in the battle. Fire was something that everyone who lived on moving cities was brought up to fear. But Max was too tired to be scared — too tired, and in too much pain from his aching muscles and blistered hands. By midnight he no longer cared much if Museion burned or not. On the whole, he thought, he rather wished it would. Then at least he would be allowed to rest.

Of the storm that was screaming around the city he knew nothing, although later, looking back, he would dimly remember looking out or up through some new opening the fire had made and seeing the sleet driving by. He hoped for a moment it might douse the flames, but if anything the wind just seemed to make them burn brighter and hotter. So he held tight to his hose, and the fire roared, and the flames leaped, and the dreadful night wore on.

24

Doom in the Doghouse

Thane Worrible was nowhere to be found. Some said he had been outside when the storm hit, which meant he was most likely dead. On the upper decks of the Hundberg, his lieutenants were beginning to squabble among themselves about who should succeed him.

The workers down below knew none of that. They only knew that the Ancient vehicle's engines were laboring harder to provide less and less speed, and that the overseers were growing distracted, more concerned with the news their messenger pups were bringing from up above than with the sweat-drenched, soot-smeared men who toiled to feed the furnaces. A warrior in a fox-fur cape barged in and began talking urgently to the chief of the overseers. Doom could not hear what they were saying over on the far side of the boiler room, but he knew panic when he saw it. He stopped shoveling. One of the other thralls, a young easterner, stopped work too, though — like Doom — he kept a firm grip on his shovel. Doom caught his eye and nodded.

"Back to work!" an overseer screamed, and a whip stung

Doom's shoulders. He was careful not to flinch. The warrior and the chief overseer had turned to look at him.

"Storm's come, has it?" Doom asked them. The engines were idling now, and all the thralls had stopped work. The wind could be heard, howling and hollering around the Hundberg's hull. "Listen!" said Doom. "That ain't no natural wind. There's voices in it. Demons, most likely. Old gods of the north, woken from their slumbers and come looking for trouble. Those Museion professors know how to call on them. They have a weather wizard, Pringle the Wise, who can summon up tempests to order. This wind's his work, I'm reckoning. It bears a fierce grudge against the Junkyard Dogs. It won't leave till you give up this hunt, and free your thralls."

The gesture he made encompassed everyone in the boiler room. The few men around him who understood translated in low voices for those who didn't, and all of them stood slightly straighter, and their eyes shone with a new light. They had long since given up hope of ever being freed. Now they looked at one another with expressions they had not used in long and bitter months. The wind sang its mad songs outside, but no one was listening.

"Kill that one," said the warrior, pointing at Doom.

The nearest overseer pulled a long knife from his belt and strode over to Doom, which was exactly what Doom had hoped would happen. He slammed the flat of his shovel into the man's face, and the young easterner darted in and grabbed the knife. Other overseers were running forward now. The warrior at the entrance drew a pistol from his holster.

"Come on!" shouted Doom. He figured that his fellow thralls would understand his tone even if they didn't recognize the words.

For a moment, it seemed they were too scared and cowed to

follow him. Doom used the shovel shaft to block a blow from a second overseer, and the easterner thrust his knife into a third. The warrior's pistol went off and Doom felt the ball flick past his head. Then, as if it had been a starting gun, everyone was suddenly moving, the thralls rushing the overseers, snatching whips, swinging shovels.

Doom felt pleased with himself. He hoped the thralls would win their freedom and maybe take over the whole fortress. But he did not plan to be their leader. That young eastern fellow seemed to be handling things all right. He had been trained, by the look of him, and he wore the remnants of a uniform. Doom guessed he was a soldier of the Anti-Traction League, captured in some skirmish on the marches of Shan Guo. Leaving him to handle things, Doom limped away from the battle down a passageway he'd spotted earlier. He didn't like skipping out on a fight, but he knew his job was to get off this battlewagon, find Tamzin, and make his way back to Hilly.

At the end of the passageway was a surprised guard and a bolted hatch. Doom punched the first and unbolted the second. But as he started to push the hatch open, the heavy, armored cover was wrenched first from his hand and then from its hinges. Doom peered out into a horizontal torrent of fist-size hailstones. For a moment he wondered if the things he had said about the storm to frighten Worrible's thugs might actually be true. The wind was bellowing like a vengeful god.

There was plainly no way out until the weather cleared, so it would be best to join the rioting thralls after all. Wearily, cursing his aching back, Doom borrowed the unconscious guard's axe and pistol and went limping back into the battle.

25

THE FROZEN WORLD

A cold wind blew gently through base tier and stirred the hanging clouds of smoke and steam. It blew on Max Angmering where he lay asleep on a heap of sodden sacks, and woke him. He did not remember how he came to be there. He had been fighting the fires, and when they started to die down someone had told him to go home and get some rest, but he had gotten lost on his way to the stairs. He must have sat down for a moment on the sacks and fallen asleep. He had dreamed of the Middle Sea, and of Posie Naphtali, the beautiful Anti-Tractionist submariner he had met there. He lay for a while, hoping sleep would come again, for it had been a pleasant dream.

But cold water was dripping on him, and the noise of people clearing wreckage echoed all around, so he rose, and wandered through the blackened and half-flooded streets. The stairways farther forward were blocked, someone told him. If he wanted to get up to the top tier he should try the stern stairs.

He went aft, and the streets were busy, full of repair teams going about their work. Several of the engines were out of action, and there was a tremendous effort underway to bring them back online. But Max heard laughter everywhere, and passersby greeted him as if he were an old friend, as if his blistered hands and soot-smeared face marked him as one of their own. *And maybe they did*, he thought. He felt an intense love now for these people and this city. They had passed through night and fire together, and fought side by side when it seemed defeat was certain, and the night and the fire had passed, and a new day had come.

Losing his way again among the charcoal passageways, he asked directions to the stern stairs from a gang of workers replacing a buckled exhaust flue. They pointed him in the right direction. "Careful, friend! It's an ice rink out there!"

There was indeed a lot of ice. Moving cautiously, Max crept out onto the open apron at the city's stern, where spindly walkways ran between the huge pipes of the exhaust system. Sunrise was happening somewhere by then, turning the fog beyond the smokestacks peachy pink. Wild sprays of ice extended from the walkway where Max stood, and from the handrail of the walkway, and the walkways above, and the stairs between them, and the cables and ducts that snaked overhead, and even from the smokestacks themselves. Foot-long icicles reached out horizontally, or hung layered like frozen waterfalls, or formed coronas around the domed cowlings of ventilators.

"Meringue boy!" called Luka Voss, and Max looked up to see the chief engineer standing above him on one of the landings of an open metal staircase that zigzagged up the city's stern.

Max waved and went to join him, going carefully up stairs fringed with icicles. Voss watched him skeptically. "Careful!" he called. "People have fallen from here before, in the dark or the fog."

But as he said it the fog thinned, and in that strange seashell light all the ice was kindled into fire. Max reached the landing and they stood side by side in a frozen explosion of light.

"It is beautiful," said Voss.

Max felt surprised, because he had thought Voss too tough and cynical a sort of person to think anything beautiful. But he had been wrong, of course. He noticed a wreath of faded flowers tied with wire to the handrail nearby, a memorial of some sort. He guessed Voss had come up here to pay his respects, or give thanks for the city's salvation.

"You did well last night," Voss said, when they had stood in silence for a time.

"I didn't do much."

"You did your best, and people noticed that. The Mayor of Thorbury's son, they said, come down from the top tier to man a fire hose like all the rest of us. Or maybe they said, look at that soft golden boy who has no idea how to hold a hose. But even the ones who said that were encouraged, because they weren't about to let you outdo them. You've got something in you that people like, Max Angmering. It gives them the courage to do things they might not be able to do otherwise. Your ancestors were warriors, and the founders of a fine city."

"But that was so long ago!" said Max, thinking of his fussy, mild-mannered father and his kindly grandpa. "I know the blood of Graf Lothar Angmering runs in my veins, but it must be pretty well diluted by now."

"Yet it is there still," said Voss. "And maybe it will be needed again, before this journey's over. Our simple plan has grown complicated, as simple plans so often do. Those war hounds have driven us far off our planned course, and they may still be out there, licking their wounds, waiting to try again. There is danger ahead of us as well as behind. Museion needs someone better than a dithering dean or a potty professor to lead it to safety."

"You could do it," said Max. "People will follow you."

"Engine-district people will," said Voss, "but not the top-tier lot. I can't go up there anyway. Even with this fog to shade me, the sun is growing too fierce. I must scurry back into my shadows before it burns me to cinders." He hesitated a moment. "Come," he said.

"I was going upstairs. I want to find out what has happened to Miss Torpenhow, and Vespertine . . ."

"And I must get back to my work," said Voss. "But I have something to show you first, and it will not take long. Come."

All night, while the storm raged and died, the stairways and chambers of the Hundberg had echoed with the sounds of violence. Now, in the silent dawn, they resounded with the noise of partying. The rebel thralls and those Junkyard Dogs who had joined them were looting Worrible's stores of wine and food, and making themselves at home in his throne room. What had become of Worrible himself, no one seemed to know. Doom did his best to explain that they needed to find the missing thane, who might be busy preparing to take the fortress back for all they knew. But the victorious slaves were not listening, or did not care.

Only the young easterner, who had been the first to help Doom in the hold, understood the danger. His name was Esan Altan and, as Doom had guessed, he had been a soldier in the armies of the Mountain Kingdoms. He had been captured when one of Hamburg's outrider suburbs devoured the fort where he was stationed. He spoke just enough Anglish to explain that, and to follow Doom's reasoning. Together, they pushed their way through the rowdy party that was developing in the throne room and kicked open the door behind the throne.

The passageway behind it led to Worrible's bedchamber, which had already been looted, and to a smaller room with magical symbols painted on its door. A man had smashed the lock and blundered in, but he now lay dead in the doorway with a black-feathered dart sticking out from his neck. The witch's lair had been protected by at least one booby trap, and it had trapped at least one booby.

Altan kept well back, murmuring in his own language a prayer against the evil eye. Doom went closer to the doorway and peered cautiously inside. There was a lot of magical clutter in there, but amid all the totems and black candles a surprisingly clean and shiny machine was sitting on a shelf. A pale glow came from little windows in its front. One of those newfangled radio sets, Doom reckoned. Quite a fancy one too. He remembered how Uncle Eagle claimed to have heard the witch talking to demons in her room. Was that how she kept in contact with her Bugtown bosses, and with whoever it was aboard Museion who was in Bugtown's pay? Doom considered switching the machine on, and wondered who would answer if he did. But he had never used a radio, and was not really sure how they worked. Besides, the witch might have rigged other traps to protect her stuff from snoopers.

They moved on through the maze of cabins and chambers at the Hundberg's stern. They found no sign of Worrible in any of the cabins, but many dead bodies. Some were warriors and thralls who had fallen in the fighting, but others were just women and servants who had simply gotten in the way, or vainly tried to protect some trinket from a man who fancied it for his own. Some were only children. War had been Doom's business all his life, and nothing that he saw surprised him, but it left him saddened and depressed. It was too easy to imagine Tamzin or Max or Hilly as dead as those poor kids.

Hoping to clear his head of the fug of blood and engine fumes that filled the fortress, he climbed the companionway to the roof, and pushed open the door at the top. A line of icicles fell from the doorframe as it opened, breaking around his feet with a sound like the chiming of tiny bells. He stepped out into dense fog, and almost went headlong as his feet slid from under him. The top of the fortress was covered with a clear sheet of ice. The lower turrets and battlements were all encased in it too. They shone coldly in the gray light, as if recently varnished. Frost-encrusted banners hung motionless from glistening flagstaffs. Apart from the faint sounds of looting and celebration on the lower levels, an awful silence reigned.

Doom made his way cautiously along the fortress's spine to the observation deck that looked out over the prow. There he found Thane Worrible, glazed with ice like everything else in that unearthly dawn. He must have been trying to crawl back inside, Doom thought, but the wind and the ice had done him in, and he had lain down here in all his frosted finery, helpless as a lost child. He tried to pull the dead man's cloak over his face but, like its wearer, it was frozen stiff.

Altan came creeping and slithering to join him and they stood together, looking down at the dead man. "We should be happy," said the easterner.

Doom shook his head. "It's not good to be happy when someone dies, even when they're your enemy. Even when they're a massive wrong 'un like Worrible. He was human like you and me. Being glad would make us less so."

"What will we do now?" asked Altan.

"Find our ways home, I guess," said Doom. "Funny thing, I never really had a home, nor wanted one. Six months ago, I'd have said I was a burned-out old codger and I might as well stop a bullet in my next fight and let that be an end of it. But then I ran into Hilly, and we suit each other so well, although we're as different as night and day, that home is just wherever she is now. Which is Museion currently, so I need to get back there. But I'll have to find Tamzin first. She's part of home too."

Altan did not speak very much Anglish. He understood little that this old barbarian said, but he recognized the word "home." It reminded him of the high valley where he had grown up, far from barbarians and their motor cities. He wished he was back there. He raised his head and looked out at the fog, willing it to part like curtains and reveal the mountains of his homeland. But instead, out there in the whiteness beyond the Hundberg's stern, he heard a grumble of great engines, and the slink and crunch of caterpillar tracks.

"Listen!" said Doom. "Hear that? That'll be the rest of the convoy, hurrying to catch up." He was already starting his slithery journey back to the companionway. "The captains of those landships are Worrible's men. Half of them will want to avenge him, and all of them will want to take his place. Let's make ourselves scarce before the fighting starts. I need to find this Bugtown place and see what's become of Tamzin."

"Look!" shouted Altan.

The fog astern was darkening as some huge shape materialized through it. It was not a landship. Clusters of lights burned green, mounted on something higher than the Hundberg. The fog tore in front of them, and Doom looked up at the huge, blunt nose of an armored suburb. He did not need to find Bugtown after all. Bugtown had found him.

"Cover! Take cover!" shouted Altan, whose experiences had left him with a healthy fear of suburbs. And, sure enough, the front of this one was starting to widen alarmingly as it swung open its hydraulic jaws. Doom caught a glimpse between those jaws into a furnace-lit dismantling hangar. Then Altan dragged him back down the companionway.

The predator surged forward. With a blast of steam and a churning rattle of gigantic chains, its jaws swung shut, and the rotating teeth with which they were lined gripped the Hundberg and dragged it in.

26

Course Correction

The grand buildings of the upper tier emerged slowly from the fog, looking like ghosts of themselves. Hilly Torpenhow, walking back from the infirmary where the dean still lay unconscious, saw that the pond in the Quadrangle had been drained to supply water for the firefighters. On its floor, the bodies of dead nomads had been laid out in rows. Groups of Museion people wandered about in dazed silence, like revelers making their way home after a wild party. Hilly noticed that half of them looked like nomads themselves now, for they had helped themselves to the armor and weapons of dead Junkyard Dogs.

Professor Stanislaus was sitting on the steps outside the Old-Tech Department, watching some students sweep up the shattered glass from the doors. He called out to Hilly as she passed, glad to see that she had been released from custody.

"You have heard about the dean?" she said. "It is pretty clear that whoever attacked him killed Rowan Bellweather and let down the ramps as well, and everyone can see I couldn't have been responsible for all those things."

"I never imagined you were responsible for any of them," said

Stanislaus. "I took shelter in the library yesterday when the nomads came aboard. It gave me time to talk with the librarians. It appears that the thefts have been going on for some months — a book here, a folio there. The stolen volumes were all about Old-Tech — instruction manuals for unknown machines, accounts of Ancient weapon systems. The librarians thought that the culprit might have been one of our Old-Tech specialists, who took them with him when he left the city. But clearly the thief is still with us, since you disturbed him the night before last."

"It seems so long ago," said Hilly. "Perhaps poor Rowan recognized him, and that was why the thief had to kill him."

"That doesn't help us much," said Stanislaus. "There are so few people aboard Museion now. Rowan would have recognized any of us."

He raised himself painfully to his feet, and they walked together through the alley that led into the Library Gardens. Vespertine was standing by the balustrade at the tier's edge, looking like a misplaced statue. Beyond her, the fog was breaking up, forming brief windows and archways in which vistas of brown plains and far-off mountains were framed.

"I can hear engines," said the Revenant.

"Voss will be turning on the ones that were shut down by the fire," said Stanislaus. "It is nothing to be concerned about."

"But some of the engines I can hear are *out there,*" said Vespertine, pointing at the passing landscape.

"More kampavans?" asked Hilly nervously. "Or perhaps the Junkyard Dogs' landship fleet has caught up with us . . ."

"Bigger," said Vespertine.

Hilly strained her ears, and so did Stanislaus. Even they heard something now: engines, and the terse sigh of big hydraulics, and a crunching, crashing, shattering, dragging noise, far off, but not nearly far enough. And then, as Museion crested a low rise, they saw it, a half mile to the north. A strange, iron-shelled, segmented place, caught in the act of eating a mass of broken timber and rusty iron.

"A predator suburb!" gasped Hilly. "Quickly! Raise the alarm!"

❁

Voss had an apartment above the control room. A strange, cluttered nest of a place, Max thought, windowless and dark. No doubt Voss liked it that way. On the wall of the living area was a framed painting of people he supposed must be Voss's parents. A bluff-looking balding man in smart red overalls, and a woman who had the same far-apart black eyes and wide, clever mouth as Voss himself, except that they looked beautiful on her. She seemed to have come from a different time or a different world from that which Voss's father inhabited. Around her neck on chains and leather thongs hung old engine parts, shards of Ancient circuit board, and the skulls and bones of birds and small animals.

"Wait," ordered Voss, and vanished through a curtained doorway into another room, where Max glimpsed a large, unmade bed. The floor trembled slightly as one of the shut-down engines started up again. Voss returned, looking solemn, and bearing a long bundle wrapped in cloth. He laid it on a table and unswaddled it to reveal a heavy, antique sword. When Voss drew it from its leather scabbard, Max saw nomad runes engraved along the blade. The iridescent edge gleamed as if it were so sharp that it was cutting the light into rainbows.

"This was my mother's," Voss said. "It came down through her family. It was forged in the north in the days of the Nomad

Empires. She said it was the same sword Blind Cluny Morvish carried at the siege of the Rostok Nest, but I do not know if that is true. It seems a heavy sword for a woman, but Cluny Morvish was a strong woman, the stories say. Whatever, it is a good sword, and it is yours now."

"Mine?" said Max, surprised. "But I couldn't — "

"It is a gift. Do you think I have any use for swords, here in my engine district? Do you think I will have any use for one if we make it to London? Do you think I would have the strength and skill to use one, even if we did? I am happy down here in the shadows, but sometimes I think it would have been nice to be a creature of the sunlight like you, and go adventuring under the bright sky. If you take the sword, then I will have some part in your adventures for as long as you carry it."

Max took the sword from him and looked at it, and felt its weight. Voss watched the reflections from the blade light up Max's tanned and handsome face, and knew that he had done the right thing, and that his mother would approve.

"What am I to do with it?" asked Max.

"Kill your enemies," said Voss with a shrug. "And wave it about to encourage your people. That is its main use. Swords are more for show than fighting with, these days."

"What enemies?" asked Max.

Voss shrugged again. "Wait and see. I have a feeling some will show up soon."

And, as if he had summoned them, the alarm bells began to ring again, and a scared messenger, bursting through the apartment door, shouted, "Voss! Predator on the starboard beam!"

Voss sprang to the door and ran after the woman. Max paused to sheathe the sword, then followed him. He considered leaving the sword behind, for it seemed too valuable to accept as a gift. But he guessed that would only offend Voss, so he carried it with him as he fled downstairs into the barely organized chaos of the control room, where bells were still ringing, lights were flashing, and Voss in his chair was shouting, "Hard a-port!"

Museion's engines screamed. The city spun about and set off at speed. "What town is out there?" Max shouted. "What town is it?"

❋

What town was it? Hilly was wondering the same thing as she stood at the balcony rail with her hands over her ears to block out the booms from the guns in nearby emplacements. It looked like a wood louse, like a centipede, with all those segments, and the track units sticking out from under its iron shell on leggy stanchions. But it seemed slow to turn, hampered perhaps by the wreckage still wedged in its half-open jaws. Steering must be a complicated business too, with all those separate tracks to control. The exhaust stacks that poked up through its shell pumped oily smoke, but there could be no room in any of the suburb's segments for engines as big as the ones now thrusting Museion forward.

A ragged cheer went up from the watchers on Museion's sides as the strange place fell astern. It fired a harpoon before it vanished, but the range was too long and the harpoon splashed harmlessly into the mud in Museion's wake. It would take them time to wind that back in, thought Hilly, and that would slow them further. But she did not let herself relax, or celebrate. Museion was running across broken country, where a shed track or a shattered axle might bring it to a halt at any moment and let the hungry predator close the gap.

She went back across the gardens to the library itself, and Vespertine and Stanislaus went with her. It was easy enough to locate a copy of *Banvard's Gazeteer of Traction Towns*, one of the standard reference books of the Traction Era. A large and improbably complicated volume, it contained details of every town and city that moved upon the land, the sea, or in the air, along with detailed steel engravings of most of them, printed on 964 tissue-thin pages. Luckily, it was possible to search for towns by track type, and there were very few with the predator's peculiar system of independent track units.

"I knew it!" Hilly said triumphantly. "That town is Crawley. One of the suburbs London built in the late seven hundreds. People used to call it 'Creepy Crawley,' on account of its slow and scuttling movement. According to *Banvard's*, it was constructed as an experiment by a radical faction of the Guild of Engineers, led by a Dr. Jago Flint. They designed it for research, not hunting. No wonder it was too slow to catch us."

"It says there that it's 'missing, presumed eaten,'" objected Stanislaus, reading over her shoulder.

"I can't help that, professor. I suppose it has been up north in the Ice Wastes all these years, or hiding in the high passes of the Tannhäuser Mountains. Perhaps this bad weather has driven it south."

"It was jolly unlucky, running into it like that," said Stanislaus.

Outside, a bell began to ring. It was not one of those jangly alarm bells, which had added so much to the unpleasantness of the past twenty-four hours, but a large, solemn, sonorous bell.

"They are summoning us to the Great Hall," said Stanislaus. "They will be choosing someone to stand in for the dean, and deciding what happens next."

"May I come too?" asked Hilly. "I could tell them about Crawley."

"I trust we have left that nasty little town far behind us," said Stanislaus. "But do come, by all means. You too, Miss Vespertine."

❁

The choosing of an acting dean proved simple. Nobody really wanted the job. It was offered to Dr. Twyne, but he said that history showed it was unwise to give a military commander too much power. The only other candidate was Professor Loomis. Loomis was the man who had brought Museion this far, after all. Loomis was the man who had recruited Vespertine, without whose help the Junkyard Dogs might have sacked the whole city.

"I am not worthy," he said modestly, but they all assured him the post was only temporary, and at last, after much persuasion, he accepted.

"Very well, then," he said, holding up his hands to stop the smatterings of applause that greeted his decision. "Acting dean I shall be, although I hope I shall be able to hand over the title to the real dean again by lunchtime."

Dr. Jaffaji looked gloomy at that, and said the dean had a serious concussion and might not regain consciousness for days, if ever. In the meantime, it was agreed, Museion must continue on its journey.

Professor Loomis called for his charts, and spread them out on the High Table. He invited the Senior Fellows to gather around. "As you can see," he said, "the nomad attack and the storm have driven us far from our course. I had hoped to have us forty miles north of here by now, making our approach to the Ravnina Gap. But somehow in the chaos of yesterday we veered southward. Now the Golgan Hills bar the way ahead. We will have to turn north and follow their eastern edge for thirty miles in order to reach the Gap."

"But if Crawley is still feeling hungry, it could cut us off on the way!" said Max.

"Quite so," agreed Loomis solemnly.

"And we may find deep snow farther north," Professor Pringle pointed out. "Museion is not equipped for deep snow."

"Quite so," said Loomis again.

"And who's to say the Ravnina Gap won't be crawling with other hungry predator towns, driven down out of the Ice Wastes by this storm?" asked Hilly.

Loomis did not say "quite so" a third time, but they could all see him thinking it.

"Luckily, there is another way," he said, "and fate has brought us quite close to it. Just a few miles southwest of here — a day's journey at our current speed — a narrow pass leads through the Golgan Hills. It is a winding way, and old, but I believe it is still navigable for a city of Museion's size. It leads to the Pons Tempestus: the Bridge of Storms."

There was an intake of breath from the rest of the faculty. Brows were furrowed, lips pursed. After a moment's silence, they all began arguing.

"What's the Bridge of Storms?" asked Max.

"I'm sure we covered it in your geography lessons," said Hilly.

"I must not have been paying attention that day."

"You very seldom were, Max."

"Please tell me again."

"Very well," said Hilly. "The Vastri River flows through the Golgan Hills. It is not a broad river, but it has carved a deep gorge for itself. In 746 the Traction City of Stormsdown dismantled its own upper tiers and used them to build a bridge across the gorge so it could go hunting in the west. The way through the Ravnina Gap was blocked by a meltwater lake in those days."

"But that was more than a hundred years ago!" said Max.

"Exactly!" agreed Professor Stanislaus, overhearing him. He turned to Loomis. "Can we be sure the bridge has not fallen into ruin, or been torn apart by scavenger towns?"

"Even if it is still there," said Dr. Twyne, "I don't much like the look of it." He leaned over Loomis's map, tracing with a finger the path that wriggled through the close-clustering contour lines of the Golgan Hills until it reached the bridge. "That pass is a bottleneck. If I was the mayor of an ambush predator, that's just where I'd lie in wait for unwary towns."

"But Museion is not unwary," said Professor Loomis. "We proved ourselves in battle only yesterday. Your gunners and fighters have passed through a trial of fire, Twyne. Our lookouts are keen-eyed. We are not some helpless farming platform, venturing blindly into the hills. And, to answer Stanislaus's query, I flew over the gorge a few weeks ago with Rowan Bellweather, on the same voyage that led to Hawkshead. The bridge was standing then. It looked as strong as ever."

"All the same," said Twyne, "we must send the *Owl of Minerva* or the *Fire's Astonishment* ahead to check the way is clear."

"Oh, dear me, no!" cried Mrs. Pringle. "That would be far too dangerous. There is more bad weather coming! Isn't there, Colin?"

"Further storms are indicated," agreed her husband.

"So what do we think?" asked Loomis, stepping back from the chart and looking at them all. "I may be acting dean, but this is too grave a decision for me to make alone. Let's have a show of hands. Shall we head north for the Gap . . . ?"

Hilly and Max did not feel they had a right to vote. They stood watching as the Senior Fellows made their decisions. It was snowing again outside, in big flakes, which looked very white against the burned-out buildings on Museion's stern. How dreadful it would be to drag themselves all the way to the Gap only to find it blocked by snow . . .

"Or shall we try for the nearer road?" asked Loomis.

The hands went up, one by one.

"Very well," said Loomis solemnly. "It is decided. I shall have my people work out a course. Museion will take its chances on the Bridge of Storms."

27

The Immortal

"False alarm," said Mortmain, unlocking the door of Tamzin's cell a few minutes later.

"What's happening?" Tamzin demanded. She had woken to sirens wailing in the suburb's corridors, and a sensation of sudden speed. There had been a lurch, a pause, and a series of rending crashes. Then Crawley was moving, changing direction sharply enough to throw Tamzin from her bunk. Now it seemed to be stationary again. She crouched against the wall of her cell and rubbed the shoulder she had bruised in the fall, glaring at Mortmain as if he had caused it all.

"Nothing's happening," he said. "We have been hunting Museion, but we lost it in the fog, and came upon the Dogs' traction fortress instead. The Head decided we should eat that, and we had barely dragged it into the digestion hangar when we *did* spot Museion. But they must have spotted us too, or heard us, for they put on speed and we lost them. Annoying. It is all right, though. They cannot escape us. Apparently, several of their engines were damaged yesterday and cannot run at full power."

"How do you know so much about what's going on in Museion?" Tamzin asked.

"Crawley has a secret agent there."

"Who?"

"I don't know. Don't make that face, Tamzin — I truly don't. The whole point of secret agents is that nobody knows who they are. It's part of their mystique. Sister Rothrock and her security people call this one by a code name: 'Lamplighter.'"

"Is that how he sends his secret messages to them? With a signal lamp?"

"Oh no, something far more sophisticated, I expect. Now, how about some breakfast? I've managed to get you classified as Threat Level Zero, which means you are allowed to come with me to the canteen. All food is served in communal canteens here. It's the way of the future, apparently."

Tamzin considered telling him where he could stick his communal canteen, but then remembered that she had not eaten since she came aboard. Besides, in some strange way, she felt glad to see him. In this place of unknown dangers, at least Mortmain was a known one.

The streets were busy. The day seemed to be just beginning, although the light in Crawley's windowless warrens never changed. People were walking briskly to their workstations, and from the forward segments of the suburb came the noise of demolition engines at work. Several passersby greeted Mortmain — "The Head Knows All!" they said brightly, in the same tone that folk on normal towns might say "Good morning!" Several looked curiously at Tamzin, for although she now wore the same white overalls as everyone else in Crawley, she still looked out of place with her olive skin and black, unshaven hair.

"We may have to call in at the barbers," Mortmain said. "The only fashionable hairstyle aboard Crawley is no hair at all."

"Is that why you all look like shaved sheep?"

"The Head regards hair as unnecessary."

It seemed to Tamzin that the Head thought most things were unnecessary. According to the book Mortmain had left her, good citizens of Crawley should not allow themselves to be distracted by music or stories or elaborate meals. They should not have close friendships or fall in love. If the Population Committee awarded them a license to have children, they should do so with the partner they were assigned, but the children must be raised in the communal nursery, and would never know who their parents were. Families were a relic of more primitive times, and had been abolished. Jago Flint predicted that this healthy and efficient lifestyle would be the way that all cities operated in the future. Tamzin rather hoped that it would not.

"Well, I think the Head is unnecessary," she said.

"Shhh!" hissed Mortmain.

"How did he get to be Head anyway? He sounds like a loon to me."

"Don't say that, Tamzin! The Head hears all! And if he doesn't, someone else will, and they'll report you. You'll get us both in trouble."

They went on in silence through the articulated corridor that separated one segment from the next, and up a metal stairway into a large, low-ceilinged space where people sat eating at rows of white tables. There was a clatter of cutlery on metal plates, and a low murmur of conversation. Mortmain made Tamzin sit and wait for him while he went to a serving hatch at the far side of the room. She did as she was told, looking around at the cheerless furniture, the stenciled slogans on the walls. At a neighboring table, a group of off-duty salvage workers were discussing the morning's catch.

"Only a traction fort. A disgusting old timber-built place."

"Still, timber will feed the furnaces."

"Not for long. We need to travel fast if we are to catch Museion."

"It'll be worth it, though."

"Oh, of course it will! I didn't mean — I hope you don't think I was suggesting — The Head Knows All!"

"The Head Knows All," the others chorused through mouthfuls of unappealing breakfast.

Mortmain returned with Tamzin's own unappealing breakfast: a heap of dry, gray patties that tasted like cardboard and despair. "They're plant-based," said Mortmain. "Made from algae. Very nutritious, apparently. There are big vats of the stuff in Segment C, tended by slaves. That's where you'd be working, if I had not requested you."

He seemed to be expecting her to thank him, thought Tamzin, but being thankful to Mortmain would leave an even worse taste in her mouth than the algae patties. She ate, and asked, "Is Segment C where the slaves from the Hundberg are?"

"You're fretting about your friend Doom, I suppose? I'll see if I can find out whether he's among the survivors we brought aboard."

Tamzin looked at him askance. "You'd do that? Why?"

"Because I am your friend too, Tamzin, if only you'd believe it."

"I don't. You aren't. You never will be. Get that through your thick, baldy head."

Mortmain ran a hand over his scalp and glanced up at the ceiling, checking that the nearest of the green lights was several yards away. Then, in a voice so low that she could barely hear him over the noise of the canteen, he said, "You asked me how Flint became our Head. Well, he always has been. He used to be a member of the Guild of Engineers aboard London. But about eighty years ago he decided that his guild had lost its way."

"He must be pretty old, then."

"Hush. Listen. Flint gathered a few like-minded comrades, and they built Crawley in the Wombs of London and set off to learn what life would be like aboard an entirely rational, scientific suburb. By the time I was born, it was up in the Ice Wastes.

"Flint was convinced that there were still Old-Tech wonders waiting to be discovered in the High North. He steered Crawley out onto the North American ice sheet — onto the Dead Continent itself! And there we found one of the black pyramids the Ancients raised in the final years before the Sixty Minute War. Inside it, like doves in a dovecot, were dozens of Revenant brains. I was sixteen by then, and a bright lad, so Flint appointed me part of the team that studied them. The nomad technomancers of old had used them to build undead armies, but Flint was certain they had far greater potential. And it turned out that he was right. His plans unsettled even me — that is one of the reasons I left Crawley. Now I am back, I find that his experiment has gone even further than I feared . . ."

"Then there are Revenants here? Stalkers?"

"Hush!"

Tamzin, glancing behind her, saw Sister Rothrock making her way toward their table. The woman's shaven head gleamed like ivory in the light from the overhead panels. She still had on her single black glove, and Tamzin's body remembered the pain in it and recoiled as she drew close.

Sister Rothrock did not notice. Her eyes were on Mortmain. "You seem very deep in conversation, Brother," she said.

"I was just telling Sister Pook about our glorious Head, and all the wonderful things he has achieved here," said Mortmain with a weak smile.

"You believe the girl will be useful to us, then? I found her rather stupid."

"Oh, she is. Very! But the Revenant Vespertine is somewhat willful and hard to manage, and Sister Pook has a way with her. With her help, I shall easily be able to get Vespertine under control once we catch Museion, and keep her calm during the procedure."

"Very good," said Sister Rothrock. She looked down at Tamzin and then, suddenly, reached out her gloved hand and grabbed Tamzin's chin. Tamzin flinched, but the glove must have been switched off, because no shock tore through her. The woman released her, and laughed lightly. "Sister Pook knows what will happen to her if she fails you. The same thing that will happen to you, Brother Mortmain, if you cannot cure the Head."

Mortmain, who had been looking surprisingly meek, straightened up when she said that, and looked for the first time like the Mortmain that Tamzin knew, full of dangerous mischief. "Sister Rothrock," he said loudly, "it would be quite wrong to say we are 'curing' the Head. That would imply that the Head is unwell, and the Head cannot be unwell, for he is perfect. I am merely trying in my small way to serve him."

Sister Rothrock's pale face reddened, and a look of alarm came into her eyes. "Of course. I have spent too long among the barbarians. I spoke carelessly. The Head Knows All."

"The Head Knows All," agreed Mortmain. "And now, if you

will excuse us, I am taking Sister Pook to the barber."

"About time too," sniffed Sister Rothrock. "All that disgusting hair . . ." But she had not quite recovered her composure. Tamzin saw her cast a nervous glance at the green lights in the ceiling.

"Those lights," she asked, walking out of the canteen at Mortmain's side. "That's how your Head watches you, is it? He's got cameras he built using the stuff from that black pyramid?"

"Yes," agreed Mortmain. "But we should not discuss this here."

"There's more, though," Tamzin said, remembering some of the things she had just heard. "Flint's old. *Really* old. *Impossibly* old. I'm guessing he's kept himself alive by using Revenant technology . . . Or he's turned *himself* into a Revenant! That's it, isn't it?" She looked up and down the corridor as if she half expected the resurrected Jago Flint to come stalking out to congratulate her on her cleverness.

Mortmain dragged her into a narrow side passage where the clattering of a badly fitting ventilation shaft cover would keep anyone from overhearing him. Green lights glowed on the ceiling. He turned his back to the nearest and looked at Tamzin with an expression that was half fear and half anger. "You were always a bright girl, Tamzin," he said. "You are right. Flint wanted to become immortal. He has turned himself into a Revenant. But he is not like the ones you faced in my Arcade. He's not like Vespertine, either. He is not like any Revenant there has been before."

"What is he like, then?" asked Tamzin. "Can I see him? Where is he, this Revenant Flint?"

Mortmain put his mouth close to her ear and said in a whisper, "You are standing inside him."

❁

Crawley stirred. Its main engines had been in danger of overheating after the failed attempt to catch Museion. A few hours of rest had given them time to cool. Now it was ready to move again. Inside it, the ant-like figures of its citizens scurried about their daily tasks. Crawley watched them coldly through a thousand green eyes. It did not care about those people any more than, when it was Jago Flint, it had cared about the blood cells that carried oxygen around its mortal body. They served their purpose, and that was all. They would keep Crawley operational until such time as it developed the technologies that would allow it to operate without them.

A faint radio signal whispered in one of the many mansions of its mind. A message from its spy aboard Museion. The city was changing course and making for the Bridge of Storms. Crawley sent a signal to its engines. The track units shuddered into motion again. The green eye clusters on Crawley's bows focused on Museion's track marks, and began to follow them westward through the thinning fog.

❁

"Crawley is Flint," said Mortmain in an urgent whisper as the engines started up. "When he died, he had us place a Revenant brain in his skull, but rather than build an armored body like the one I gave Eve Vespertine, he had himself plumbed into Crawley's central control system. He runs the engines, the tracks, the electrical generators. Cameras inside and out stream images straight to his brain. The Planning Committee has no say anymore in where this suburb goes or what towns it hunts. Flint is Crawley: a Revenant-suburb that travels where it will, and hunts whatever takes its fancy. But it has become unstable. The Committee members believe there is a flaw in the brain they used to resurrect Flint. That's why they dragged me back here, to make repairs."

"And that's why you need Vespertine?" asked Tamzin. "You're going to take her brain apart and use the bits to fix this thing?"

Mortmain nodded, then shrugged. "Yes. That's the plan I sold the Committee. Between ourselves, I doubt it will work. There's something wrong with Crawley that can't be fixed by just stuffing fresh circuitry into the Head. Tamzin, I believe this suburb is insane . . ."

28

FOOTHILLS

Museion limped on its way. Smoke still rose from the buildings that had burned, and dirty water dripped from the ceilings of the engine district. Everyone aboard seemed dazed, as if they had all just awoken from the same bad dream. But there was much to be done: wounded to be tended, rubble to be cleared, dead Junkyard Dogs to be heaved overboard, captive ones to be guarded. The base tier resounded all day with the sounds of the repair crews, but the auxiliary engines remained offline. Track-maintenance gangs were reporting damage to most of the linkages on the port side.

That afternoon, in the fire-damaged Temple of Peripatetia, Professor Pott-Walloper conducted a funeral for all those Musonians who had lost their lives in the battle. Professor Loomis took time from his work to give a moving eulogy for Rowan Bellweather. Then, while the choir sang their threnodies, an ornate sacred elevator called the mechanical catafalque bore the shrouded bodies down a shaft into the Number Four furnace. The mourners could at least console themselves with the knowledge that their loved ones' cremations had added a little extra energy to Museion's engines. But even with that grim fuel to help it, the city's top speed was less than fourteen miles per hour.

❁

After the funerals, Professor Stanislaus went to his office in the building next door to the Archaeological Collection. It had a musty, shut-up smell about it. He had not set foot in there for months, and had not really expected to ever use it again. But someone had to discover who the traitor was who had killed poor Bellweather and attacked the dean, and since everyone else was too busy with the running of the city, Stanislaus was still determined to do it himself. He would become a detective, and make himself useful to Museion one last time. The office would be his base of operations.

He busied himself for a time finding a fresh notebook for the writing down of clues, and wondering if a magnifying glass would be needed — and where one might be found. Then there was a heavy knocking at the door. Vespertine entered, carrying her cat.

"They said you wished to speak with me," she said.

"Miss Vespertine," Stanislaus said, offering her a chair and then regretting it, because the chair had always been one of his favorites, a gorgeous antique from the Bickering Citadels Era. He doubted it would support a Revenant's weight.

But Vespertine preferred to stand. Stanislaus fidgeted with the blotter on his desk, then looked up searchingly into her blank, green gaze. "Do you remember her?" he asked.

"Remember who?"

"The person whose body you inhabit. The person you were before you — before she — before you were so tragically . . ." He paused, shook his head, then asked her the question he had been wanting to ask since their first meeting. "Vespertine, what is it like to die?"

The green lamps of her eyes flared softly with their glowworm light. She said, "I have never done it. I am not Eve. But I remember what being Eve was like. I remember that death was a surprise to her. Even while it was happening, she did not really believe that she was dying."

"I see," said Stanislaus, adjusting the blotter again. Then he said, "I am dying, Miss Vespertine. Another few weeks and I shall be gone. Even if we survive this journey. Even if we reach London. I will cease to exist. All my thoughts and memories will be less than smoke on the wind. I never found time to marry, or have children, and I have never been a friendly person. There will be no one to remember me."

"Yes," agreed Vespertine. But as she stood there, with the old man looking up at her, she realized that something more was called for. He was very frightened. She felt sorry for him. She put Small Cat down on a bookcase and went around the desk. As Stanislaus rose from his chair in alarm, she stooped and put her arm around him, crushing him against her steel breastplate.

"This is called a hug," she said helpfully.

"Nnff," said Stanislaus, and tottered back as she released him.

"It would work better if I still had two arms," Vespertine said.

"Nevertheless," said Stanislaus, "it is the thought that counts. You are most kind, Vespertine. Surprisingly kind, considering . . ." He sat down again, rubbing his bruised ribs. "Do you think there is anything afterward? After death, I mean? Heaven or Hell or Nirvana or the Sunless Country . . . Do you think Eve went to a place like that?"

"I do not know," said Vespertine. "She died, and then there was me."

"Perhaps you are the only afterlife there is," said Stanislaus, and a strange, almost hungry look came into his face. "They say the Stalker brains the Ancients placed in their black pyramids were remembering devices. If we could get the Stalker brain out of your skull and into mine, then it might remember me as it now remembers Eve. I would be saved. Something of me would survive."

"Perhaps," agreed Vespertine.

"But no," said Stanislaus. "No, what am I thinking? That would mean killing you, or erasing you, or whatever the correct term is. That would be very poor behavior. What would Small Cat do without you?"

Vespertine was relieved. She had not liked the idea, although she still felt sorry for Professor Stanislaus.

He shuffled the papers on his desk, businesslike again. "Forgive me," he said, waving a sheet of foolscap at her. "I was distracted. What I really wanted to discuss with you is this. It is a report from Voss's people. They say the cargo ramp was lowered deliberately during the chase. That can only be done from a control cubicle above the main cargo holds — a cubicle that is kept locked, and to which only Museion's senior staff have a key. And whoever killed Bellweather had a passkey to the library, which suggests that they too were on the senior staff. I mean to speak with all my colleagues, and find out what each of them was doing at the time of the incident, and whether any of them has had their keys go missing recently. And I should like you to act as my assistant, Miss Vespertine. People are far more likely to tell me the truth if I have you looming at my side. You are so very good at looming."

❁

The fog seemed reluctant to clear away entirely. Separating into clumps and clots, it slunk down into the hollows and low marshy places of the land and lay there sulking for the remainder of the day. Museion left it behind, toiling its way up on to the lower slopes of the Golgan Hills, whose snow-clad shoulders reared up ahead of it into clouds from which more snow fell.

This was the beginning of a chain of cold winters that would last for almost fifty years. Later, historians would agree this mini ice age marked the end of the Golden Age of Traction. But Hilly Torpenhow, watching from Museion's observation balconies, knew only that it was very cold. She was far more concerned with Crawley, whose smoke she could see in the east, staining the evening sky. The nasty, scuttling suburb was still following Museion, although it was clearly unable to catch up. Perhaps its masters were hoping that Museion would break down. Or perhaps the traitor who was still on the loose aboard the city had assured them that it definitely would . . .

One of the young militia women came hurrying up, looking rather alarming in a nomad's helmet and armored jacket. "Miss Torpenhow," she said, saluting. "Dr. Twyne sends his compliments and asks you to meet him in the lockups. He has been questioning the prisoners. He has some news about your friends."

❁

The lockups were Museion's jail. They had seldom held any prisoners more dangerous than drunken students, arrested for stealing porters' bowler hats on Moon Festival night. Now security around them had been strengthened, with a whole squad of the militia on duty at the entrance. Max was waiting there too, having just arrived with Dr. Twyne. Hilly noticed that he was wearing a splendid old sword, and she thought how well it suited him, and wished his father could have seen him. He looked every inch an Angmering.

"Tamzin and Doom are alive!" Max said excitedly when he saw Hilly.

Dr. Twyne held up a hand, gesturing for caution. "We can't know that, Max. We only know that they were alive yesterday morning. These Junkyard Dogs are a sullen lot, and that's pretty much all we've got from them. But one of them was wearing this . . ."

"Oh!" said Hilly, taking it from him. It was the brass sun disc that Tamzin always wore around her neck, her good-luck charm, and her only memento of her lost family. "Oh, poor Tamzin!"

"It seems that she and Mr. Doom were captured and taken aboard the Dogs' traction fortress."

"And where is the fortress now?" asked Max. "We could take the *Fire's Astonishment* and fly there . . ."

"We do not know. Behind us, somewhere."

"Let me speak to the prisoners," said Hilly.

Twyne unlocked the massive main door and he, Max, and Hilly entered a corridor lined with cells. Behind their wire-mesh doors, captive nomads lay on straw-filled pallets, or sat about in various postures of boredom and defeat.

"Which of you is in charge here?" Hilly asked in her most teacherish voice. The Junkyard Dogs paid her no heed, until one young man pushed his face against the mesh of his door to leer at her.

"I reckon it's me," he said. "Stoat, I am. I was first aboard your city. I'd've took it from you too, if your Nekroteknik hadn't stopped us. Cheating, that is. Nasty, letting the dead do your dirty work."

"I am hoping for news of Oddington Doom and Tamzin Pook," said Hilly, ignoring his tone. "Dr. Twyne tells me they were captured . . ."

Stoat laughed. "I took 'em up myself. Easy as scooping up blind baby rabbits. We were told they were coming, and we were waiting for them. They're in the Hundberg now, unless they're dead."

"Someone told you they were coming?" asked Hilly. "How could anyone have known?"

"Worrible's witch knows stuff like that," said Stoat.

"And who, pray, is 'Worrible's witch'?"

"A gift to Thane Worrible from the Thane of Bugtown."

"Bugtown? You mean Crawley?" asked Hilly.

Stoat shrugged. "It's a slinking beetle of a place, so we call it Bugtown. It don't matter anyway. The witch said she could see everything, but she didn't see your pet Stalker, or, if she did, she kept it to herself. When I get back to the Hundberg, I'll kill her quick, and then I'll kill Worrible slow, and then I'll be Thane Stoat and the Dogs will do some proper hunting."

Hilly had heard enough. She and Twyne moved back toward the door. But Max could not ignore the challenge in the young nomad's tone. If he left now, he thought, they would jeer at him, and think him a coward. He could already hear some of them snickering. So he stood his ground and said, "How do you think you're ever going to get back to the Hundberg?"

Stoat looked scornfully at him. "You reckon you can keep us caged? We are the Junkyard Dogs. Hounds of the war gods, us. You should have killed us all when you had the chance, but you were too soft, weren't you?"

"Not too soft to send a lot of your friends to the Sunless Country," said Max.

Stoat grinned at him, pressing his face against the metal mesh that separated them. "You ever killed a man, townie? Killed him close, when it was just you or him? I have. Last time we raided the Frying Pan. My first kill. The best day of my life that was. It's lit up all glorious in my memories. I stuck my spear under his ribs, and the light in his eyes went out like I'd flicked a switch. Then I felt the boy I used to be creep away and hide forever way deep down inside of me, because I had become a man at last. Do you know how that feels, townie?"

"No," said Max. "Because I'm not a maniac."

"Because you're not a man," said Stoat. "But we are. Even Yanna over there is more of a man than you. There's no cage that can hold us, townie boy. Soon or later, we'll be out of here, and then what do you think will happen? Do you think we'll spare you because you spared us? That's how you think, but we ain't like you. When I'm out, I'll take your pretty head for a hood ornament on my new kampavan. We'll kill all of you townies, except the ones we choose to keep for thralls. Then we'll turn this stinking town around and go find our friends."

He threw back his head and howled, and the others copied him, until the howling and the echoes grew unbearable. Max could not think of any more to say, and couldn't have made himself heard if he had. He turned and strode with as much dignity as he could muster back along the corridor to the doorway where Hilly was waiting.

"That nomad's right," he said as he went with Hilly back up the stairs to top tier. The handrails were decorated with carved whales, elephants, and dogs. He remembered Tamzin talking about them, far more delighted by cute wooden animals than you would think a hardened Arcade fighter could be. Suddenly he missed her terribly, and was filled with a hot and entirely useless hatred for the youth who had kidnapped her, stolen her sun pendant, and sent her off to be a slave, or worse. "We should have killed that lout Stoat and his friends when we had the chance," he said angrily. "It's not safe, keeping them aboard."

"It might have been better if they had died in the battle," agreed Hilly. "But they didn't, and if we were to kill them now we would be as bad as them."

"Maybe we need to be as bad as them, if we're going to survive," said Max.

"Now you sound like Gabriel Strega. I refuse to believe that we have to abandon all our standards. Those misguided young people will be safe enough in the lockup until we find a humane way to be rid of them. In the meantime, I am more worried about this so-called witch. How did she know Tamzin and Oddington were on their way? Could someone aboard Museion have signaled to her somehow?"

"We'll take the airship and fly back east," said Max. "Vespertine can batter a way into the Hundberg for us . . ."

"But you heard what Professor Pringle said about more bad weather on the way. It would be no help to anyone if we end up wrecked in the Out-Country, or blown halfway to the Sea of Khazak. Besides, I think we may be needed here in the coming hours."

They walked out onto one of the observation balconies that jutted from the port side, near the infirmary. The city was laboring up a long, stony slope, with still-steeper slopes rising ahead. Fog hid the lower-lying country behind, but the chimneys and upperworks of Crawley poked out of it, perhaps ten miles astern.

"It is horribly persistent, that little town," said Hilly.

"But it's farther behind each time we look," said Max. "It can't catch us, can it? Not unless our engines fail, or we get stuck in the Golgan Hills. And Loomis says the way through the hills is passable, and Voss will never let the engines fail."

"I am sure he won't," Hilly agreed. "And you are right. Professor Loomis knows his business."

But Crawley's horrid persistence still unsettled her. She had a feeling that Museion was being driven into a trap.

29

Stanislaus and Vespertine Investigate

The navigation suite, right at the top of the Ivory Tower, was perhaps the most beautiful of all the beautiful rooms aboard Museion. Ringed by tall windows, it commanded fine vistas of the landscape ahead of the city and to either side, while sternward the Quadrangle and the grand buildings of the upper tier were laid out like a street plan, all the way to the exhaust stacks. At present several of the windows were boarded up, having been shattered when the storm hit, but glaziers were busy repairing them. On the huge mahogany table in the room's center, Professor Loomis and his staff had spread out their charts. Across the largest of these, a young woman was pushing a model of Museion while a student with a compass called out the city's precise position.

"What is it?" asked Professor Loomis tetchily when Stanislaus came in. "I am exceedingly busy now that I am both dean and chief navigator . . ." But something about Vespertine's green gaze as she ducked through the doorway to stand behind Stanislaus made him reconsider and he said more affably, ". . . but I'm sure I can make time."

"Excellent looming, my friend," said Stanislaus, patting

Vespertine's arm. She stood by the door and watched as he went over to the table, studying the maps laid out there. She watched the glaziers, and the girl at the chart table, who had blonde braids and owlish spectacles and wore a black armband on the sleeve of her crisp white blouse. She felt a strong urge to protect Stanislaus, just as she wanted to protect Small Cat. But Small Cat was safe at the house with Miss Torpenhow and Max Angmering, who had promised her they would look after him. Professors were considerably more difficult to take care of.

"This Crawley place," said Stanislaus, watching Loomis's assistants place a second, smaller model on the chart, twelve miles behind Museion. "Should we be worried?"

Loomis shrugged. "I don't see why. It's a small-time scavenger, and it falls farther behind us with every passing hour. It will give up the chase soon. I daresay the only reason it is still following is in the hope of grubbing up any debris we throw out."

"Have you been aboard it at all? In all your travels?"

"Crawley?" said Loomis. "Never."

The young woman at the chart table glanced at him, and seemed about to speak, or so it seemed to Vespertine. But she did not, and then Stanislaus said, "Anyway, Loomis, I did not come here to talk about Crawley. Might I have a word in private?"

Loomis sniffed irritably, but he roused himself from his chair. "Take over, please, Barley," he told the young woman at the chart table. "Barley Bellweather, poor Rowan's sister," he confided, as she crossed the suite to take his place. "She is very young, but just as capable as her late brother. It was she who steered Museion for a time, during the attack. I had been making observations up at the stern when the ramp was lowered and the nomads boarded us. I was lucky to get back here in one piece."

When the girl had installed herself in his seat and Loomis was satisfied that she understood his instructions, he led Stanislaus and Vespertine down a short, private staircase into his office on the floor below. Those sections of the office walls not lined with drawers and bookshelves were paneled in autumn-colored wood, and the circular window commanded nearly as good a view as those upstairs.

Loomis gestured vaguely to a chair. Stanislaus sat down gratefully and said, "I was reading Twyne's report. It seems you were the one who raised the alarm about poor Bellweather's death."

Loomis glanced uneasily at Vespertine as she stooped in through the low doorway and came to stand behind Stanislaus. "So have you and this monstrosity teamed up to fight crime?" he asked. "I should have thought you would both have more important things to do."

"If the killer is still at large, and preparing further acts of sabotage, then I can think of no matter more deserving of my attention, Loomis. No matter at all."

"Quite so," said Loomis, and frowned, as if the seriousness of the situation were only just becoming clear to him. "And yes, yes, it was I who raised the alarm about the murder. I happened to be passing the library on my way back to my quarters when I noticed that the front door was ajar. I went up the steps, looked inside, and saw my poor young friend lying in a pool of blood. Naturally, I assumed nomad raiders had gotten aboard the city, and I ran to fetch Twyne at once."

"I see, I see," said Stanislaus. "And there was no sign of anyone else?"

"Only that Torpenhow woman. She was there when I came back with Twyne and his people."

"But you don't believe Hilly Torpenhow to be the murderer?"

"Of course not. It was I who brought her to Museion. It would reflect pretty poorly on my judgment if she were to start knifing navigators."

"So who do you think was responsible?"

Loomis spread his hands hopelessly. "I am a geographer, Stanislaus, not a psychologist. Who aboard our city would want to help the Junkyard Dogs destroy us? It could be anyone. What about Professor Waghorn? He is always bleating on about how the nomads are misunderstood . . ."

"That is just a pose," said Stanislaus. "Waghorn thinks it impresses the students and makes him seem sophisticated."

"A worker from the engine district, then. Who else would have had access to the control cubicle, to lower that ramp? Half of those lower-deck types come from other towns. You hear a dozen different languages being spoken in those grubby little streets around Dark Park. They aren't loyal to Museion in the way you or I are. Some of them might be former nomads themselves for all we know. Have you tried pursuing your inquiries in the engine district?"

"I plan to do so tomorrow," said Stanislaus, rising to his feet. Vespertine noted how carefully he stood up, and how, as he turned his back on Loomis, his face changed. He was in pain, she realized, and trying to conceal it. She did not feel pain herself, but Eve whom-she-had-been had known it sometimes. She remembered the idea of pain.

"You should rest, Professor Stanislaus," she said as they went down the long stairways of the tower and out into the cold sunlight.

"I don't have time to rest, Vespertine." Stanislaus took a pill box from his pocket, tipped two white tablets out, and swallowed them. The city rocked, scrambling up a slope of tumbled boulders. Students were shouting to one another as they repaired the defenses. Stanislaus leaned against a statue of some bygone dean and waited for the pills to take effect.

"How beautiful it all is, in the winter sun!" he said. "I do love this old place. It would be a shame to think of it torn to pieces, dismantled in the gut of some scavenger town. Did you know that the Lord Mayor of London has promised to keep some of our old buildings intact? They will be taken apart with great care, and reassembled on London's upper tiers to house the Guild of Historians' new museum. I do not have very much time left, but if I can use it to make sure this city gets safely to its rendezvous with London, that would be something, wouldn't it? They might put up a statue of me, after I'm gone, and then people will be able to lean against my pedestal in years to come and say, 'I wonder who that old fellow was?'"

"They will say, 'Here is a statue of Gilbert Stanislaus, the Great Detective,'" said Vespertine.

"Vespertine, was that a joke?"

Vespertine grinned. The effect was unsettling, but Stanislaus knew she meant well. "They will not remember either of us as very great detectives if we cannot unmask this saboteur," he said, standing upright with an effort. "Come, Vespertine: The game's afoot!"

He set off across the Quadrangle. Vespertine followed him. She was glad that he had liked her joke, but it pained her to think that he was dying. She was beginning to understand that the world, which had seemed so new and fresh and interesting when she first awoke into it, lay always in the shadow of an immense sadness. The same thing that was happening to Professor Stanislaus would happen sooner or later to Small Cat, and Miss Torpenhow, and Tamzin Pook, and indeed to all the people Vespertine cared about. Death would come in the end for everyone — even, perhaps, for her.

30

Doubt

Evening revealed the hidden beauty of the hills. There was a reddish cast to the granite they were built from, and as the westering sun lit up the rugged faces of the crags, they glowed a rich red-gold. It was snowing again, and the fresh-falling flakes took on the same warm hue, until it might have been a shower of rose petals drifting down over Museion's battered rooftops. People laughed and talked as they made their way toward the Great Hall for the evening meal. Some of the militia were training with captured nomad weapons in the Quadrangle. From hanging valleys on either side of the pass, small predator towns peered down greedily at the passing city. But they saw how many guns it carried, and sensed something fierce and desperate in its manner, and decided to let it go by unmolested.

Max was helping to repair fortifications on the stern of the top tier when Professor Loomis appeared, waving a large envelope. "Mr. Angmering!" he said. "Would you pop these down to the engine district for me? Revised charts of the way ahead, for Luka Voss. You can tell him I'm sorry they're late. I was delayed by Stanislaus, who's busy playing at detectives with that Revenant of yours."

Max slung the sandbag he had been carrying on the top of the emplacement and took the envelope. "Vespertine is not mine," he said. "And it's not exactly playing, is it?"

"Well, you can tell Miss Vespertine from me that she won't find our saboteur on the upper tier."

"Where, then?" asked Max.

Loomis hesitated, then started to say something, then stopped again and shook his head.

"What is it, Professor?"

Loomis looked troubled. "Luka Voss has a key to the ramp controls," he said.

"Luka? Of course he has. He's chief engineer."

"Indeed. And I'm sure he was at his post in the control room when the ramp was lowered?"

Max hesitated. He remembered how Voss had appeared so suddenly outside the cargo hold that day. But that did not mean . . .

"You know he only became chief engineer because his father died," said Loomis, conversationally. "Poor old Troutbeck. He fell off the stern stairs one dark night and broke his neck."

"The stern stairs?"

"A terrible business. Young Luka stepped into his old man's shoes while they were still warm. The lower-deck people love him, of course, but I have often wondered if the Senior Fellows were altogether wise to appoint him as our chief engineer. He is so young, and — well, he has so much nightwight in him."

Max felt himself blush. He wished he was one of those people who went pale when they were angry — it was so much more dignified. As it was, he could feel his ears turning red. "Just because Luka's mother was a nightwight doesn't mean he's not loyal to Museion! You can't think he deliberately lowered that ramp? If he was in league with the Junkyard Dogs, he could have just shut down all the engines and let them catch us."

"Oh, I agree. I just think it's *odd* — that's all. Something to bear in mind. Anyway, dinner in the Great Hall at six. I shall see you there."

Carrying the envelope, Max went briskly down the stern stairs. They looked bleak and businesslike now, with none of the magic they had held when the ice was on them. At the landing where he had talked with Voss he stopped to look at the faded wreath wired to the handrail. Sure enough, it was a memorial to Voss's father. This was the exact spot from which Mr. Troutbeck had fallen. But the handrail was high, too high to simply tumble over, surely? Unless the poor man had jumped. Or someone had pushed him.

Max stood there a moment, telling himself that he was being ridiculous, then hurried on down into the engine district to find Luka. But he was not in the control room, and no one seemed to know where he could be found.

"Repairs going on all over," said his deputy. "Luka could be with any of a dozen crews."

Max gave the charts to her, then returned to the upper tier by one of the internal stairways. He did not want to go past Mr. Troutbeck's memorial again. He did not want to think the thoughts about Voss that were crowding in on him. He remembered the picture in Voss's apartment. How different from each other the engineer's parents had been. He found himself wondering whether Mr. Troutbeck had loved his spooky-looking wife, and whether she had loved him back. Even if he had treated her well, she might have resented him using her knowledge to improve Museion's engines (and taking the credit for the improvements himself, no doubt). Perhaps she had spoken of her resentment to young Luka, and he had grown to hate his father. Perhaps he had grown to hate Museion itself. Perhaps, as the last of the nightwights, he had grown to hate all human beings . . .

It couldn't be him, Max told himself. It simply couldn't. But where had Luka been on the day of the battle, when the ramp went down and the fires broke out? What had he been doing, up there above the cargo holds? Had his friendliness afterward been only an attempt to throw Max off the scent?

On the top tier, night was falling and the first stars were twinkling. High on the passing mountainsides the age-old walls and crumbling stone towers of some forgotten static kingdom showed dark against the snow. Above them, the aurora spread its faint, green stains across the sky.

Dinner was well underway in the Great Hall. Max hurried to the High Table where the Senior Fellows and their guests were eating. Hilly was deep in conversation with Professor Stanislaus, but she broke off when she saw the look on Max's face.

"Max? What's wrong?"

"I've worked something out, I think."

"What is it?"

Max settled himself in an empty seat between Stanislaus and Professor Waghorn. "I think I know who dropped the ramp. And started the fire maybe . . ."

"Who?"

"I think," said Max, "I think — well, Luka Voss was down near the cargo hold when the ramp was opened."

"Voss has a key to the control cubicle," said Waghorn.

"But why would he put his own city at risk?" demanded Hilly.

"Because it isn't his city. He is half nomad. Half nightwight.

His mother came from beyond the Tannhäusers. Maybe she was an agent of Crawley or the Junkyard Dogs all along, and trained little Luka to succeed her . . ." replied Waghorn.

"I don't know if that's true," said Max, because now that his concerns had escaped the confines of his head and other people were taking them seriously, he was starting to feel a perverse desire to defend Voss.

"He could not have been responsible for Bellweather's murder and the attempt on the dean's life," said Professor Stanislaus. "He was down below on both occasions."

"We can't be sure of that," said Waghorn, who had never liked Voss. "Does he have an alibi? There are all sorts of rat runs between the engine district and the top tier known only to him and his staff."

"And his staff worship him!" agreed Mrs. Pringle, cottoning on. "I believe they would do anything he asked of them."

"Even murder?" asked Max.

But no one was listening. The news about Voss was spreading along the table, and Nesrine Pott-Walloper was shouting to some of the students to run and find Dr. Twyne. "Voss is the traitor!" Max heard people yelling. "Voss is the murderer! Arrest him! Quickly!"

He stood up, his hand on the pommel of the sword Voss had gifted him. People were hurrying to the main door, leaving their dinners unfinished as they wandered out into the frosty Quadrangle. Max wondered if he should call for calm.

"I hope you are certain of your facts, Mr. Angmering," said Professor Stanislaus, the only one left at the High Table. Max reached out to help him stand, but Stanislaus waved him away. "It is a serious matter to accuse someone of treachery and murder."

"I know," said Max.

"I am sure you do. Forgive me. Vespertine and I have been looking into this affair all day, and perhaps I am a little peeved that you have found the answer before us. I had planned to interview Voss this afternoon, but he said he was too busy to meet with me. A sign of guilt, perhaps. If you are right, you have saved our city. Voss must know a hundred ways to shut our engines down and make it seem an accident. Perhaps he planned to wait until we were high in the pass, then strand us there while Crawley catches up."

Max went outside. People were gathering at the head of the stairs to watch as Dr. Twyne and some of his militia went hurrying down into the engine district. Pushing past the onlookers, Max followed the squad downstairs.

Voss was eating dinner with some of his assistants and their families in a crowded dining area behind the main engine room. It was a jollier affair than dinner in the Great Hall, thought Max, or at least it had been until Twyne and his people barged in, with Max slinking behind them. Then the talking and the laughter stopped and people stood up from the tables in alarm. Voss rose too, looking questioningly at the newcomers.

"I'm sorry, Luka," said Dr. Twyne. "There have been accusations. Questions about your whereabouts on the day of the battle, and the night before it, and your actions since . . ."

"You think I am the traitor?" said Voss, and started to laugh. A murmur of shock and disbelief ran through the room. One of the children started to cry.

"I am here to bring you to the Ivory Tower," said Twyne. "You'll be held there until we can get to the bottom of this."

Voss's laughter had just been for show. It stopped, and left him looking angry and perhaps a little scared. "Who made these accusations?" he said. "Who asked these questions?" His black eyes scanned the faces of the militia lads lined up at Twyne's shoulder, and stopped when they reached Max. Max looked away.

"This is madness!" one of Voss's companions was shouting, shaking his fist at Dr. Twyne. "Luka's all that's kept this city moving. He'd never betray us! We won't let you take him!"

The men and women around him agreed. Some picked up the knives they had just been eating with, as if they planned to fight. But Voss held up his long, pale hands and called for calm. "This is what the traitor wants," he said. "To turn us all against one another. I will go with these fools and answer their stupid questions, and while I'm gone you will keep the engines running and the wheels turning. Mr. Vladich, you'll take over my duties in the control room while I'm upstairs. Miss Kreva, you can take Vladich's place in engineering."

They were not happy about it, but they shuffled aside, and Voss walked to the door, where Twyne and the militia gathered around him. As he passed Max, their eyes met again, and there seemed to be no anger in Voss's gaze at all, only hurt and a terrible disappointment. Max did not want to follow the squad as they marched their prisoner back up the stairs, but nor did he want to stay below and face Voss's angry people. So he tagged along, hanging back far enough that he hoped Voss would not see him there, and at the top of the steps when Twyne led his prisoner forward toward the Ivory Tower, Max turned aft instead, and went miserably out onto the burned-out balconies behind the Temple of Peripatetia. On either side of Museion, the steep flanks of the Golgan Hills rose black against the glowing sky. Behind it, looking like a minor constellation fallen to the midnight earth, the clustered lamps of Crawley glittered with a greedy light.

If I am right about Voss, thought Max, *then I have done the right thing*. But he could take no pride in it, because if he was wrong he had betrayed a friend, and robbed Museion of its most brilliant engineer in the very hour of its need.

31

The Lightning Gun

Vespertine and Small Cat were guarding the airships again. Voss was being held under arrest in the Ivory Tower, but Hilly thought it possible he had accomplices who might try to flee the city before they were discovered. So she had set Vespertine to stand watch in the hangar overnight, "since you're the only one of us who doesn't need to sleep."

Vespertine did not mind. It was true, she did not need sleep. But she could not help feeling disappointed. She had liked solving crimes with Professor Stanislaus. Now the saboteur had been caught, life seemed far less interesting.

But something still worried her. Her memories of the day were very clear, and she sorted through them for a while until she found the thing that was nagging at her. It was the look on the face of Barley Bellweather, up in the navigation suite, when Loomis was talking about Crawley. Stanislaus had asked him if he had ever been aboard the suburb, and when Loomis had said, "Never," the young woman had glanced up at him with — what? Surprise? Interest? Doubt? Vespertine was not always good at reading the emotions that flickered so rapidly over once-born faces. But she could tell that Barley had felt something. And why should that be? Why should she feel anything at all, if Professor Loomis had simply been stating a fact?

She stood pondering on it for a time, then kissed Small Cat on the top of his head and set him in his basket. He snuggled down there like a little curl of fluff, in that way that always made Vespertine feel strangely warm inside. “Sleep well, Small Cat,” she said, and went across the hangar to where the *Owl of Minerva* was berthed. The gondola door was locked, but the lock was weak, and had not been designed to keep out Revenants. The green glow from Vespertine’s eyes swept over the lockers on the cabin walls and the cupboards under the control console. She opened each in turn, until she found what she was looking for.

❁

Professor Loomis was already in bed, they told Vespertine when she had climbed the many stairs to the navigation suite. It was very late by then. She wondered if she should wake Professor Stanislaus, or Hilly, but decided to let them sleep until she had found out the truth.

The lights in the sky had swirled and shimmered as Vespertine crunched across the crisp snow in the Quadrangle to Loomis’s home, in a street of houses behind the library. After she had rung the bell, waited, and rung again, she wondered if she should simply push the door in. But Loomis came at last: bleary-eyed, wearing a dressing gown over striped pajamas, and a nightcap on his head.

“Revenant?” he said, opening the door a crack and scowling at her through it. “Who sent you here? Is there some fresh emergency?”

“Nobody sent me,” said Vespertine. “There is something I wished to ask you. It is about the information you gave to Professor Stanislaus earlier today.”

Loomis blinked sleepily. “What? Can’t it wait?” He glanced down at the leather-bound book she clutched in her huge hand. “What do you have there?”

“It is the logbook from the *Owl of Minerva*.”

Loomis yawned. Vespertine stood patiently on the doorstep, frost settling on her armor. She could hear the aurora; it made soft, sky-filling sounds: cracklings and rustlings. She wondered if Loomis heard it too. Perhaps once-born ears were not sharp enough.

“You’d better come in,” he said at last. Vespertine followed him into his cluttered and comfortable living room. “Now, what was it you wanted to know?”

Vespertine opened the book and held it out to him. “When Professor Stanislaus asked if you had ever been to Crawley, you said, ‘Never.’ But your assistant looked surprised. I think her brother had told her about the voyages he took with you, and he had mentioned something about Crawley, and that was why your answer surprised her.”

“Extraordinary, the way that brain of yours works,” said Loomis acidly. “Almost intelligent.”

“The *Owl of Minerva*’s logbook lists all the air harbors she has called at,” said Vespertine. “Look: It says that she stopped at Crawley. See, here is the stamp from their harbor office. It says you stopped there for two days.”

Loomis took the book and peered at it. “So it does,” he admitted. “More than three years ago. It must have slipped my mind. But, yes, I do remember now . . . It was before our present troubles began. I was on a survey voyage north of the Tannhäusers, way up in the Ice Wastes. Bellweather and I must have set down at half a dozen different towns and suburbs on that trip. I had quite forgotten Crawley was among them."

Vespertine could hear his heart going *pitter-pat, pitter-pat* inside his chest, as if he had a hamster running on a little wheel in there. She had seen a hamster running on a wheel like that in the window of a pet shop in Thorbury, and Small Cat had watched it with an intent interest. Vespertine watched Loomis with an intent interest now. "I am surprised you forgot," she said.

"Human memories don't work the way yours does, Revenant," said Loomis irritably, and turned away. He went to a set of shelves in the corner of the room and took down a wooden box. "We don't all have Old-Tech gadgetry wedged into our heads. Most of us have to make do with ordinary, fallible human brains. Will there be anything else?"

"No," said Vespertine, sensing that he was dismissing her. She turned toward the door, then stopped. "Yes. There was just one more thing . . ."

Loomis had opened the lid of his box. Something shiny inside it cast shifting reflections on his face as he glanced up at her. "What?"

"I heard Miss Torpenhow talking about the night the dean was injured," Vespertine said, and sifted quickly through her clever mind for Hilly's precise words. "She said you heard it happen, and ran down to investigate. You met the others on the landing outside the dean's office."

"Yes, yes," agreed Loomis. "That is how I remember it. I heard a crash from the office, and the dean cried out . . ."

"Miss Torpenhow says it was the other way around — the cry first and then the crash."

Loomis shrugged. "Who can be sure? It was such a wild night. We had just lost all those windows in the navigation suite. I may not have been paying full attention to noises from below."

"How could you hear them at all?" asked Vespertine. "The navigation suite is four floors above the dean's office. I do not believe you could have heard the sound of his window breaking. And how could you have arrived outside the office at the same moment as Miss Torpenhow and the others, who had come up from the Senior Common Room? Could you descend four flights of stairs in the time it took them to climb one?"

"Probably," said Loomis, looking annoyed. He busied himself with the thing in the box — a big silvery flashlight. "What are you suggesting?"

Vespertine was surprised. She had thought her meaning was perfectly obvious. "You attacked the dean," she said. "When the storm came, you went downstairs with one of the hailstones, which had broken the navigation suite windows, in your pocket. You struck the dean with some heavy object, then smashed his window and left the hailstone there to make it look as if the storm had done it. As you were leaving, you heard the others coming up to investigate, so you joined them, and pretended to be as shocked as they were. And if you are responsible for the attack on the dean, it is likely that you are the one who let the nomads aboard. You said you were making observations on the stern when the attack began, but you could easily have gone down from there to the control cubicle and used your key to gain access and lower the cargo ramp. And you are also the murderer of Rowan Bellweather. You must have been stealing books from the library when he recognized you, so you killed him."

Loomis straightened up, holding the flashlight. "Theft, assault, sabotage, and murder, eh? And why on earth would I have done all these things?"

"Because you are in the pay of Crawley," said Vespertine. She was working it out as she spoke.

Loomis laughed again. "Remarkable!" he said, as if he were denying it, and then, growing serious, "Remarkable," as if he had been impressed by her reasoning. "No wonder they're so keen to get hold of you."

Vespertine didn't understand what that meant. "I will warn the others," she said.

"You will do nothing of the sort," said Loomis.

He raised the flashlight, and Vespertine saw that in place of a bulb and a lens it had only a blank disc of metal. Loomis pointed it at her, and lightning blazed from the disc in a screeching blue-white arc. It struck her in the center of her armored chest and sheathed her whole body in a crawling scribble of cold fire. She saw Loomis's furious face lit up by the electric crackle of the weapon. She tried to reach toward him, but the lightning seemed to hold her back. She thought sadly about Small Cat, and wondered who would look after him now. Then she toppled backward, and lay in the wreckage of Loomis's coffee table.

The lightning stopped. Loomis looked down at her. Vespertine's vision came and went. When he saw that she could not move, Loomis started to grin. He started to caper. He threw off his solemn, professorial manner and danced a little jig on the hearthrug, waving the silver gun above his head. "I fooled them all! I fooled them all!" he crowed. "For years and years! All those professors and doctors, all those world-renowned experts in this and that. 'Make us a chart, Loomis,' they'd say. 'Set us a course, Loomis.' Looking down their bony noses at geographers all the while. And not one of them guessed I was robbing them blind! A book here, a machine there, whatever those baldy-headed nerds in Crawley need! Soon I'll rob their whole town out from under them. And I would have gotten clean away with it if it hadn't been for you, you meddling mechanical."

He kicked Vespertine in the place where her ribs used to be before her armored exoskeleton was built. The pain of his stubbed toes changed his mood. He cursed and aimed another kick, but thought better of it. "Well, I can't wait here for Crawley to catch up," he muttered. "Not now that you've wrecked everything. Stanislaus will come looking for you in the morning. But by the time he drags his old bones out of bed, I'll be long gone. And you, you tinned monstrosity, you're coming with me."

He raised the gun again. Vespertine felt afraid of it, but she could not speak, or raise her hand to fend the lightning off. She could only lie there watching the ceiling as it came and went in the stuttering glare, until the lightning ceased, and darkness fell.

32

Betrayed

No one aboard Museion noticed the hangar's outer doors roll open. No one heard the engine-grumble of the departing airship, lost as it was within the louder grumble of the city's progress. Loomis kept the *Owl of Minerva* low, a bubble of deeper night against the darkness of the midnight hills. Not till she was far astern did one of the lookouts spot her. By then it was too late to do much.

The city, which had only recently gone to bed, woke up again as the clatter of alarm bells filled its streets — a wearyingly familiar sound by then. Max and Hilly, stumbling out from their house into the frosty Quadrangle, heard from some passing students that an airship had been seen leaving. They ran with them to the hangar and found to their relief that the *Fire's Astonishment* was still there. But the *Owl of Minerva*'s berth was empty, and Vespertine was absent.

Dr. Twyne was questioning a trio of indignant air-dock workers in the harbor office. "It was Loomis who took the ship out," he said when Max and Hilly joined him. "These fools fueled the ship for him, and opened the doors . . ."

“’Tweren’t our fault,” declared the foreman. “Loomis said he was on a secret mission, on the orders of the dean himself — the acting dean, that is.” He rummaged in the back pocket of his overalls and produced a crumpled memo with a spidery signature.

“Loomis *is* the acting dean!” said Twyne.

“Well, how was we to know? So many blemmin’ changes these past days — we can’t keep up with all of ’em. Whichever way you look at it, Prof Loomis is an important man. ‘Fuel the ship,’ he tells us. ‘Fill the gas cells.’ It weren’t our place to argue. ‘Open the hangar doors,’ he says. ‘Carry this here crate aboard . . .’ We just did as we was told.”

“Crate?” asked Max. “What crate?”

“A tea chest full of valuable books and Old-Tech knickknacks, I expect,” said Hilly. “The coward has flown off to save his own skin and taken some valuables so he can set himself up in style aboard another city.”

“Oh, ’twere bigger than a tea chest,” said the foreman. “A big packing crate, big as a wardrobe. Heavy too. He had us fetch it down here from his house. Equipment, he said it was. There was quite a weight to it. Big as a coffin, it were.”

“Where is Vespertine?” asked Max.

❁

They went to search the hangar. The big lamps on the ceiling bathed it in a light as cold and bright as a winter’s morning. Under the *Fire’s Astonishment*’s gondola, Max found Small Cat cowering.

“Vespertine would never have left her cat behind,” said Hilly.

Max thought of the crate, big as a wardrobe, big as a coffin. “She has been kidnapped.”

A gray dawn was breaking as they trooped after Dr. Twyne

e Quadrangle to Loomis's house. Th was locked, neone fetched a key. The house was empty, and showed very sign of a hasty exit having been made. Loomis had taken books and papers, his hat and boots, and his best overcoat. A coffee table had been broken, as if he had dropped some heavy weight on it in his hurry. He had left some half-burned documents crumpling into ashes in his stove, and an open wooden box from which — to judge by the heavy lock and the negative shape embossed in the red felt lining — something gun-size, flashlight-shaped, and quite valuable had been removed. Another box, hidden under Loomis's bed, held a silver contraption covered with dials and switches.

"I am no expert in Old-Tech," said Hilly, "but I should say that is a radio set. Some of the smarter airships are starting to use them. I expect that is how Loomis kept in touch with his masters aboard Crawley, and how he sent word to Crawley's agent among the Junkyard Dogs to tell her Oddington Doom and Tamzin Pook were coming. Loomis has been our traitor all along."

"So the game has been rigged against us from the very start," said Twyne, sitting down and putting his head in his hands. "Loomis! I would never have believed it!"

"The harbor crew said he didn't take much fuel," said Hilly. "I wondered at it, and now it makes sense. Crawley is only a few miles behind us. Loomis has fled there to join his masters, so he will be in no danger when they rip Museion apart."

"But why take Vespertine with him?" Max asked. "Also, while we're on the subject, *how*? I can't imagine making Vespertine go anywhere she didn't want to."

"As to the why," said Hilly, "remember that Crawley is a town run by engineers. A working Revenant in tip-top condition would be a fine prize to bring home to his masters. And, fo[illegible] don't suppose this radio set is the only bit of high Old-[illegible]ow, I supplied him with. What was in that empty box? Perhaps he[illegible] some gadget that could threaten even Vespertine."

"Why did he bring Vespertine here instead of taking her straight to Crawley?" wondered Twyne.

"Because his masters needed him here, as their eyes and ears aboard Museion," said Hilly. "He could not fly Vespertine to Crawley without revealing his treachery. And he did not need to: If Crawley had eaten Museion, Vespertine would have been part of its catch."

"But it was Loomis who hired us," said Max. "Why would he hire us to protect a city he wanted to see get eaten?"

"When he first saw Vespertine at Hawkshead," said Hilly, "he wanted to buy her from us. Don't you remember how angry we were at the suggestion? He only hired the rest of us because we would not part with her. And, I suppose, as he had been sent out to find help for Museion, he had to bring *someone* back with him. He reckoned we would not be very good at it. I fear he was right."

"Speak for yourself," said Max. "If Loomis thinks we can't look after ourselves, he's got another thing coming. I'm going after Vespertine."

"You're not," said Twyne and Hilly together.

"We've lost Tamzin, we've lost Doom," shouted Max. "I'm not losing Vespertine too!"

"Vespertine is bulletproof," said Hilly firmly. "You are not. Anyway, the Crawley people will see you coming and blast the *Fire's Astonishment* out of the sky before you reach them. It's not safe, Max. I'm sorry. It is brave of you to suggest it."

But it wasn't brave, Max knew. It was cowardly. Flying to Crawley on a hopeless rescue mission was a terrifying prospect, but it was not half so terrifying as the prospect of apologizing to poor Luka Voss. He guessed that Loomis had deliberately seeded the idea that Voss was the traitor in his mind to hide his own guilt, but that did not make Max feel any better. He had swallowed Loomis's poison like the fool he was. He had accused poor Luka of betraying his own city, and of murdering his own father. He did not see how the engineer could ever forgive him.

The wrecked room swayed, adding to Max's rising nausea and to the sense they all felt that the world had grown suddenly unstable. A bottle of hair tonic, which Professor Loomis must have dropped in his hurried packing, rolled out from beneath the dresser. The floor, which had been sloping steeply uphill toward the city's bows all night, leveled off briefly, and then slowly tilted downward. The bottle of hair tonic went trundling back again.

"We have crossed the summit of the pass," said Dr. Twyne. "We are heading down into the gorge, toward the Bridge of Storms."

"The route Loomis chose for us," said Hilly. "The route he promised us was safe. What were his promises worth, I wonder?"

"You think it is a trap?" asked Max.

"I am quite certain of it."

"Trap or not, it's too late to turn back now," said Twyne. "We shall strengthen the defenses on the stern. We don't have much ammunition left, but if Crawley means to corner us and eat us, we can at least give it a bloody nose. And I suppose we shall need to appoint yet another acting dean."

33

Lamplighter

Tamzin had not believed Mortmain at first. A conscious suburb? Who would build anything so bizarre and so dangerous? But she had thought about it while the barber clipped her hair off, and decided that it explained all too well the weirdness of the place. Now, as she followed Mortmain down the steeply sloping corridors toward one of the rear sections, she found it impossible not to think of Crawley as a living thing. A dragon, perhaps, with tracks for feet, and engines for a heart — and Tamzin Pook just a frightened little flea, scurrying around beneath its armored hide and hoping that it would not notice her.

She had no idea what time of day or night it was. Mortmain had come to her cell again and told her they were needed in Section H, and nothing else. She had not asked where they were going, for she was afraid to ask anything now. *The Head Sees All, The Head Hears All.* How it saw was obvious: those green lights everywhere, like the eyes of watchful Revenants. It must have ears too, microphones hidden in the walls or ceilings, but Tamzin did not know where, or how to spot them.

At last, while they waited in a noisy area to board an elevator,

Mortmain paused just long enough to look back at her and say, "Something's gone wrong. Our agent Lamplighter has fled Museion. His ship docked ten minutes ago."

When they stepped off the elevator, a breath of fresh air reached Tamzin, refreshing after the hot, mineral-scented fug, which was all she had breathed since she'd boarded Crawley. She followed Mortmain across an articulated section into another segment of the suburb, and he slid open a door to reveal a broad platform open to the sky.

It was dark, and the air felt startlingly cold on Tamzin's newly shaved scalp. She saw steep hills passing on either side, and black crags slashed with snow, very close to the suburb's flanks. She was so busy wondering if she could run and leap off the side and land safely on one of those rocks that it took her a moment to realize that the platform she was standing on was the apron of a small air harbor. A ship she knew was moored there.

It was Professor Loomis's *Owl of Minerva*. A group of Crawley people in their white coats were clustered around the gang-plank. Sister Rothrock was there, overseeing things. A couple of her underlings were dragging a big crate out of the ship. Beside her stood Professor Loomis himself.

"It is not my fault!" he was saying as Tamzin and Mortmain approached. "That fool Stanislaus kept poking his nose in. I had to leave. But I have brought you the Revenant . . ."

"Professor Loomis!" Tamzin said, and he glanced around and saw her. He had the decency to look a little ashamed. "It was you? You are the traitor?"

Loomis shook off his shame and put on a look of haughty indifference. "Miss Pook. I am glad to see you in one piece. I am not a traitor, merely one who sees sense. Museion will inevitably be devoured on this mad dash into the west. I simply took steps to ensure that the end would come sooner rather than later."

"And that you would make a tidy profit from it," added Mortmain. He was more interested in the crate than in Loomis. He shooed away the men who had been handling it and stooped to unfasten the lid. When he opened it, Tamzin saw Vespertine lying inside. The Revenant's eyes were lightless, and her gray face had no expression.

"Is she dead?" Tamzin asked. "I mean, dead*er*? Deader than usual?"

"I'd say your friend Loomis has shot her with a lightning gun," said Mortmain, examining a blackened patch on Vespertine's armor. "It has much the same effect as the electric blade you used in the Arcade. Vespertine's systems have shut down. Not dead, but sleeping."

"We must restrain the unit before it restarts," said Sister Rothrock. She snapped her fingers and signaled to the men who had dragged the crate down the gangplank. "Take it to security."

"No," said Mortmain. "Vespertine is to be taken to my laboratory. It is important that I examine her at once. I have laborers from the slave barracks standing by to transport her."

Two men in gray overalls who had been waiting in the shadows came forward at his command. They were pushing a metal trolley, and they heaved Vespertine up on to it and stood back, ready to wheel her away. The hard lights of the air harbor fell upon their faces then. One of them was a young easterner, who looked alarmed at being so close to a Revenant, even a sleeping one. The other was Oddington Doom.

Tamzin let out a cry of surprise, and managed just in time to disguise it as a sort of hiccup. Doom glanced at her then, and she saw him recognize her, but he was too wise to show it. He looked away, then glanced back at her and winked. Or maybe it was just a blink — it was hard to tell, since he had only the one eye.

Luckily, Professor Loomis had not recognized Doom. He was busy talking to Sister Rothrock. "I should like to be on my way before you eat Museion. It would be awkward to meet my former colleagues in your slave holds. Besides, if I hang around here too long you might shear my hair off, like poor Miss Pook, and that would not suit me any better than it suits her, ha ha ha! So if you could just see your way to paying me the amount we agreed, and refueling my ship, I will take off at first light."

"Of course, professor," said Sister Rothrock. "I do agree that your usefulness to Crawley has reached its natural end. You are quite certain Museion cannot escape us?"

"There is only one road through these hills," said Loomis gravely. "They must either follow it to its bitter end, or turn back into Crawley's waiting jaws. I have set them on the path of no return."

"Then you have performed most satisfactorily. Please, let me shake you by the hand . . ."

Sister Rothrock held out her hand to him. "Don't!" Tamzin shouted, but Mortmain hushed her and it was too late anyway. Loomis's fingers were already closing on the black glove. That kicked-hive sound came from it, and he cried out and flailed as if he were desperate to get away, but quite unable to let go. Sister Rothrock gave a little hissing laugh. They stood like that until thin wisps of smoke started to come from their clasped hands. Then Sister Rothrock touched some control on her belt, the buzzing stopped, and Loomis fell lifeless to the deck.

Crawley was tilting very steeply now, and the two security men had to stop Loomis's body rolling away into the shadows under the mooring gantry. Sister Rothrock turned her icy smile on Tamzin. "A reminder," she said, "that your services are expendable, however much Brother Mortmain may value you."

"The Head won't value any of us for long if we stand here nattering instead of getting Vespertine to the lab," snapped Mortmain. "Come, Pook. You men, we are heading for Segment E, Sublevel Six. I'll show you the way . . ."

❁

Once again, Tamzin kept quiet as she hurried after Mortmain back up the steep corridors. But Oddington Doom had not worked out the nature of the suburb yet. As he pushed the trolley bearing Vespertine ahead of her he kept glancing back and grinning. "I'm gladder than I can say to see you safe, Tamzin. My new friend here is Altan. He's a soldier of the League, fallen on hard times. But for him I'd have been crunched flat when the Hundberg got gobbled up. I thought we were stuck aboard this Crawley dump, for its slave-holds are far better run than Worrible's and there seemed no chance of escaping. But then the two of us got sent up here. How did you manage to get us assigned to this job?"

"I didn't," said Tamzin, careful not to meet his eye. And then, in case the Head was listening, she added loudly, "I don't know what you're talking about, old man."

Doom cottoned on. They went in silence after that, until they came to a corridor where the noise from the engines was loud enough that Mortmain thought it would drown out their voices. There he called a halt. "Something amiss with that front right wheel," he said, and crouched down, pretending to make adjustments to the axle.

"What are you playing at?" whispered Tamzin.

"I rescued Mr. Doom from the slave-hold, as you asked," Mortmain replied, looking at the wheel instead of her. "I thought it might convince you that I actually am your friend."

"You aren't."

He glanced up at her, annoyed. "You may not like it, Tamzin Pook, but in this suburb I am your *only* friend. I hate this place at least as much as you do. It was bad enough growing up here, but to be dragged back, now that I know all the pleasures and luxuries I could be enjoying on a normal town, is unendurable! Chances are, the Committee will bump me off as soon as I have done what they want, anyway. You saw what happened to Loomis. So I mean to escape. In a few hours, Crawley will reach Museion, and the Head's attention will be taken up with catching and eating it. Everyone else will be busy too. Then we shall sneak back to the air dock, get aboard one of the ships there, and be off. You can fly an airship, I believe?"

"That's what you need me for? That's why you made me your assistant?"

"Not just that, no," snapped Mortmain, taking a small wrench from one of his pockets and pretending to tighten the nut that held the trolley wheel in place. "I mean to start a new life on some more appealing town, and I thought you might care to tag along. You're the best Revenant fighter I ever trained. You could be the star of a new Amusement Arcade . . ."

"You must be even more deranged than the Head if you think I'd want that," said Tamzin.

"And we can't just fly off!" protested Doom. "What about Hilly? What about Max?"

But Mortmain's imaginary repairs to the trolley wheel were

complete. He sprang up and hurried on his way, shouting for the others to follow. They had reached Segment E now. He opened the doors of a freight elevator and ordered Doom and Altan to wheel the trolley in.

Even in the elevator there was a green light, shining down from the ceiling. It reflected in Vespertine's unseeing eyes, as if to remind Tamzin that there was still a spark of life in her dead friend.

34

At the Bridge of Storms

The night passed, and a pale, watery sun rose above the summits of the Golgan Hills to pierce the shadows in the gorge. The battle-weary people of Museion were finally able to see what lay ahead of them. Max, making his way to the Prow Gardens in front of the Ivory Tower, joined a small crowd who had gathered there, waiting to catch their first glimpse of the bridge.

The Vastri, slow and patient, had carved itself a deep, snaking channel through the hills' granite. A mile to the south, a plume of rising vapor caught the sun where the river went plunging over the falls at Heklafoss before curving away westward and descending cataract after cataract to join the Wassermauer at Flussenkreuzung. Here, where the pass descended to meet it, the gorge was so deep that it remained as a line of ink-black shadow even when the sun had risen high enough to light the stony slopes on either bank. Across it, rust red in the morning light, stretched the Bridge of Storms.

Rust red. The cheers that broke out in the Prow Gardens when the climbing sun first touched the bridge faltered and died away as the watchers saw it clearly. Vast and grand it was, for Stormsdown's civic engineers had stripped whole tiers from their city to construct it. It was three times the length of Museion's chassis, and half again as wide, supported by massive, arching girders, which had their footing on piers cut from the living rock. But years of rust had gnawed at the struts that supported it. Rust stains had run like spilled blood down the sheer walls of the gorge. Rust had chewed holes in the roadbed, and whole sections had gone missing, scavenged by passing towns, or fallen into the fierce waters of the Vastri, which raged unseen in shadows far below.

"It doesn't look very safe," someone ventured.

"It must be," said another. "The Senior Fellows wouldn't have come this way if it weren't."

"The navigation report says it's passable . . ."

But the navigator who made that report had been Professor Loomis, Max thought, and Professor Loomis was a traitor. Loomis had sent them this way knowing full well that they would not be able to cross.

From the moment Loomis's betrayal was discovered, Twyne and the others had guessed they were driving into a trap. Yet what could they do but keep going? The high hills hemmed them in on north and south, and if they turned back east they would run straight into the jaws of Crawley. Museion's only option had been to keep moving west, and hope that by some miracle the bridge was still sound.

Now they confronted the brutal truth. Barley Bellweather, the new chief navigator, issued an order to stop. Down in the engine district Luka Voss, restored to his throne in the control room, signaled his crews to back all the engines and apply the brakes. For the first time since it had left the Frying Pan, Museion came to a halt, a quarter mile or so uphill from the ruined bridge. Silence did not exactly fall — there is never real silence aboard a Traction City — but the wheels were stilled, the engines idled, and it felt like silence compared with the ceaseless din that had accompanied the journey west.

Max heard the voice of the river rising up out of the gorge — the rush and rumpus of the hungry water — and the crash of giant boulders tumbled in the flood. He stared at the remains of the bridge and wondered how much weight it could bear. He wished he could go down below and see what Voss made of it, but he had not spoken to the chief engineer or even seen him since he was released, and he guessed he would not be welcome anymore in the control room.

He ran instead to the Ivory Tower and climbed the long stairs to the navigation suite, to find Hilly and most of the Senior Fellows already there.

"We are done for," Professor Waghorn was shouting as Max burst in. "We can't cross that!"

"It doesn't look as if it would bear the weight of a wheelbarrow, let alone a city," agreed Professor Stanislaus.

"This is why bridges fell out of fashion," wailed Professor Pott-Walloper. "We should never have come here!"

"What do we do now?" wondered Hilly. "Turn around?"

"We can't!" said Barley Bellweather, who was having a stressful first day in her new job. "There isn't room to turn here!"

"Well, if we can't cross the bridge, and we can't go back," said Professor Pringle, the new acting dean, "all we can do is wait for Crawley to catch up with us."

He went to peer out of the sternward sweep of windows. Most of the others followed him, as if there were safety in numbers. Behind the city, the road it had just traveled reached back in a series of steep zigzags toward a distant ridge, dark against the morning sun. There, as they watched, the skyline seemed to grow spines, and the spines turned into the chimneys and upperworks of Crawley, dragging itself over the summit of the pass. It seemed to pause there, panting for breath perhaps, staring greedily down at its cornered prey.

"Dr. Twyne," said Hilly. "Can we hope to fight a town like that?"

Twyne had been sitting disconsolately in a swivel chair beside the chart table. He took a moment to collect himself before he came to join the others at the window. "No," he said. "That suburb is well armored, and we used up most of our ammunition on the Junkyard Dogs. They played their part well, herding us here. Now Crawley will move in for the kill."

"So all we can do is wait to be eaten?"

"Yes," said Twyne.

"I fear so," said Pringle.

"No!" said Max.

They all turned to look at him. "No," he said again. "Museion might not get across the bridge, but we can. On foot."

"What good would that do us?" demanded Professor Waghorn. "Even if we didn't fall through the holes in the bridge, we would just end up stranded on the other side, townless, watching Crawley eat our home."

"On the bare earth!" agreed Professor Pringle.

"I have walked on the bare earth," said Max. "Several times. And I came to no harm."

"That is true," said Mrs. Pringle, taking her husband's hand. "Don't you remember, dear, our journeys in the mountains?"

"As a young man," said Stanislaus, "I spent many months on

foot, exploring Ancient sites. If we evacuate Museion and walk across the bridge, we could make our way down to the plains beyond. Perhaps we might find a friendly town or city there to take us in."

"Or an unfriendly one that will enslave us," grumbled Waghorn. "We might as well take our chances with Crawley."

While they were arguing, Hilly wandered back to the forward windows and peered down critically at the bridge. She had not bothered to look hard at it before, but had trusted the others when they said it was impassable. Now, seeing it properly for the first time, she pursed her lips thoughtfully. "I may not be as clever as you professors," she said, "and maybe some of Oddington's natural optimism has rubbed off on me, but I believe we may not have to abandon Museion after all."

"You can't mean we should try to cross that rusting wreck?" cried Professor Pringle. "It isn't safe."

"Oh, it certainly isn't safe," Hilly agreed. "We must get everyone we can spare off the city and send them across on foot, as Max says. But once they're safely on the far bank, there might be enough bridge left that a skeleton crew of volunteers could try getting the city over too."

"And then knock the bridge down behind us so Crawley can't follow!" said Max.

Hope crept into the faces of the Senior Fellows, like the first glimmer of day after a dreadful night.

"It is worth a try," said Barley Bellweather.

"I'd sooner end up in the river than in Crawley's slave-holds," said Professor Waghorn.

"Max," said Hilly, while they were still deciding, "get downstairs and start spreading the word. Tell everyone who isn't needed to grab a coat and whatever they can carry and head to the forward exits. But do be careful on that bridge — even the bits that don't look rusted through may still be treacherous."

"Aren't you coming?" asked Max.

Hilly shook her head. "It was my idea. I can't expect anyone else to volunteer to stay aboard if I do not do so myself."

She gave Max an affectionate hug, and sent him on his way. Then she returned to the sternward windows. Crawley still squatted motionless at the top of the pass, like a spider that had caught a fat fly in its web and felt it could take its time eating it. *What was it about that suburb?* Hilly wondered. She had the strangest feeling it was *watching* her.

35

In the Belly of the Beast

Sirens were wailing again in Crawley's depths as Doom and Altan wheeled Vespertine out of the elevator. Tamzin helped them as they followed Mortmain along more dripping passageways. The suburb was tilting so steeply on its way downhill to the bridge that it was all the three of them could do to keep Vespertine on the trolley and the trolley from running away with her. A harsh, mechanical voice rang through the corridors, ordering work crews to clear the digestion yards and prepare the jaws.

"Here we are! My little kingdom," Mortmain announced, stopping outside a door marked with yellow warning chevrons and a sign saying KEEP OUT. "It's a bit of a comedown, but positively luxurious by Crawley's standards."

The room he let them in to was large, but low and dimly lit, and cluttered with weird machinery. At its center stood a massive metal table, and he directed Doom and Altan to lay Vespertine on this. Two young Crawley people watched suspiciously from among the waiting machines: a man and woman, pretty much identical with their white coats and bald heads.

"My assistants," said Mortmain, gesturing vaguely at them.

"Brother Carmody and Sister Walker. Or is it the other way around? They're very reliable, anyway. Loyal servants of the Head. Sister Rothrock vetted them herself." He looked meaningfully at Tamzin, warning her not to trust this pair, then turned his attention back to Vespertine. He secured her wrist and ankles with thick leather straps whose ends were bolted to the table. "Sister Pook will be observing the procedure," he told his assistants. "She has experience with the Vespertine unit. And these two gentlemen will be staying too. Just in case the restraints fail." He glanced meaningfully at Tamzin.

Sister Walker and Brother Carmody, eager to help, began unspooling thick cables from the machines that surrounded the table. Mortmain, pulling off Vespertine's bobble hat, plugged the cables into ports on her misshapen skull.

"What are you doing to her?" asked Tamzin.

"Please stay back, Sister Pook. I am checking she has not been damaged by Loomis's shenanigans," said Mortmain. "If we are to use her brain to repair the Head, we need to be certain it's in tip-top condition. Come, Sister Walker. It's time to wake the patient."

Sister Walker glanced uneasily at Brother Carmody. Neither of them approved of Brother Mortmain's lighthearted way of talking. To them, the thing on the table was a subject, not a patient. No doubt Brother Mortmain had picked up his disconcerting sense of humor during his years of exile. They both rather wished that he had stayed exiled, and that the Head had not allowed him to return. But they dared not say so, even to each other. The Head knew all. And everyone said Mortmain understood Stalker brains better than anyone in Crawley.

Sister Walker pressed a switch on one of the waiting machines. Tamzin, watching over Mortmain's shoulder, saw two tiny far-off stars of green light appear in the depths of the Revenant's eyes and slowly grow. Mortmain leaned over Vespertine, looking expectantly into her face.

"You are not Professor Loomis," said Vespertine.

"Excellent," said Mortmain, stepping back. "Eyes are working, memory too. Make a note of that, Brother Carmody. Patient revived at six thirty a.m., bright-eyed, bushy-tailed, and ready for anything."

Subject restarted at 06:30 hrs Brother Carmody scribbled on his notepad. *Functioning within acceptable parameters.*

"You are Dr. Mortmain," said Vespertine, studying the face that hung above her.

"Good girl," said Mortmain. "Welcome to Crawley."

Vespertine moved, trying to rise from the table, but the leather straps held her tight. "I must return to Museion," she said. "My friends will miss me. Small Cat needs me."

"As for your friends," said Mortmain, "one of them is here already: Look, there is Miss Pook. And I have no idea who Small Cat is, but I doubt he or she needs you as much as Crawley does. Well, not *you* so much as that brain of yours. It's one of the best-preserved Stalker brains I ever worked on. You've not been using it for very long, so it should still be in prime condition. We're just going to whip it out of you and reuse the parts to repair another, rather more important Revenant."

Vespertine's eyes dimmed and flared uncertainly. "And what will happen to me?"

"Well, your consciousness will be deleted, of course," said Mortmain. "Don't worry — it won't hurt a bit. You just lie there and relax."

"But I do not wish to be deleted," said Vespertine. The thought that she was going to suddenly stop being herself — that she was going to stop being anything anymore — was very disagreeable.

This is fear, she thought, lying there on the table while Mortmain adjusted the restraints on her wrist and ankles and his assistants fussed with their machinery. *This is how Professor Stanislaus must feel. This is death. I am going to die.*

"Tamzin Pook," she said, "I do not wish to be deleted."

Tamzin went to stand beside her.

"Please step aside," snapped Brother Carmody, trying to push her back, but Tamzin ignored him and reached for Vespertine's big, cold hand. She looked at Mortmain, wondering what his plan was, and whether he really meant to take out Vespertine's brain. It seemed quite likely. But then why had he insisted on Tamzin being present? Why had he asked Doom and his new friend to stay? To control the patient, he had said, but surely the restraints would do that?

"Tamzin Pook," said Vespertine. "I am afraid."

"Don't be," said Tamzin. She remembered the way Mortmain had looked at her when he talked about the restraints failing, and guessed what he wanted her to do. For once, she felt happy to fall in with his schemes.

Sister Walker was testing an electric bone saw that looked like a motorized pizza cutter. While the device whined, Tamzin leaned down so that her face was close to Vespertine's and whispered, "Those straps are not strong enough to hold you. You must break free."

Vespertine tried moving her arm. She had not been able to move it an inch before, but now, to her mild surprise, the restraint holding it to the table shifted slightly. She remembered Mortmain tinkering with it while he talked to her. She had assumed he was tightening it, but it was looser than before. It was very mysterious.

"Brother Mortmain," said Carmody nervously, "I think it is trying to get loose!"

"Nonsense," scoffed Mortmain, glancing around at Tamzin and trying to semaphore some urgent message with his eyebrows.

"Vespertine, now!" shouted Tamzin, and sprang back just in time as Vespertine wrenched her arm and legs free, sending the bolts that had secured the leather straps to the table pinging around the laboratory like stray bullets.

"It is free!" screamed Brother Carmody, as Vespertine stood upright. Sister Walker ran to a cabinet and produced another of those blank-ended guns like the one Professor Loomis had used, but Vespertine knew all about those now. She lunged across the lab and smashed Sister Walker aside before she could fire, caught Brother Carmody as he tried to flee and slammed his head into the low roof, then spun to grab Mortmain by the throat.

"Vespertine, no!" said Tamzin.

"But it is Mortmain," said the Stalker, squeezing.

"Guurk!" Mortmain protested.

"He's a friend!" said Tamzin.

"No, he isn't. He is Mortmain."

"You mean this Mortmain is *that* Mortmain? *The* Mortmain? *Mortmain*, Mortmain?" asked Doom, who had never actually met Margate's Master of Amusements.

"What is a Mortmain?" asked Altan.

"He is our one hope of getting off this place," said Tamzin, grabbing Vespertine's arm.

The Revenant released Mortmain, and he dropped heavily to the deck, gasping for breath. "Get back on the table!" he croaked. "Before the Head sees!"

"Do as he says," said Tamzin, and Vespertine meekly lay down on the table again. Mortmain clambered to his feet and started fussing with the cables that linked her to his machines, replacing the ones that had been jerked from their ports when she broke free. From time to time, he shot quick glances at the green light on the ceiling. "The Head Sees All," he explained hoarsely, "but the Head doesn't actually concentrate on all. There must be a thousand cameras feeding images from every part of Crawley into his brain. He can't watch all of them all the time. If we keep things looking as normal as possible here, there's a good chance he may not see what we are up to. Get those two dimwits out of sight, and gather around."

Doom checked on Brother Carmody and Sister Walker and found they were both alive, though one was unconscious and the other was pretending to be. With Altan's help, he dragged them into the shadows behind one of the cabinets, bound their hands with spare cables, and gagged them with electrical tape. Tamzin joined Mortmain, fiddling with the machines around Vespertine's table and trying to look as if she knew what she was doing.

"So if he's your actual Mortmain," asked Doom, "why is he helping us?"

"He's not," said Tamzin. "He's helping himself. He's just using us to get his way."

"I'm helping all of us," said Mortmain irritably. "I am the tide that lifts all boats."

"Bit of a coincidence, us running into you again like this," said Doom.

"Of course it isn't," said Mortmain. "I learned months ago that you'd adopted my Revenant and set up as buccaneers. And since Crawley needs a Stalker brain and the best one I know of is in Vespertine's head, I told them to find her. If Crawley's air patrols had picked her up, they would have killed the lot of you and brought her straight here. Luckily for you it was that fool Loomis who spotted her first.

"I wasn't expecting her to come aboard tonight, but when she did I realized that with Tamzin to control her she could be a useful ally in my brilliant escape plan. I am improvising, you see. It is a mark of my genius. You don't think we can just waltz aboard an airship and leave, do you? Even while Crawley's busy eating, there will be guards at the air dock. We'll have more chance of getting past them with Vespertine on our side. All we have to do is wait until the Head is thoroughly occupied with Museion, and then make our way aft."

"Sounds good to me," agreed Doom. "What do you reckon, Altan?"

Altan made a helpless gesture. He had no idea what these barbarians were talking about, but it seemed to involve leaving Crawley, and that was fine with him.

But Tamzin said, "No."

"No what?" asked Mortmain.

"No, we can't leave."

"Why not? Are you planning to stop around and see the sights?"

"Crawley is going to eat Museion," said Tamzin. "It's going to use Museion's engines to make itself faster, and Museion's Old-Tech knowledge to make itself stronger, and when it comes down out of these hills it will be a match for any city in the Hunting Ground. And Crawley is a monster." She turned to Doom. "It has a mad mind of its own, and a burning hunger that will drive it to eat town after town after town. But we can stop it, and if we do, then Museion may be saved too."

"Fool of a Pook!" cried Mortmain in disgust, and then, recalling that the Head might hear, went on in a strangled whisper, "We are not here to save the world! Saving our own skins will be hard enough. You think you can stop Crawley? You would have to destroy the Head himself!"

"How do we do that?" asked Doom.

"You can't! The Head is housed in an armored silo in the central segment. The staff there are all loyal to him, and his inner sanctum is patrolled by two Revenants that I built for him myself, back in my younger days. I called them the Raptor Twins. Rather catchy, I thought at the time. They will tear apart any intruder."

"You made us fight things called Raptors in the Arcade one season," said Tamzin, recalling nights of blood and terror.

"The design is similar, but these two are much tougher, and the Head controls them directly. You can't fight them."

"I can if Vespertine is with me," said Tamzin.

"We are a team," explained Vespertine.

"Are you sure about this, Tamzin?" Doom asked.

Tamzin thought about it. She put her hand to her chest, touching her sun disc for luck, as she always did before a fight. The disc was gone, of course. Maybe her luck had gone with it. *Even so,* she thought, *someone has to do something about Crawley,* and she was the only one in a position to do it. If she did not act now, the Revenant suburb might rampage for years before someone better suited had a chance to stop it. Maybe no one ever would, and the grim future of which Jago Flint dreamed would come to pass.

"I think we have to try," she said. "Even if we can't destroy the Head, we might distract him long enough that he slips up and lets Museion get away. If we can't save the world, we could at least save Max and Hilly."

"And Small Cat," said Vespertine.

"All right," said Doom. "You're on." He didn't fully understand this Head business, but he had learned to trust Tamzin's judgment. If she said Crawley needed dealing with, then deal with it he would. He glanced at Altan. "Are you up for a bit more trouble, my friend?"

The young man spread his hands helplessly. "I wish only to return to my own country. But I am a soldier of the Anti-Traction League. I swore an oath to fight all mobile cities. Yes, I will stand with you."

Doom slapped him on the shoulder. "Good fellow. You needn't fight 'em all — just this one. Then we can see about getting you home. What will we need, Tamzin?"

Tamzin looked around the laboratory, wondering if anything could help her battle Revenants. "Do you have an electro-blade?" she asked Mortmain.

"Of course I don't have an electro-blade!" Mortmain hissed, panic-stricken. "This isn't the Amusement Arcade! It wouldn't help anyway! Don't you understand? That was just show business. The Arcade Revenants were designed so that even a flimsy girl like you could defeat them. These Raptors I built for the Head are designed so that no one can. This is madness!"

Maybe it was, Tamzin thought. But it felt good to be taking charge of things at last, and better still to be telling Mortmain what to do. The fearful, cowering way he looked at her made her feel good. Even if she achieved nothing else this day, she would make the Master of Amusements find out how it felt to be forced into deadly danger.

36

Rust

The evacuation of Museion had begun. The access ramps between the front wheels — seldom used and rather rusty themselves — had been lowered, and down them was pouring most of the little city's population. Max, waiting at the foot of the ramps, was surprised at how many Museion still contained, and how many children, how many dogs and cats, how many songbirds in cages and goldfish in bowls and small aquariums. Many of the children were crying, and many of the adults too. They had never set foot upon the bare earth before. They had never imagined leaving the safety of their city. And they thought it probable that they would never be able to return.

From behind them, on the steep eastern slopes of the gorge, came the snarl of engines and the clatter of dislodged boulders. Crawley was barely a mile away now. Ignoring the zigzag road that Museion had taken hours to traverse, it was winding its way downhill between the crags like a fat and sinister worm. It had already unlatched its jaws and swung them half open in anticipation of its coming meal. The watchers on the city below could see the red glow of furnaces deep in its gullet.

The first groups of refugees quailed and bunched up at the bottom of the ramps. As if leaving the safety of their city were not terrible enough, the bridge that stretched out before them was so rusty and so dotted with gaping holes it looked certain to give way beneath them. Max was afraid they might be right, but he knew they could not stay where they were, huddled on the eastern bank with Crawley creeping down on them. *Someone needs to lead them across,* he thought. *If one person is brave enough to make the crossing, the rest will follow.* And that reminded him of something Luka Voss had said.

He drew the sword that Voss had given him, and held it up so that it shone in the sunlight. The people around him fell quiet at the sight of it, and the quietness spread through the whole crowd. It was as Voss had said, thought Max. They needed someone to follow. They did not know that Max was just as scared as they were.

Holding the sword high, he stepped out on to the bridge before his courage failed him. To his relief, the bridge felt sturdier than it looked. There were those horrible gaping holes to be avoided, and sections where the rusted metal sagged sickeningly underfoot, but most of the way across he might as well have been walking on the firm deckplates of a city. Stormsdown's engineers had underpinned their work with massive girders. The changeable weather of the Golgan Hills had eroded them until they looked like the vast rusty bones of some prehistoric monster, but they were still strong enough to bear the weight of all Museion's people.

But what about Museion itself? Max wondered as he reached the western bank and turned to see the crowd of refugees following him. People could get across all right, but would the bridge support a whole city?

Once the last group on foot was safely across, the tractor from the Air Staithe came trundling down the ramp. It had been converted into a makeshift ambulance, and made several crossings, ferrying Dr. Jaffaji's medical supplies and those patients from the infirmary who could not rise from their beds, like the dean and Lamorna Fey. When it returned to Museion to fetch the final load, Max rode with it.

Professor Pott-Walloper, who had been organizing the evacuation, stood at the top of the ramps with Dr. Jaffaji and some of his colleagues. "Well done, Mr. Angmering!" she called, as Max jumped off the tractor. He laughed with pride, and with the excitement of doing great things, and helped the doctors aboard with the last of their supplies. But as the tractor rolled back down the ramp to begin its final crossing he noticed Luka Voss watching him. The chief engineer had been standing in the shadows, invisible until Max's eyes adjusted to the darkness of the lower deck. It was the first time Max had seen him since his arrest.

"Meringue boy," said Voss. "You have been avoiding me, I think."

"No," said Max. "It's just that I have been so busy . . ." But he was lying to himself as well as Voss. Of course he had been avoiding him. What did you say to someone you had falsely accused of being a traitor to their own city? "Sorry" would hardly cover it. His pride and his excitement died away. He felt ashamed.

He unbuckled his sword belt and held out the sheathed sword to Voss. "You gave me this," he said, "but I think you were mistaking me for someone else."

Voss's black night-adapted eyes watched him coldly. He did not reach out to take the sword. He said, "So you would insult me by returning my gift?"

Max hesitated.

Voss snorted. "That was well done, getting the people across. But now we have a city to move, and a city is heavier, and not so easily encouraged by handsome young men waving swords about. I do not like the look of this bridge."

He turned his back on Max and went stalking off down the streets that led into the engine district. Max buckled the sword back on and ran after him. "You don't think Museion can get across?"

Voss stopped, waiting for him to catch up. "I did not say that. I said I did not like the look of the bridge in front of us. But I like the look of that suburb behind us even less. I do not like the thought of my beautiful engines being junked and recycled in its belly. And the rest of you might be able to walk to safety, but not me, because the sun will blind and burn me. So I am going to order the engines to full ahead slow. In a few more minutes, Museion will either be on the far side of that river, or at the bottom of it."

"Let me help," said Max.

"I thought you would be going up to the navigation suite with your friends."

"I'd sooner be down here. In the heart of things."

"You are no engineer. What can you do?"

"I can do what I'm told."

Voss raised an eyebrow. "Very well. Then come with me."

The skeleton crew Voss had selected were at their stations in the engine district. They cheered him as he walked by, and the staff in the control room clapped as he took his seat. A woman reported the latest observations from the Ivory Tower. "Crawley is at eight hundred yards and closing. Men are preparing harpoon launchers in bunkers above her jaws."

"Then if we are crossing this bridge, we had better cross quickly," said Voss. "Main engine start."

"Main engine start," someone said into a speaking tube, and Max heard the order taken up by other voices, fainter and fainter, like echoes running away from him into the warrens of the engine district.

Museion woke, and purred.

"All ahead slow," said Voss.

Again the echoes fled away. The city trembled and started inching forward. As its front wheels rolled from the stone of the pass on to the metal of the bridge, a weird, half-musical moan came drifting through the streets, startling everyone aboard. It was the voice of the Bridge of Storms, protesting as it felt Museion's weight.

37

Control

The mind that controlled Crawley did not care about the people who scurried about in the warrens of its streets. It needed them, as a human brain needs muscles, blood cells, and gut flora to keep it moving around and putting its thoughts and desires into action, but it cared nothing for them otherwise. Among its deepest, most secret dreams, it nursed a long-term plan to have the whole population replaced with Revenants, all slaved directly to itself. But, for now, these fragile and fallible once-born would have to suffice. Its voice rang from speakers all over the suburb, telling them to fire up the engines, increase speed, and ready the harpoon launchers. The cameras that were its eyes fed it flickering images of the scene ahead. It was so busy studying them that it paid scant attention to the internal camera feeds. Had it not been so focused on its prey, it might have noticed Tamzin and Mortmain walking toward the central segment, followed by two laborers pushing a trolley on which a sheeted figure lay.

The central segment was a complicated maze of interlinked control rooms where shaven-headed men and women peered at screens and barked instructions into speaking tubes and telephone receivers. Security officers stopped the party several times, but each time Mortmain told them he was there on urgent business for the Head, and since they knew him, and what his business was, they let him through. Door after door opened before them and closed behind until they came to an antechamber at the core of the segment where one last door would let them into the Head's silo. A woman sat at a desk there, monitoring readouts on the banks of screens and dials that carbuncled the walls. The door behind her was oval, and stenciled with the single word "CONTROL." Tamzin supposed that the Revenants that patrolled inside the silo were so dreadful there was no need to have guards outside too.

"You cannot make repairs now, Brother," the woman said when Mortmain stated their business. "The Head is concentrating on the hunt. Look — his brain activity is massively increased. You will have to wait until Museion is eaten." She came and twitched back the sheet that covered Vespertine. "This is the unit you are using for spare parts?" she asked, looking in surprise at Mortmain and his companions. "It is still whole!"

"That is because Brother Mortmain is not here to repair the Head, but to destroy him," said Sister Rothrock, stepping into the room behind them.

Tamzin reached for her knife, then realized it was hopeless. On her way into the central segment, Sister Rothrock had collected half a dozen of the guards Mortmain had breezed past earlier. The men stood behind her, guns held ready.

"I have never trusted you, Brother Mortmain," Sister Rothrock said. "Luckily, I thought to take a look in your laboratory just now. Where I found your assistants tied up and gagged."

"What does this mean?" asked the other woman.

Sister Rothrock smiled. "It means Brother Mortmain is a

traitor," she said. "And we know what happens to traitors, don't we, Brother Mortmain?" She flicked a switch on the power pack at her waist.

"Not me!" shrieked Mortmain as her gloved hand reached for him. "It's them you want! They made me do it!"

He scrambled backward, and the glove missed him. Sister Rothrock hissed and raised her hand to strike again, while the men behind her pushed forward, raising their guns, shouting.

But Vespertine was ready for them. The gunmen fell back in horror as she rose from beneath her shroud. Sister Rothrock rounded on her, but before the electric glove could touch her armor, Vespertine simply picked the woman up and hurled her to the far side of the room. Meanwhile, Doom and Altan dealt with the men at the door, knocking the leaders down, taking their guns as they fell, and turning them on the men behind. There were shots, ricochets, sprays of sparks and smoke from shattered screens. Mortmain shrieked. Vespertine moved in, surprisingly swift, surprisingly graceful. A man shot her at point-blank range and the bullet made a silver scar on the breast of her blue armor. Then his gun was in her hand and she swung it like a bat to knock him down. She sprouted a foot-long spike out of her elbow and drove it through another man who was aiming his gun at Tamzin. The survivors fled, shouting for help as they went.

Altan crouched down by Mortmain, who was whimpering and clutching his shoulder. Tamzin looked around for Sister Rothrock, saw her crumpled and unmoving in a corner, and turned to the other woman. Doom tossed a dead man's gun at her, and she caught it and pointed it at the woman's face. "Let us through," she said.

The woman was lean and brown, about Doom's age. Like many

of the senior engineers, she wore a red cogwheel on her brow. She looked at Tamzin, then past her at the dead men and the shifting veil of gun smoke in the doorway. She said, "Have you really come to destroy our Head?"

"Yes," said Tamzin, hoping she would not have to harm her. "Let us through."

"I am glad," said the woman. "I have been waiting for someone to move against him. I am Sister Yarrow. I will help you if I can."

Tamzin wasn't sure whether to believe that or not. She glanced at Mortmain to see what he thought, but he was too busy grizzling about his flesh wound. "Why should I trust you?" she asked Sister Yarrow.

"There's no reason why you should. But a lot of us here in Central feel the same. We hear what he whispers to himself, down there in the silo. We have grown afraid. We believe the Head is insane."

"Increase speed!" brayed the too-loud voice of the suburb, crackling out of speakers in the ceiling. "Museion is attempting to cross the bridge. We will secure them before they are destroyed. Increase speed."

"Security teams will be coming for you," said Sister Yarrow. "And inside the silo there are dreadful things."

"I can deal with the security men," said Doom. "Dreadful things are more in Tamzin's and Vespertine's line."

"The Raptors that guard the Head are directly controlled by the Head," said Sister Yarrow. "They are Crawley's hands, if you will. Or, to use a more accurate analogy, they are antibodies that Crawley uses to fight off dangerous microbes."

"Forward harpoons," bellowed the voice in the ceiling, "target the rear chassis. Adjust for windspeed. Fire in three, two . . ."

Tamzin thought she felt the floor jolt as the harpoons fired, but there was so much other jolting and rattling going on that it was hard to tell. She tossed her gun to Altan, reasoning that it would be more useful against human guards than against whatever was waiting for her beyond the silo door. The suburb lurched and tilted, hurrying down some final steep slope toward the Bridge of Storms.

"I will let you through," Sister Yarrow said. "But I will have to close the door behind you. I cannot risk the Raptors getting loose."

She typed a series of numbers into the Old-Tech pad on the wall beside the oval door, and it rolled aside to reveal a passageway bathed in green light. Tamzin turned to Vespertine. "After you," she said.

But before either of them could reach the door, Sister Rothrock sprang up, scrabbled her way through it, and ran into the green light, screaming, "Head! O Head! They are coming to harm you!" The light flared and fluttered as she fled along the passageway. For a moment the violent movements of the deckplates subsided as Crawley's attention switched from its prey to what was happening in its own insides. That hard voice screeched from the speakers, ordering extra security teams to the central segment.

Vespertine strode through the door in pursuit of Sister Rothrock. Tamzin yelled at her to come back, for she could not see how they could win this fight now that the element of surprise was gone. But Sister Yarrow was shouting at her that the Head was overriding the door controls, and she could not let Vespertine face the dangers in there alone, so she ran through too.

The door slammed shut and locked itself behind her. She was trapped in the inner sanctum of the Head.

38

Harpoons

Hilly had said she wanted to be useful, so they gave her a flag and sent her out to stand upon the Bridge of Storms. It was not a real flag, just somebody's old shirt, tied by both arms to a broom handle. Other people with similar flags stood spread out in a line across the width of the bridge. Their job was to walk slowly in front of the city as it crept across, and wave their flags to signal "left a little" or "right a bit" to observers on the bows, who relayed their instructions to the control room and the navigation suite.

The second set of wheels rolled cautiously onto the bridge, and again the ancient girders groaned, and again the people waiting on the western side of the gorge gasped, and the green lamps on the jaws and upperworks of Crawley seemed to flare with an evil light.

A section of the roadbed gave way as the bridge twisted under Museion's weight, opening a yards-wide hole through which Hilly saw the falling piece go end over end, down into the gorge until it smashed apart on black rocks in the shadows there and the rushing river swept the pieces away. Museion rolled on. The track units at the city's rear end were edging on to the bridge now, one slow link at a time. Behind it, Crawley was negotiating a difficult bend around one final crag. In five minutes, it would be on the approach to the bridge, and within harpoon-shot of Museion.

Hilly waved her flag urgently to steer the city to the right, away from a patch of rust through which she could see daylight. Museion obeyed her, and she thought for a moment how strange it was that she, Hilly Torpenhow, was controlling this vast edifice by flapping a shirt in the air. She felt rather pleased with herself.

But the city had steered too far to the right. The front wheels scraped the parapet at the bridge's edge, the parapet gave way, and at the same moment the entire bridge twisted and tilted. Thrown off her feet, Hilly rolled almost to the edge of the nearest hole before she could stop herself. Her dropped flag went through the hole and down, a bright bird flying through the blizzards of fluttering rust flakes. The voice of the straining girders under the bridge was like whale song, bellowing mournfully along the gorge.

Whimpering with terror, and terribly glad there was no one nearby to hear her, Hilly clawed her way up the forty-five-degree slope of the roadbed, while rust and loose stones slid past her to begin their own flight to the river. Around her, fist-size rivets popped out of their sockets like squeezed blackheads as the bridge twisted again. Hilly reached the southern parapet — the upper parapet, you might call it now, since the bridge was skewed so steeply out of true. She clung there and looked back and saw that all her fellow flag-wavers had lost their footing too, and were clinging on like her, or crawling on all fours across the shuddering rust. She did not think anyone had fallen off, thank the gods. Museion, steering blind, had its whole weight on the bridge now, but it was canted over at such an angle that she thought it must surely overturn, or simply slide off sideways into the gorge.

But no. It kept coming, edging like a novice tightrope-walker along that flimsy ribbon of rust, while Hilly and the others found their feet again and backed away before it, until they reached the bridge's end, and scrambled gratefully up into the rocky outcrops there to watch with everybody else as Museion's vast front wheels rolled slowly, slowly off the bridge.

The sudden series of bangs that echoed across the gorge then sounded at first like the supports giving way. The watchers cried out in horror, for Museion was still mostly on the bridge, and would plunge backward into the abyss if it gave way.

But the bridge held. It was almost a relief to discover that the bangs had been only the reports of Crawley's harpoon-launchers going off, and the sound of the harpoons slamming into Museion's stern.

Several of the harpoons had missed their mark and fallen uselessly on to the bridge, but three had penetrated deep into the city's upperworks, and stuck there. As Museion edged forward toward safety, the heavy cables attached to the harpoons went taut, and Crawley started to haul its prey backward into its waiting jaws.

❁

"Harpoons!" someone in the control room shouted as the whole engine district shuddered under the impacts. A moment later, the city's slow, steady progress stalled, and it started to roll backward.

"More power to the engines," ordered Luka Voss.

"But, Luka," said one of his staff, "the vibrations could shake the bridge apart."

Voss shrugged. It could not be helped. "More power," he said, and, looking around for someone not already busy, remembered Max. "Cut the harpoon cables," he told him.

It would take more than a flashy sword to do that, Max

thought. The hawsers of the harpoons were made from braided steel, as thick as the trunks of giant trees. But in the hallways around the control room he found workers waiting, all hoping to do their bit to get Museion to safety.

"Luka wants the cables cut!" Max shouted at them, and some scattered to fetch tools while others followed him toward the stern, through the blackened streets where they had fought the fires two nights before.

They were passing the cargo holds, heading for the open apron at the city's stern, when they found their way barred. At first, when he saw those raggedy figures swaggering out to bar his way, Max thought it was some of the militia come down from the top deck to lend a hand. He had forgotten the Junkyard Dogs till then. But here they were. In the confusion of the evacuation, some too-kind guard had let them free, or they had forced their way out anyway, and with Stoat at their head they were making their way to the control room. Some had helped themselves to hammers, wrenches, and lengths of pipe on their journey from the lockup. Stoat was hefting a fire axe with a bright red blade.

He grinned in triumph as Max and the engine district crew skidded to a halt in front of him. "This city's mine now," he said.

"You fool," Max shouted. "Don't you know where we are? Can't you feel what's happening? We're all in this together now! This is the Bridge of Storms. The whole city could fall if we don't cut ourselves free of those harpoons!"

Museion was shaking like a frightened animal, straining to pull itself forward while Crawley strained to drag it back. The nomads behind Stoat looked uneasy. This was news to them. Shut up in the dark since the fires broke out, they had no notion of where Museion was going, or that it was so closely pursued. They knew the Bridge of Storms, though. The Dogs had crossed it often in former years. It was no place for a city to linger.

But Stoat just shouted, “Lies!” and swung his axe. “You’ll have to do better than that, city boy!”

And Max, leaning backward as the blade whisked past his face, could do nothing except draw his sword and fight.

39

Armed and Dangerous

"Well," said Tamzin. "This is nice."

Vespertine's big shape filled the passageway ahead of her, her head almost brushing the pipes and ducts that formed the ceiling. She turned to look at Tamzin and said, "We are a team."

"We are a good team. Pook and Vespertine."

"Vespertine and Pook."

"Watch out," warned Tamzin. "It's not just the Revenants we have to worry about. Sister Rothrock is in here. That glove of hers would probably do you no good if she touches you with it."

"I will be careful," promised Vespertine.

Tamzin reached for her sun disc and felt annoyed at herself for forgetting yet again it wasn't there. Together, she and Vespertine moved along the passage. It turned a corner, and opened onto a metal walkway that ran in a ring around a deep, circular chamber. A handrail guarded the walkway's edge. Tamzin leaned over it, and looked down into an open pit two or three stories deep, its depths filled with machinery. There was a tangled forest of pipes, ducts, cables, and tubes down there, and a lot of green lights shining like diseased jewels. A narrow ladder led from the walkway down into the pit. But the ladder was on the far side of the silo, and between it and Tamzin stood Sister Rothrock.

"Fools!" the woman said, moving toward Tamzin and Vespertine along the curve of the walkway. She held her gloved hand toward them and it buzzed with angry power. Blood was running down her face from her collision with the wall. In the dim green light the rivulets looked black, like cracks spreading across a porcelain mask.

"Do you think I will let you harm our Head?" she said. "Jago Flint is a genius, and you are nothing. He is immortal, and you are as good as dead. He looked at the universe with clear, cold eyes and saw there were no gods, so he made himself a god. Soon all the world will worship him."

Tamzin pulled the knife from her belt and wondered if there was some way she could duck under Sister Rothrock's guard without the deadly glove touching her. Beside her, Vespertine unsheathed her own blade. Sister Rothrock paused. Her eyes flicked from one to the other of them, wondering if she could tackle them both. "Head!" she said loudly. "Head! Unleash your angels of death upon these trespassers!"

Behind her, something unfolded itself out of the crisscross shadows between the pipes. It was vaguely man-shaped, but a good deal larger, and it seemed to be made of knives.

Sister Rothrock glanced back at it and let out a wild laugh. "Punish them!" she cried.

But the Head was angry with her for letting saboteurs get inside the silo. Or perhaps he could no longer tell one human being from another. The knives flashed. Sister Rothrock's laugh became a scream. She turned and lunged at the thing with her black glove and it sliced her arm off just above the elbow. Blood splattered blackly in the green light. Sister Rothrock reeled back, whimpering. She hit the handrail, and toppled over it. Her scream went trailing after her, and ended abruptly down in the pit.

The Raptor forgot her and came stalking toward Tamzin and Vespertine. Tamzin checked behind her just in time to see a second, identical machine emerge from a kennel or cubbyhole and begin stalking the other way along the curving walkway to cut off their escape. She shifted her knife from hand to hand, getting used to its weight and feel, and wondering what earthly use it could be against these things.

The Raptors were chromium-plated dinosaurs, and they moved as prissily as wading birds on their long, backward-bending legs. They had clawed feet, long tails held out behind them for balance, and small green-eyed heads that flicked quickly to and fro on snaky necks. Every inch of them was bright as a mirror, and every edge and corner razor-sharp. Tamzin, who had always had a knack for knowing what the Revenants she faced were thinking, could tell that these two didn't think at all. They were just spiky puppets being operated by something that lived down in that pit, something that was powerful and cold and infinitely more clever than any Revenant she had faced before. It was watching her and Vespertine through the Raptors' eyes, but also through all the emerald lights that clustered on the walls and ceiling of the silo. She sensed it was amused by Tamzin and her dinky little knife. Her stomach felt empty, as if those chrome claws had already gutted her.

"Tamzin Pook," said Vespertine, "you cannot fight these things."

"I'm not leaving you to fight them alone," said Tamzin. She went into a fighting crouch, back-to-back with Vespertine. "We're a team, remember?"

The first Raptor sprang at Vespertine, chrome spines splashed black with Sister Rothrock's blood. Vespertine seized the bladed fist it drove at her, swung up a foot to kick it backward, and ripped off its arm. There were sparks, and a spurting and splashing of dark hydraulic fluids. Vespertine wheeled and shouted, "Duck!" and hurled the arm at the head of the second Raptor as it ran at Tamzin. Both machines drew back, surprised at Vespertine's strength and speed, reconsidering their plan of attack.

"You cannot harm these Revenants," said Vespertine. "I will fight them. You must find the brain that drives them."

The Raptors were moving in again, more cautious this time. One swiped at Tamzin and she dodged and tried to parry the blow with her knife, striking sparks from the Raptor's blades. The knife was jarred from her hand; she heard it clatter on the deck somewhere. Then, before the Raptor could strike again, Vespertine's big hand caught her under one arm and lifted her out of its reach, swinging her out over the handrail. She dangled helplessly above the pit of plumbing.

"Good luck, Tamzin Pook," said Vespertine, and let her go.

Falling, Tamzin glimpsed both Raptors closing in, claws slashing at Vespertine's armor. Then she bounced off a bit of pipework and landed hard on the floor of the pit. She lay there for a moment with everything hurting, wondering what was broken. Nothing seemed to be, except maybe some ribs, so up she got, the way she would have in the Arcade.

Keep moving, Pook, she told herself, like the trainers used to yell at her in practice fights. She forced her way through thickets of ducts and cables and around big metal pipes. Sometimes, looking up, she caught glimpses of heavy metal carnage happening on the walkway. Vespertine had a Raptor by the head and was trying to squeeze it to death by the look of things. But where was the other?

She looked left, then right, and saw it. It had left its twin to deal with Vespertine and it was coming into the pit after Tamzin, creeping down the ladder like a lizard on a wall. Its small head twisted this way and that on its long neck, scanning for her. Its arms were long too, like the arms of an ape, and bladed all over. All Tamzin could hope to do was avoid it long enough to find and kill the thing controlling it.

Just then, something black swung past her face like a fat spider. She yelped and flinched away from it. It was Sister Rothrock's severed arm, still in its long black glove. It was dangling from the armored cable that connected the glove to a power pack on Sister Rothrock's belt. The woman's body hung just above Tamzin's head, snagged in a sagging web of wires and cables. The glove still buzzed faintly. As it swung past her again, Tamzin saw the silvery mesh covering the palm and fingers, through which the current ran. Afraid that it would brush her when she went past it, she reached up to the power pack on Sister Rothrock's belt and switched it off.

The power pack was just like the power packs of the electric knives Tamzin had used in the Arcade, and the familiar feel of it gave her an idea. Standing on tiptoe and reaching up, she disconnected the power cable. The severed arm fell to the deck, the cable snaking down after it. Tamzin imagined the Raptor reacting to the sound, tilting its triangular head on one side like a dog, trying to pinpoint the source. As quickly as she could, she unbuckled the dead woman's belt, cinched it around her own waist, reconnected the power cable, and picked up the severed arm. She had somehow imagined it would be stiff and cold like the arm of a shop-window mannequin, but it was still warm, soft, and very horribly armlike.

She had been planning to pull the glove off and wear it, but a stealthy metallic sound behind reminded her that there was not time. The Raptor was stalking her through the ducts, and she guessed its eyes were better than hers in the green gloom of the pit. The weight of the power pack against her hip was familiar and reassuring. She thumbed the switch and pressed forward toward the center of the pit, holding the arm out in front of her. The dead hand flopped limply on the dead wrist and the black glove buzzed.

I am armed and dangerous, Tamzin thought.

And suddenly she stepped into a kind of clearing among all the ducts, and there before her was the Head himself.

40

Duels

Fighting an axeman, Max discovered, was mostly a question of keeping out of the way of the axe. All the fancy fencing he had been taught in Thorbury was useless here. He just had to dodge Stoat's vicious swings, and do his best to get a blow of his own in before it was time to dodge the backswing. His hope was that Stoat would get tired and make a mistake, but so far Stoat just seemed to be enjoying the exercise, while Max was tiring quickly himself. Already the axe had nicked him once, a flesh wound in his left thigh that had felt like nothing when it happened, but which was starting to throb now.

"We are wasting time!" he shouted as he fought. "If the bridge goes, we'll all die together! If Crawley eats us, we'll all be its slaves! Stop this. Help me get the harpoons free!"

As before, the watching nomads looked uneasy. As before, Stoat just laughed. "You think I fear death, city boy? The war gods will welcome me with honor if I take your head. Your soul will be my slave in the Sunless Country . . ."

They circled each other, feinting with axe and sword. Max's leg was numb. The growing crowd of Museion people looking on now included several men with guns, but they dared not use them for fear of hitting Max. He wondered if he should fling himself to the floor, and if the gunmen could shoot Stoat down before he buried his axe in Max's body. He doubted it, and he did not want Stoat shot by someone else anyway. It would feel unfair somehow. This thing was between the two of them.

An anger rose in him. This was the lad who had shot at the *Fire's Astonishment*. This was the brute who had bragged of capturing Tamzin and Doom and sending them into slavery, or worse. This was the thief who had helped himself to Tamzin's precious sun disc. This was the maniac who had started the fires. He shouted something that had no words in it, just rage. He thrust his sword at Stoat's heart, and his foot slipped in the growing puddle of his own blood.

Down he went, and up went Stoat's red axe to finish him. But in the same moment, before Stoat could bring his axe down or Max's followers could train their guns on him, Museion lurched backward and sideways. Some vital support beneath the Bridge of Storms had given up the ghost, and as it collapsed the whole city canted steeply to one side. People screamed and prayed, nomads and Museion folk alike. Stoat's swing missed Max. The axe head thudded into the charred timbers of a tier support. Stoat started to tug it free. And Max, seeing his one chance, forced himself upright and drove his sword into Stoat's chest.

Stoat left the axe where it was. Max pulled the sword out of him and stood wondering if he should stick it in again. Blood welled from Stoat's wound, and tears welled from his eyes and trickled down his startled face. He had thought he was the hero of this tale, and that a thousand wild adventures lay ahead of him. Now it was already ending.

"I'm sorry," said Max, and he was, for his rage had gone far away and it seemed a terrible thing that he had done. But he knew there had been no choice, for the wildness in Stoat could never have been reasoned with, or tamed.

Stoat was not listening to him. Stoat was not listening to the cheers of the Museion folk or the cries of woe from his Dogs either. Stoat was hearing the voices of his ancestors, calling to him from the Sunless Country. He fell on his knees, then on his face. He sighed once, and lay still.

Then Max turned and saw the watching faces of Stoat's friends, and wondered what chance there was against them all, and what would happen to Museion while they wasted time fighting. The city swayed with the swaying of the bridge, and edged forward a few inches toward safety, and was dragged back again. Loose things rolled in tilting streets above Max's head.

He wiped his sword on his tunic, but did not put it away. The Junkyard Dogs respected swords. But he held out his free hand to them and said, "Help us. Please."

Tamzin was slightly surprised to find that the Head really was just a head. She had been expecting something more along the lines of Vespertine: human-shaped, and maybe sitting on a throne. But all that was left of old Jago Flint was his bald head. Detached from his body when he died, fitted with a Stalker brain, and then linked up to more pipes, wires, and tubes than she could count, it sat like a gruesome grayish meatball in a bowl of Old-Tech spaghetti. Some kind of gel oozed over it from a nozzle above, so that it glistened wetly. There were no eyes in its eye sockets, but fat cables snaked out of them and plugged into one of the various machines that stood around it. Tamzin knew it was watching her through all the flaring green lamps in the chamber, just as other lamps were watching Vespertine up on the walkway and Mortmain outside in the passageway, and the progress of Museion across the bridge.

When the Head spoke, its voice came not from its dead mouth (although the mouth did open, horribly, upon yellowed teeth and a black slug tongue) but from speakers in the ceiling, and probably from speakers in every ceiling, all over the suburb.

"I am Crawley," said the Head. "You will obey me."

"You are Jago Flint," said Tamzin. "And you're as mad as a brush."

"Flint," said the Head in a thoughtful way, and just for a moment Tamzin wondered if she had triggered its memories of its former life, like the memories that seemed to come from time to time to Vespertine. She wondered if it was recalling Jago Flint's childhood, or his first love. Maybe it would grow sentimental, and she could talk to it and persuade it to end its city-hunting and take up flower arranging or some sort of charity work instead?

But Jago Flint had been a horrible child, and in all his long life he had never loved anybody except Jago Flint. "You are an obstacle in the path of Crawley," said the Head. "You will die."

"How? You're just a head. What are you going to do? Bite me?"

A stealthy reflection shifted in one of the silvered tubes. Tamzin glanced behind her. The Raptor was easing its way through the duct forest, reaching out its nightmare hands, readying itself to spring at her.

"I am immortal," said the Head. "I am Crawley. I am the future."

"You're history," said Tamzin, thinking that Hilly would

approve of that, and hoping that she would remember to tell her about it if they ever met again.

She slammed Sister Rothrock's hand down on top of the Head's bald, slimy scalp and kept it pressed there. The Raptor lashed wildly at her, missed, and kept on flailing and thrashing, its blades severing tubes, which spewed steam, or sparks, or goo. The Head howled, and still Tamzin kept pressing the black glove down on it, until smoke rose between the fingers, and the gel trickling over Flint's face started to bubble. Then one by one, at first all over the silo and then all over Crawley, the green lights flickered and went out.

41

Tug of War

On the Bridge of Storms, a struggle was taking place that would be sung about for centuries afterward. Museion, with both sets of wheels on the firm stone of the western bank, was struggling to pull itself forward off the bridge. Crawley, with the front half of its segmented chassis on the bridge and the back half still on the eastern bank, was struggling to drag it far enough backward that its jaws could close upon Museion's stern. And between the city and the suburb, the three harpoon cables stretched taut and sang in thin, high tones that rose above the roar of straining engines and the clamor of stressed metal.

And the bridge itself, that soaring catenary arc, which had spanned the abyss for so long, swayed and shivered under the adversaries' weight, while shards the size of falling trees and hunks as big as houses were shaken loose from it and went tumbling down and down into the Vastri's foam.

Max, his bad leg bandaged with someone's neckerchief, scrambled out on to the gantries at the city's stern with a mixed-up band of nomads and Museion folk. They reached the place where the first of Crawley's barbed harpoons had lodged itself in the deckplates. Some set to work with crowbars and angle grinders, trying to free it from the hole it had punched. Max ran past them up the harpoon's shaft to where the cable was attached and started hewing at that with Stoat's axe.

"Too dangerous!" a man yelled. "If it snaps, it could . . ."

But what could it do, thought Max, that could be worse than dragging Museion into a suburb's gut or the cold embrace of the river? So he hacked at the cable, blunting the axe, jarring his aching arms, until others came to join him with power tools. Then he jumped clear and stood watching the sparks gush upward until first one strand of the cable parted, then another, and suddenly the cable was gone, severed, whipping backward out of Museion, felling an exhaust stack on its way.

They were a tight band now, united by their victory, and Max felt sorry that Stoat could not have been with them as they ran together through the shadows and the smoke to where the next harpoon was wedged. And the city lurched, and the bridge moaned, and the smoke rose, and the engines roared, and high in the Ivory Tower Professor Stanislaus looked down — straight down, through the starboard-side windows — into the gorge, and thought, *This is it. This is the end of everything* . . .

The second harpoon was not so heavily embedded. Only one of its barbs had pierced Museion's deckplates. They started cutting it free, and sprang out of its way as it pinged suddenly backward, flying across the bridge and slamming into one of those blockhouses on the jaws of Crawley with a wrecking-ball violence that made everyone cheer. Max noticed then that the green lights on Crawley's bows seemed to have been turned off, but there was no time to wonder what that might mean. He ran with the others to the final harpoon.

This one was bedded deep. It had gone right through the deck and down into the chassis so only the cable showed, stretching away eastward into the dust and smoke that hung between Museion and its tormentor. The cable sang like a plucked harp string as the suburb and the city strained against each other. Max stood looking at it, wondering if there was time to go down into the crawlways on Museion's underbelly and find where the harpoon itself had lodged.

No, he thought. He snatched an angle grinder from someone, fired it up, and started hewing at the bundled steel. A heavy tool, and hard to use, but he just had to hold it down and let it do its snarling work. He climbed out on to the cable so that the blade could bite deeper. And when the cable snapped — more easily and more suddenly than he had expected, cracking like an immense whip — he thought that it would take him with it, but hands reached out to catch him as he fell. Some caught him by his injured leg, and the pain was so intense that tears came into his eyes. But he was laughing too, for the cable was tumbling away in useless loops like a beheaded dragon, down through the sunlight into the shadows of the gorge, and as it fell Museion went surging forward, clawing its way on to firm ground at the gorge's western edge.

The Bridge of Storms gave way behind it. Down it went in rust-red ruins, and down with it went the first few segments of Crawley, dragging others behind them until the whole front half of the articulated suburb was dangling over the cliffs, and its jaws lay shattered in the river.

❁

All Tamzin knew of this, deep in Crawley's central segment, was a shuddering jolt that hurled her against a wall and went on and on. But it stopped at last, and she lay there in blackness, breathing hard. The lights had gone out, but sprays of sparks were spurting from various pipes she'd severed, and by that intermittent glow she saw that the Raptor that had been reaching for her was motionless now, collapsed against the plumbing with its eyes gone dark. The Head lay gaping in its steaming pool of gel, and smoke rose from the charred glove-print on its brow.

Tamzin groped for the power pack and turned it off, although the black glove had stopped buzzing and seemed to be spent. She unbuckled the belt and let it drop. Crawley's engines seemed to have cut out, but the suburb still moved occasionally in a jerking, uncontrolled way. The silo was filled with the sounds of stressed metal and distant shouting, mixed with occasional muffled bangs, which might have been gunfire.

"Vespertine?" Tamzin called, fearing there would be no answer.

On the catwalk above her something stirred. A single green lamp shone down at her. "Tamzin Pook," said Vespertine.

The Raptor that Vespertine had been fighting lay in pieces, like a model kit awaiting assembly. It had done some damage before Vespertine dismantled it: There were deep claw marks on her armor, and her left eye was smashed and lightless. Something nasty dribbled from a gash in her side. But she came to the ladder head and helped Tamzin up the last few rungs. Together they limped back along the passage. The oval door through which they had entered was still locked. Vespertine hammered on it with her iron fist, but no one came, so she kicked stubbornly at it until it came off its hinges.

A thin mist of gun smoke hung in the passage outside. Altan gave a cry of alarm and swung his carbine at Vespertine as she stepped over the wrecked door, but Doom had seen her too and held his hand up to stop the younger man from shooting her. They were crouched in the doorway behind an overturned locker that they had been using as a barricade. Sister Yarrow knelt nearby, fussing over Mortmain, who sat propped against the wall.

"They've been coming in waves," said Doom, gesturing past the locker to where the passageway was clogged with sprawled heaps of Crawley's security men. "Small guns at first, then bigger ones. I thought we were done for till the lights went out. How's the Head?"

"Dead," said Tamzin. "He's a dead head. I dead-headed him . . . Sister Rothrock lent me a hand." She felt a little drunk, like she had sometimes in the Arcade after a fight: adrenaline and relief and the pain of busted ribs. "I killed him," she said. "I killed Crawley. I'm a suburb slayer. I'm a town killer." She shouted so it echoed under the low roof, "I'm TAMZIN POOK!"

Vespertine, meanwhile, stooped over Mortmain, who was clutching his wounded shoulder, his face as white as a floured dumpling. "You are not to die, Mortmain," she warned him. "I need repairs. I require a new eye and a new arm."

"Brother Mortmain is a great man," said Sister Yarrow. "He has been telling me how he hatched this plan. Many of us have longed to rid ourselves of the Head these past few years, but we never mustered the strength or the courage. If Brother Mortmain had not brought you here, we would never have had the means."

"This wasn't Mortmain's plan," protested Tamzin. "He just wanted to run away and save his worthless skin! It was me and Vespertine and Doom and Mr. Thingy here who did this . . ."

But no one was listening to her, because Crawley was suddenly on the move again, sliding forward with a sickening motion that got faster and faster and then stopped with a jerk. Vespertine put her large steel hand on Tamzin's shoulder. "We have done good work here today, Tamzin Pook. But now we should leave. I think something has gone very wrong with this suburb."

Vespertine gathered the moaning Mortmain up and slung him over her shoulder, then started back along the darkened passageways, helping Tamzin, Altan, and Sister Yarrow to find their way by the light from her remaining eye. The control rooms of the central segment seemed abandoned. There were signs of panic everywhere, and signs of fighting too. It was hard to make out what was going on until a group of engineers came by and happily turned out to be Sister Yarrow's friends.

"The bridge is down," they said. "The forward segments of Crawley are hanging in the gorge. We plan to sever the couplings and let them fall, before they drag the rest over the edge. Then we'll take what remains for our own. Crawley will rise again! No Head this time! We shall elect a new mayor, a man of reason. Or a woman — you should stand for election, Sister!"

"Perhaps I shall," said Sister Yarrow. But as they climbed through other segments toward the stern, she muttered, "Crawley will rise again, but I think I have had enough of it. May I leave with you aboard your airship, Mr. Doom? I presume Museion can use another engineer?"

They waded through a shin-deep river of plant-based slurry leaking from the algae farms. The rear segments had been taken over by slave workers escaping from the barracks there. A fearsome old man named Uncle Eagle was their leader, and it seemed to Tamzin that he was far more likely to end up as the new mayor of Crawley than any of Sister Yarrow's comrades. The rebels had been joined by a lot of Crawleyites and they were doing all the things that were traditionally done in such situations — breaking stuff, looting the canteens and food stores, and parading their former masters' heads around on sticks. But they quieted down when they saw Vespertine coming. The Revenant and her friends walked toward the air docks on a path that opened silently before her, walled on either side with wary faces.

Tamzin still did not really understand what had happened to Crawley. Trapped in its windowless rooms, never having seen so much as a picture of the Bridge of Storms, she did not appreciate the depth and grandeur of the gorge until the *Owl of Minerva* lifted off from the air dock. Only then did she understand what had happened to the suburb, and the meaning of all the slitherings and lurchings she had felt when she was deep inside it became clear. The central segment had come to rest right at the brink of the gorge. The segments in front of it hung over the edge. Engineers, apparently still unaware of the rebellion that had broken out at the stern, were busy trying to cut the dangling forward sections free. As the ship swung overhead, Tamzin could see them down there, tiny figures in white coats and welding masks, with oxyacetylene torches burning blue-white like stolen stars. But their work was hampered by the fires that had broken out in the foremost segment, and the oily smoke that poured up the cliffs. Crawley's jaws lay half submerged and tangled with the carcass of the bridge, whose wreckage had clogged the gorge and partly dammed the river.

Tamzin guessed that she would be hearing poems and songs about Crawley's fall and Museion's salvation for the rest of her life. She wondered whether she would get a mention. It was hard to be sure how much of a part she had played in everything. Wouldn't it all have happened anyway, whether she had killed the Head or not? Or had she distracted Crawley at a crucial moment, and made it miscalculate the strength of the bridge?

There seemed no way of knowing. But at least Museion was safe on the western bank, with all its people clustered around to watch the *Owl of Minerva* come home. And she was alive, and the Head was defeated, and Vespertine was no more dead than before. And Mortmain, who had cast his shadow over her life for all those years, was reduced to nothing: a feeble, whimpering little jelly of a man, who would do whatever Tamzin told him to do.

When the ship settled on to the Air Staithe, the first people she saw as she went down the gangplank were Hilly (running to throw her arms around Oddington Doom), and Professor Stanislaus, who had brought Small Cat to greet Vespertine.

Just behind them, limping along on a crutch made from a repurposed broom, was Max. He seemed changed in ways that Tamzin could not quite explain. He looked battered and battle-stained, but wiser, and more certain of himself, as if he had grown years older in the few days they had been apart.

For a few seconds, he did not know what to say, and Tamzin started to wonder if he even recognized her, in her strange Crawley clothes and without her hair. Then he reached in his pocket and said, "This is yours," and took out the sun disc that she had thought was lost. He had fitted it on a new cord, and he reached out and put the cord over Tamzin's head so that the disc hung against her chest, where it belonged. And, although she was not a huggy sort of person, Tamzin hugged him, and let him hug her back, and as they stood there in the sunlight holding each other she thought for just a moment that she should kiss him, and that he might not mind it if she did.

But she had used up all her courage for that day, so she just pressed her face for a long moment into his shoulder, and stepped back, saying, "This is Sister Yarrow, who helped us, and this is Esan Altan of the Anti-Traction League, who is very brave, and Mortmain is in the gondola — yes, *that* Mortmain. I know. I suppose we will have to carry him to the infirmary."

42

As If I Were Never Here at All

West of the Vastri, the Golgan Hills descended in a series of long, sloping ledges to the plains of the Central Hunting Ground. Museion made the journey slowly, for much damage had been done during its battering upon the bridge. Luka Voss and his repair teams labored night and day to fix ruptured steam pipes and to prop up fallen smokestacks. Meanwhile, Max's wound healed, and so did Tamzin's scrapes and bruises. Her shaved scalp sprouted a fine black stubble, which soon grew soft and velvety, as if her head had been flocked. Tamzin was embarrassed by it, and wore a hat whenever she could, but secretly Max felt it suited her.

There was not much work for warriors during those days, so Oddington Doom enjoyed a well-earned rest, and spent all his time with Hilly. She showed him around all the city's galleries and collections, and when he grew tired of looking at old artifacts and fancy paintings he looked at Hilly instead, delighted by the delight she took in those old things.

"I've had an interesting life," he told her, "and surprisingly long, all things considered, but you're the best thing by far that ever happened to me."

Hilly felt the same way. "We are so lucky to have found each other," she said. "Whatever happens, let us never be parted again."

Professor Pott-Walloper married them the very next afternoon, in the Temple of Peripatetia. The temple was fire-scarred and missing its roof, the feast was sparse, and Tamzin and Vespertine made an odd pair of bridesmaids, but everyone agreed that a wedding was a hopeful thing after all those funerals. The sun shone down between charred rafters to illuminate the happy couple, and Professor Pott-Walloper declared it a sign that the goddess blessed their union, and that she would also bless Museion's union with London.

❁

Slowly, the hills fell astern, and the wide, rolling plains of the Hunting Ground stretched out on all sides, with just a rumor of rough country on the southern horizon where the vast lava flows of the Sculpture Garden lay. They crossed the river Wassermauer, which earlier in the year and farther south had formed an impenetrable barrier to towns trying to escape Thorbury's rampage. Here in its northern reaches it was broader, and flowed slowly in winding braids between long banks of gravel. At its deepest point, it barely reached up to Museion's axles. Small mobile villages had gathered in the shallows, slurping up water for their boilers through gutta-percha hoses. A slab-sided fuel town was resting nearby, and Museion met with it and refilled its coal bunkers and oil tanks.

While that was happening, one of the stern ramps was lowered, and the surviving Junkyard Dogs departed. They had helped tremendously on the Bridge of Storms, and would have been welcome to stay aboard, but the girl Yanna, who spoke for them now, said they would miss the old ways too much. With Voss's help, they had cobbled together two new kampavans from the wreckage of their own and some vehicles taken from the collection, and in those they set out north, hoping to pass the Ravnina Gap before winter closed it, and meet up with the landships and barges of their scattered pack. Whether they found them or not, no one aboard Museion ever knew.

That night another blizzard blew in, and as the wind howled around the walls of the infirmary and hail rattled at the windows, the dean suddenly opened his eyes, sat bolt upright in his bed, and said, "Goodness gracious! Have I missed anything?"

❁

Sister Yarrow settled in easily to life aboard Museion. Despite her shaven head and curious ideas, the Senior Fellows found her to be very much their sort of person. They consulted her about some of the documents in the Old-Tech library, which meant nothing to them. Did she think London's Guild of Engineers might be interested in these parchments, on which tech-monks in the Black Centuries had painstakingly copied out the operating instructions and wiring diagrams of Ancient washing machines and record players? Or in this fragmentary account, possibly fictional, of a cobra-headed death-ray called MEDUSA? Sister Yarrow studied the old documents intently: She thought they very much might. She believed her colleagues aboard London might have much to learn from Crawley's discoveries too. In that way, she hoped, the wanderings of the experimental suburb might turn out to have been not wholly in vain.

Mortmain made a surprisingly fast recovery. "London, eh?" he said, when he heard where Museion was bound. "A man could make a name for himself in London." Dr. Jaffaji recommended he remain in the infirmary, and Tamzin insisted that he was not to leave, but from his sickbed Mortmain was able to instruct Sister

Yarrow in the building of a replacement arm for Vespertine, and the repair of her broken eye and other wounds. Her new hand, while not as strong as the old one, was far more sensitive. ("Now I have a hand for fighting and a hand for stroking Small Cat," said Vespertine, flexing her new fingers in a satisfied way.) As for her eye, it never shone with quite the same shade of green afterward, but Hilly assured her that odd-colored eyes had always been a way to tell that someone was particularly favored by the gods.

❁

Professor Stanislaus found that he had almost enjoyed the events of the past days. Terrible as they had seemed at the time, they had taken him out of himself. It had been one last adventure, most unexpected, and really rather welcome. During the crossing of the Bridge of Storms, he had felt more alive than at any time in his life. And then when the *Owl of Minerva* appeared so unexpectedly, bringing Vespertine and the others home, and turning catastrophe so suddenly into joy . . . Well, it had all been most invigorating.

But, now that it was over, he was left feeling immensely weary. He slept a lot, and whenever he woke, his body was full of low, insistent, ominous pains. He felt that he should press on and do things, but there did not seem much left to do. When he gathered the strength to go outside, he found the city so altered that it no longer felt like the Museion he had known. The dear old buildings still stood, most of them, but there was a new spirit among the students and the fellows — they were more confident, less bound by old traditions. All very natural and proper, Stanislaus supposed, but personally he had *liked* the old traditions. Their absence made him more aware than ever that his time in the world was coming to an end.

One morning he made himself walk to the Archaeological Collection, then crossed the Quadrangle to the house where Tamzin and her comrades stayed. Waiting at the door for someone to answer his knock, he looked behind him and saw the line of his own footprints in the snow. What a doddery, wavering path he had left! And how swiftly it was being erased by the big, fluffy flakes of a fresh snow shower . . .

Tamzin let him in. She was alone in the house that morning. Stanislaus sat down in the warm kitchen and caught his breath while he pretended to drink the tea she made him.

"Miss Pook," he said when he was ready, "I remembered that on the day we first met, you were inquiring about one of the relics in the collection. I'm afraid I was upset, and rather rude, and did not give you a proper answer." He had brought the relic with him: the bronze disc with the smiling sun and the cryptic lettering. He set it on the tabletop like an expensive coaster.

"I have one like it," said Tamzin, taking out her own disc, which, when set beside the museum's version, turned out to be a cheaper sort entirely. The sun-face was the same though: a kind smile, and the rays reaching out all around.

"I looked in the museum records," said Stanislaus. "This was brought back sixty years ago, by one of our Fellows who made an expedition to the Caribbean rafts, and the ziggurat cities of the Nuevo Maya."

"What does the writing mean? 'Apollo Nuevo' and 'Thursday?'"

"Thursday is a god they have in those parts. His servants were talking birds, and sometimes he is pictured as a bird himself since he understood the mysteries of flight. Because of that, and because he came from the eastern sea, where the sun rises, he was taken to be a reincarnation of the sun god Apollo Nuevo, whose fiery chariot carried Niall Strongarm to the moon in the days of the Ancients."

"My parents left me this," said Tamzin, running her fingertips lightly over the face on her own pendant. "Do you think that means Thursday was their god? Perhaps they came from the raft cities? Or Nuevo Maya?"

"Perhaps," said Stanislaus. "Or perhaps they were simply daring travelers, like yourself. At any rate, Tamzin, I would like you to keep our disc. No, no, I insist. If we reach London, all our treasures will be absorbed into the Guild of Historians' museum, and it will end up in a dusty drawer with half a dozen other curios. But if you take it — well, perhaps your journeying will lead you one day to those places, and you will learn more about the Thursday cult than our historians ever found out. And, if not, it doesn't matter. Thursday is supposed to bring good luck to aviators."

When he went to rise, he found that he couldn't. He had grown too weak. Tamzin sent for Vespertine, and the Revenant lifted him gently in her two arms and carried him back across the Quadrangle to the infirmary. The footprints he had made in the snow were completely gone by then.

He thought, *It is as if I were never here at all.*

❁

The Hunting Ground was vast: a rolling gray-green sea from which hills and mountains jutted up like scattered islands, and on which sometimes another town or city showed far-off in the distance, like a passing ship.

Not all of those towns and cities were friendly. A week after the crossing of the Wassermauer, a pack of small predator towns emerged from their lair in a scumble of deep track marks and gave chase. Dr. Twyne used the last of Museion's ammunition to fire a few shots from the stern guns, disabling the leader, and the rest of the pack broke off the hunt to feast upon their crippled comrade. But a few days later a larger predator appeared, a town that *Banvard's* listed as Wee Glasgey. It had tartan armor, and hideous skirling sounds came from the long black funnels on its stern as it raced after Museion, only giving up once Luka Voss brought the auxiliary engines online and showed it a burst of speed it could not match.

The next day, a more serious threat appeared. Whether it had heard of Museion's plans and lain in wait, or whether it was just ill fortune that had brought it to that particular portion of the Hunting Ground on that particular day, there was no way of telling, but it was a large town, almost a city, and its extendable jaws looked perfectly capable of swallowing Museion whole.

"It is called Hay-on-Wye," said Hilly, studying it through Doom's binoculars between the passing snow showers. "Its founders were the descendants of people marooned at a literary festival when the Sixty Minute War broke out. They called themselves the Booklords, and made it their business to collect as many books as they could. But when they motorized their town, there was not room for every book, so they decided that they should keep only the best ones, and destroy any that they deemed inferior or offensive. And gradually, over the years, they came to class more and more books as offensive, until they decided that the best thing would be to destroy them all, just to be on the safe side. That pale smoke from the chimneys amidships is probably from the furnaces where they are burning the contents of a library they have lately captured. That is what will become of all Museion's books and manuscripts if they catch us."

There was nothing to be done but run, and pray no other predator appeared to bar the way. The engines were almost at full capacity again, and kept Museion well ahead. But from then on, whenever anyone looked back from the stern, Hay was lumbering along in Museion's wake, sometimes just a smudge upon the snowfields, sometimes close enough that sharp-eyed observers could read the slogan "Be Kind" painted in rainbow colors on its jaws.

❁

Fifty miles from the coordinates where it was due to rendezvous with London, Museion ran into fog. That part of the Hunting Ground was low-lying, and the fog filled it like thick gray soup filling a bowl. There was nothing to do but cut the city's speed, and the only consolation was that Hay, five or ten miles astern, would have to go just as slowly. The charts showed no mountains or dangerous rivers ahead, but fresh track marks might have been made since the charts were drawn. A city pitching unwarily into one of those could bust an axle or shear off a wheel, leaving it as a helpless involuntary buffet for every hungry predator in the region.

The fog was not as icy as that which had enveloped Museion on the day after the Junkyard Dogs' attack, but it was damp, and clammy, and in the windless air it mingled itself with the engine smoke that hung around the city and became a choking smog that crept through open doors and the cracks in window frames. Every flat surface bore a fine covering of soot, and a grayish haze hung in the air of every room. Outdoors was worse. People groped their way to the infirmary with injuries they had suffered from bumping into walls in the whiteout, or were carried in with ankles they'd sprained by pitching down the stairways.

Dinner in the Great Hall on the third night of the fog was a dismal affair. The rose window had been shattered in the fight with the Dogs and was boarded up. Half the chairs at the High Table were empty, and half the chairs below too. Museion had lost a lot of good people on its journey west, and of those who were left there were many who did not care to risk the snowy, fog-bound streets. Dinner, when it arrived, turned out to consist of nothing but a few rather elderly potatoes and some tinned meat.

"Boiled spuds and luncheon meat," said the dean gloomily, and he wondered if it would be too ironical to ask his traditional, "Are we well fed?" at the end of the meal.

"I hear poor Stanislaus is fading fast," said Professor Pott-Walloper. "I pray the goddess will guide his soul down to the Sunless Country."

"Perhaps we are all in the Sunless Country already," said Professor Waghorn. It was exactly the sort of clever remark that had made him so popular with his students and so unpopular with everybody else. "It is hard to imagine any country more sunless than this. Does anyone remember when this infernal fog began? Perhaps we are all dead, and did not notice."

"No call for that sort of talk, Waghorn," pleaded the dean, who thought Waghorn's remarks in very poor taste. "Where there's life there's hope. Isn't that so, Mr. Doom?"

Oddington Doom speared a boiled potato with his fork and studied it as if it were an old friend whom he had been rather hoping not to meet again. "What's that? Yes, yes: If the Booklords nab us, we can fight."

"But it won't come to that," said Hilly firmly. "We must be nearly at the meeting place by now. We shall find London soon, and then all will be well."

"It will be the end of Museion either way," said the dean sadly.

"I hope we can spot London in the fog," said Max. "We might roll past a few feet from its tracks and never notice it."

"The fog will clear tomorrow," said Professor Pringle. He and Mrs. Pringle were the only ones who seemed to be enjoying their meal, and he beamed brightly at the others as he spoke. "The pressure is dropping. There'll be a wind from the north by noon, and we shall have sunny intervals, and scattered showers."

❁

Early the next afternoon, a few patches of watery blue sky showed above the city, but the fog was slower to clear than the Pringles had promised. Max and Tamzin climbed up to the navigation suite, hoping that from there they might catch a glimpse of the land ahead, and perhaps of London itself. But the forward windows of the suite still looked out only onto fog, as thick and gray as wet toweling.

"I don't know how we'll ever see London in all this," Max grumbled.

"City to starboard!" shouted one of the assistant navigators suddenly. Everyone rushed to the starboard windows, but the fog had closed in again as thickly as before. "I'm sure I saw it," the man said, not sounding sure at all. "The fog lifted for a moment and there were rooftops and chimneys . . ."

"London?" asked Tamzin.

"It must have been . . ."

"The wind is rising," said Barley Bellweather.

Outside, the damp flags and pennants that had hung so limply these past days had started to bestir themselves. They were not fluttering yet, but they looked as if they were thinking of fluttering, or at least starting to remember that fluttering was a thing that flags and pennants could do. Off the city's starboard quarter, an acre or two of wet heathland appeared, and the water in an old track mark blazed a sudden silver and there was the other city, an angular blur coming slowly into focus as the breeze began to clear the fog aside. Tamzin saw the tracks first, then buildings piled above them, and then — because the city was at right angles to Museion, moving toward it — the jaws, with the words "Be Kind" painted across them.

"That's not London!" she said. "That's Hay!"

But already alarm bells were ringing, and everyone else in the navigation suite was scrambling to their stations. After a few breathless moments, Max and Tamzin felt the city tremble as the engines surged and the starboard tracks went into reverse, swinging Museion toward Hay.

"Wrong way!" Tamzin shouted, gripped by a sudden, dreadful fear that Barley Bellweather was as treacherous as her old boss had been, and was steering them straight into Hay's jaws. But Max said, "No. This is good. If we turn to port and run, the predator just chases us; if we go starboard, we'll go past them and they'll have to turn before they chase us."

They were passing Hay as he spoke. The lookouts in its town hall must have been as surprised as anyone aboard Museion to find their prey so close. Max could see people running up and down stairways there, and smoke starting to spew from the big sternward chimneys as more engines came online. Then Museion was back in the fog and running west, out of whiteness into whiteness. But the fog was thinning now, and through the gaps that opened and closed in it, the upperworks of its pursuer showed, barely a mile behind and gaining fast.

43

This May Not Be the End

Professor Stanislaus opened his eyes. He had been mostly asleep for the past few days, drifting in and out of odd dreams and surprisingly intense memories of his childhood. It took him a few moments to work out where he was. Ah yes, the infirmary, of course. A small white room that Dr. Jaffaji had set aside for him. Beside his bed sat Vespertine, like a carven angel keeping watch over a tomb. Except that most angels did not wear bobble hats, or keep small cats curled up asleep on their shoulders.

"Vespertine?" he said. "Have you been here all this time?"

"Yes," said Vespertine.

The room lurched as the city went bucketing across rough ground. Things fell from shelves in a neighboring room, and someone cried out.

"Can you tell me what is happening?" asked Stanislaus.

"Museion is being hunted by a city called Hay-on-Wye," said Vespertine. "It is very close behind us."

"And is there no sign of London? We were supposed to meet London, I think. Wasn't that the purpose of this journey? Or did I dream it all?"

Vespertine shook her head, careful not to disturb Small Cat. "We are at the rendezvous point, but London has not been seen."

"Changed their minds, perhaps," said Stanislaus. "Vexing, very. To come so far, and make such efforts, and for it all to have been for nothing. Eaten by Hay. What a shame. The Booklords will burn up all our libraries, you know."

"They have not caught us yet," said Vespertine.

"That's the spirit. While there's life there's hope." Stanislaus groped about on the bedcovers until his frail old hand found her strong new metal one, and he held it tight. "I am glad you are here with me, at the end."

Vespertine raised her head for a moment. Outside the window, thin wintry sunlight was turning the fog to watered gold. Her keen ears caught a new sound, hard to decipher through the competing thunder of tracks and engines.

"This may not be the end," she said.

❁

The sunlight strengthened, bathing Museion's upper tier in gold, kindling reflections from the gilded decorations on the facade of the library and the Archaeological Collection, shining on the battered paneling of the Ivory Tower. A wind from the east was ushering the fog away, and as the land astern came into view the people gathered on Museion's balconies saw that it was not just Hay behind them but two other towns as well: rusty, hungry-looking predator platforms that must have been driven out of their usual territories in the Frost Barrens by this sudden winter. A glance through *Banvard's Gazeteer* confirmed that one of the towns was called the Snackdragon. The other had enlarged itself with bits and pieces torn from so many luckless mobile villages that it was impossible to identify.

Up on the city's stern, Oddington Doom was trying to make people stop staring at the onrushing towns like frightened rabbits and start loading one of Museion's few remaining guns. "There's no shot left," he bellowed, grabbing students by their collars and shoving them toward the emplacement, "but we'll find something — bowling balls, nuts and bolts, cutlery — anything we can pack down that gun's throat and shoot at Hay . . ."

Hilly took his hand and hushed him. "It is useless, my love," she said. "A few cannon shots will not stop three hungry towns. It would only anger them, and make them more likely to treat Museion's people cruelly when they take us. It is allowable perhaps when one is being hunted by nomads, or by a piratical suburb like Crawley, but as a general rule it is considered very poor form for cities to fire off guns at one another. Municipal Darwinism was intended to put an end to that sort of thing. No, we should run for as long as we may, and then surrender to whichever of these towns is the fastest and boldest."

As if it had heard her, the Snackdragon put on a sudden burst of speed, almost overtaking Hay, but Hay swerved to nudge it aside, determined not to be cheated of its prey. On Hay's jaws, figures armored in the leather bindings of burned books could be seen preparing their harpoons.

"You're right," said Doom bitterly. "But it stinks, to have fought so hard and come so far, just to be gobbled up by one of those dumps. We should find the others and get them down to the *Astonishment* . . ."

"Leave, you mean?" Hilly was shocked. "It would feel awfully cowardly, sneaking away while all our friends are eaten."

"It's that or be eaten with 'em," said Doom. "Vespertine's at the infirmary, but where have Max and Tamzin gone?"

❁

Max and Tamzin had gone right to the city's bows. They had not meant to. They had come out of the Ivory Tower meaning to look for Doom and Hilly. But such a crowd of people was hurrying forward in the desperate hope of sighting London that they were carried like twigs in a torrent all the way to the Prow Gardens. There was no view from there of the pursuing towns, so all they knew was what the people around them were saying — that there were three, four, half a dozen hungry cities snapping at Museion's stern.

The fog still lay upon the land ahead. But it was clearing steadily as Museion plowed toward it, drawing aside like a series of veils, or the curtains in an immense theater. And suddenly, very high in the sky, the sunlight gleamed on a cluster of windows, and buildings appeared around the windows, and other buildings around those, and Tamzin realized she was looking at a city.

"London!" she shouted, because she knew it could be no other.

London, first and greatest of the Traction Cities of the earth! The fog was thinning quickly now, revealing each of the seven famous tiers, the green parkland on their brims, the brightly painted buildings, the red and blue and gold of the massive tier-supports, the partially reconstructed Temple of St. Paul blazing brilliant white upon the very summit. And down below, still half hidden by sluggish wraiths of fog, the vast wheels turning, the rust and mud and steam and brute weight of a metropolis on the move.

And suddenly everyone in the Prow Gardens was shouting, and Tamzin was shouting with them, "London! London!" As if just yelling it could somehow make their poor straining city go faster. For how awful it would be to be caught now, when the safe harbor they had come so far to find was within sight! "London!" they screamed. "London!" as if the people up in the navigation suite might not have noticed it yet.

But they had, of course, and already Museion was altering course, running toward the oncoming city. And so had the navigators of Hay and the two other predator towns. None of them knew that Museion had arranged this meeting. They knew only that they had wandered within reach of one of the great predators of the Hunting Ground, and they had no wish to end up in its belly. Hay was the first to break off its chase, swerving across the path of the other two and fleeing south. The others slowed, then turned and followed it. If they could not feast upon Museion, perhaps they would snack that night on Hay instead.

Max and Tamzin pushed their way back through the gardens and ran out across the Quadrangle. Everyone else was still on the observation balconies. In its sunlit emptiness, the old city looked more beautiful than ever, battered and fire-scarred though its buildings were. Tamzin wished it did not have to be eaten. She was glad that she had been able to see it before it was.

Max took her hand. Already London walled off the sky ahead. "We'd better get to the airship," he said.

"What about Hilly and Doom?"

"They'll be on their way, I expect."

"What about Vespertine?'

"We'll stop by the infirmary on our way to the hangars."

❁

"London is here," said Vespertine, who could hear nurses and other patients talking about it in the corridors outside Professor Stanislaus's quiet white room.

She thought Stanislaus understood her, because his eyes

moved behind his papery eyelids, and his mouth twitched in a little smile. But he was very far away from her, and going further all the time, and after she had sat holding his hand for another five minutes she realized he was no longer there at all.

She wished then that she could cry. But the stupid eyes that Mortmain had given her were not equipped for tears. She had never understood crying before, but she needed to do it now, very badly, and she couldn't. She wondered if punching a hole in the wall would help. But that would only scare Small Cat. So instead she stooped and kissed Professor Stanislaus's forehead very gently, and said, "I will remember you."

She hoped that, wherever he had gone to, it was not so far away that he could not hear her.

When she stood up, she found Tamzin and Max watching her from the doorway. She did not have anything to say to them. It was all too big and sad to talk about. But they understood that, and Vespertine was glad they were with her. She took their hands, and they walked together to the Air Staithe.

❁

Hilly and Doom were supervising the ground crew as they prepared to let the *Fire's Astonishment* depart. The airship's gasbags and fuel tanks were filled, and so was the cash box in the compartment under the gondola floor. Altan was hauling crates of provisions up the gangplank. The Senior Fellows had even presented Hilly with some lovely but unimportant artifacts, which they said might as well go to her as to London.

"We're headed for the warm south," said Doom when Tamzin, Max, and Vespertine arrived. "We'll drop Altan off at one of the Tyrolean statics where he can get transport back to the Mountain

Kingdoms. After that, we can go wherever we want. Trieste . . . Ashkelon . . . the Hellenic Conurbation . . ."

"Cairo," said Hilly. "Memphis. Hot days and warm nights and the wine-dark sea! Oranges you can pick straight off the tree!"

"Posie Naphtali," said Doom, nudging Max.

Max thought of the Middle Sea glittering in the warmth of the sun, and it was a good thought. But he found that his memories of Posie Naphtali had faded somewhat. He had not thought about her for weeks, and when he tried to call up her face he kept thinking instead of Tamzin, as Tamzin had looked when she stepped off the *Owl of Minerva*: bald as a coot, with an incongruous pink bandage on her brown face, short and plain and scruffy and somehow adorable.

"Where do you want to go, Tam?" he asked her.

"The Caribbean rafts," said Tamzin, without hesitation. "And the ziggurat cities of the Nuevo Maya."

She sounded so certain about it that they were a little surprised. But after a moment Hilly said, "Well, why not? If we can go wherever we wish, why not brush the dust of this tired old continent from our heels and find out how the others are getting on?"

The sun that was shining on the Great Hunting Ground that day gave little warmth, but it lit Museion like a painting as the *Fire's Astonishment* rose and turned above the Quadrangle. Few of the people on the observation balconies noticed her leave. Who could blame them, for London towered above them now with its enormous jaws spread wide in welcome. But as Doom swung the airship across Museion's stern, Max looked down and thought he saw Luka Voss on the stairway there, braving the sunlight to stand

and raise one hand in farewell. And Vespertine bowed her head and remembered Professor Stanislaus, and Tamzin fingered the sun disc he had given her and wondered how long it would take to fly to the Caribbean, or to South America.

Then Museion, battered but dignified, with all its flags and pennants streaming on the breeze and its dean and Senior Fellows gathered in the Prow Gardens in their formal robes, drove proudly up the broad tongue-like ramp that extended from London's jaws, and the jaws closed behind it with a deep and sonorous clang.

"Congratulations, everybody," said the dean, adjusting his feathered hat as his city drew to a halt in the cavernous Dismantling Yards, next to the gantry where welcoming committees from London's guilds stood waiting. "We are all Londoners now!"

And, outside, the *Fire's Astonishment* soared higher, up through the sunlight, past the crowded observation decks where bunting had been strung and hand-painted banners read LONDON WELCOMES MUSEION, until, somewhere over Circle Park, the north wind met her, and bore her away toward the warm south, and the promise of new adventures.

ACKNOWLEDGMENTS

Many thanks to my editors at Scholastic: Lauren Fortune, Samantha Stewart, and Wendy Shakespeare in the UK; Emily Seife in the USA; Scholastic's UK Art Director Jamie Gregory, and everyone else who has worked on this book. Ian McQue's cover art gets better and better, and I'm grateful to him for finding time among his Mileships to keep illustrating my stuff.

Many details of the world Museion wanders in are inspired by Jeremy Levett, or actually dreamed up by him when we worked together on *The Illustrated World of Mortal Engines*.

And finally, thanks and salutations to Philippa Milnes-Smith, who has been my agent since the days of *Fever Crumb*.

ABOUT THE AUTHOR

PHILIP REEVE lives in Devon, England, with his wife and son. His first novel, *Mortal Engines*, was published in the UK in 2001. Three sequels followed, the last of which, *A Darkling Plain*, won both the Guardian Children's Fiction Prize and the *Los Angeles Times* Book Award. Philip later wrote three prequels to the Mortal Engines Quartet — *Fever Crumb*, *A Web of Air*, and *Scrivener's Moon*.

He has also written a novel set in dark age Britain called *Here Lies Arthur*, which won the Carnegie Medal, a stand-alone novel called *No Such Thing as Dragons*, many illustrated younger fiction books with illustrator Sarah McIntyre, and a YA trilogy, Railhead. He is the coauthor, with Brian Mitchell, of two stage musicals, *The Ministry of Biscuits* and *Lord God*. He has also made a short film called *Gwenevere*, which you can find on YouTube.

Learn more at philipreeve.com.

EXPLORE THE WORLD OF MORTAL ENGINES!

THE ORIGINAL SERIES!

THE PREQUEL SERIES!

MORTALENGINES SCHOLASTIC and associated logos are trademarks and/or registered trademarks of Scholastic Inc.